"This mystery is rock star exciting—Nick and Nora are a hoot. I was hooked from start to finish!"

—Laura Childs, *New York Times* Bestselling author

"Nick and Nora are a winning team"

—Rebecca Hale, *New York Times* Bestselling author

"A fast-paced cozy mystery spiced with a dash of romance and topped with a big slice of 'cat-titude.'"

—Ali Brandon, *New York Times* Bestselling author

"Nick and Nora are the purr-fect sleuth duo!"

—Victoria Laurie, *New York Times* Bestselling author

"Excellently plotted and executed—five paws and a tail up for this tale."

—*Open Book Society*

"Nick brims with street smarts and feline charisma, you'd think he was human . . . an exciting new series."

—Carole Nelson Douglas, *New York Times* notable author of the Midnight Louie mysteries

"I love this series and each new story quickly becomes my favorite. Cannot wait for the next!"

—*Escape With Dollycas Into a Good Book*

"I totally loved this lighthearted and engagingly entertaining whodunit featuring new amateur sleuth Nora Charles and Nick, her feline companion."

—*Dru's Cozy Report*

Books by T. C. LoTempio

Nick and Nora Mysteries

Meow If It's Murder
Claws for Alarm
Crime and Catnip
Hiss H for Homicide
Murder Faux Paws
A Purr Before Dying

Urban Tails Pet Shop Mysteries

The Time for Murder is Meow
Killers of a Feather

Cat Rescue Mysteries

Purr M for Murder
Death by a Whisker

A Purr
Before
Dying

A Nick and Nora Mystery

T. C. LoTempio

BEYONDTHE**PAGE**
PUBLISHING

A Purr Before Dying
T. C. LoTempio
Copyright © 2023 by T. C. LoTempio
Cover design and illustration by Dar Albert, Wicked Smart Designs

Beyond the Page Books
are published by
Beyond the Page Publishing
www.beyondthepagepub.com

ISBN: 978-1-960511-02-7

Acknowledgments

As always, thanks go to my agent, Josh Getzler, and his assistant, Jon Cobb. Also a very special thanks to my wonderful editor, Bill Harris, who really went above and beyond this time. Many thanks for keeping me on track!

And I always want to give a special shout-out to my cousin, Paul E. Ferrante, who has been a dedicated supporter of the Nick and Nora series and all my books.

Finally, a big thank-you to all the readers and fans who buy the books and support the series. Without you, there would be no Nick and Nora! We hope to entertain you for many more volumes to come.

Dedicated to the memory of my cousin, Paul T. Ferrante, and to his son, Paul E. Ferrante, two of Nick and Nora's biggest supporters!

Chapter One

"I can't believe it! You're actually going to be cooking meals every day for two weeks for Preston McLintock! It's like a dream come true. You are *so* lucky!"

Myra Bassett, who was eighty if she was a day, pressed her hands together and rolled her eyes toward the flat-screen TV above my front counter with what I could only describe as a rapturous look. The show of choice right now was the super-popular cable soap opera *All the Days of Tomorrow*, and at the moment the forty-inch screen was filled with the image of a tall, handsome blonde man—shirtless—embracing a very pretty brunette wearing a lacy bra and a skirt that was practically nonexistent. The cast and crew of the show were set to arrive tomorrow for two weeks to do a location shoot in my hometown of Cruz, California, and I'd campaigned along with several other local venues for the honor of catering the food for the shoot's duration. My competition had been in the food business a lot longer than me, so no one was more surprised than I was when I'd been notified that the specialty sandwich shop I'd inherited from my mother, Hot Bread, had been deemed the winner. Especially in light of the fact that I could count the times I'd actually seen the show on one hand.

Nan Webb, the curator of the Cruz Museum, handed my assistant, Mollie, a crisp twenty for today's breakfast special: the Preston McLintock, of course, named in honor of my new catering gig, which in actuality was a ham and cheese scramble on a toasted bagel and medium coffee. "Luck had nothing to do with it, Myra," she said. "Everyone knows Nora inherited her talent for cooking from her mother. I'd have been surprised if she hadn't won."

Myra leaned both elbows on my counter. "I hear Amos Greene was particularly upset." Amos managed Chomps, a deli at the other end of town. She gave a loud sniff. "I don't see why he should be, though. His grilled corned beef and Swiss on rye is good, but it can't hold a

1

candle to yours, Nora. Especially those mini pies you make. They are soooo good."

I laughed. "I'm sure Amos wasn't the only one upset. It's going to be a lot of work, true, but there's a lot of money involved. And, as caterers in Cruz go, I'm pretty much the underdog."

"Oh, piffle." Myra waved her hand dismissively. "You couldn't be an underdog if you tried, Nora Charles. Anyway, everyone in Cruz is pretty excited. We've never had anyone from Hollywood film anything here, ever."

"I'll tell you who's not excited," I remarked with a chuckle. "Our estimable head of Homicide, Dale Anderson. She was in here yesterday complaining about the streets they want her to close in the wee hours of the morning for filming. They were very specific about wanting police guards cordoning off the shooting area to prevent spectators from disrupting the filming." As I said this I couldn't resist throwing Myra a sidelong glance. I had no doubt that given the opportunity, the feisty senior would make every attempt to catch a glimpse of her favorite stars.

"Well, with Tom Maloney and Ben Halleran both on sick leave, our Cruz PD is a bit shorthanded," Nan admitted. "Still, the TV crew's presence here should be a boost to the Cruz economy."

"Maybe not. The way I understood it, their shoot schedule is so rigid they have hardly any free time to browse in our shops. A few of them are staying at the Cruz Inn, and some have private trailers out at Sweeney Park. As a matter of fact, the first few days of filming are out there."

"Oh, that's at least a half hour from here." Nan clucked her tongue sympathetically. "How will that impact your catering?"

"The director told me they're setting up a special commissary tent at Sweeney Park with state-of-the-art appliances. I had to fax him a list of supplies I'll need. He promised me a fully stocked kitchen not only there but at all the shoot locations."

Myra beamed like a schoolgirl and clasped her hands in front of her. "After this, Hot Bread is going to be even busier than it is already. Oh, and by the way, Preston is going to be on this shoot, right?"

"Oh, really, Myra," Nan said, rolling her eyes. "Nora doesn't watch the show every day like you do. You have to tell her the actors' names, not the names of their characters."

Myra's bottom lip thrust forward in a petulant pout, and I could tell from the set of her jaw she was ready to argue with Nan. "It's okay," I said quickly, reaching into the middle drawer and pulling out a list. "They're cross-referenced on here. I guess they figured most fans might refer to the actors by the roles they play on the show."

Myra shot Nan a triumphant look. "See that," she chortled. "The TV people know how we fans think, all right."

I scanned the typewritten list and looked up at Myra with a smile. "Mark Emerson, the actor who plays Preston McLintock, is listed. There are some others here that might interest you too. Ardis Malone, Emily Van Horn . . ."

"Yes! Ardis's character is Preston's current flame, Rachel Potts, and and Emily plays his ex-wife, Eva." Myra's sullen expression softened and she rubbed her hands together in anticipation. "Wow, that should be good for a catfight or two. Frankly, he should have stuck with Eva. I don't know what he sees in Rachel."

"No? I think it's pretty obvious." Nan laughed and pointed toward the TV screen, where the brunette had shed her bra and miniskirt and was now sprawled in a provocative pose across the bed, clad in only a towel.

"Hm," snorted Myra. "That's just sex. Won't last." She regarded me over the rims of her glasses. "Who's directing? Henry Bourne, I hope. He almost always has Preston take his shirt off."

I ran my finger down the paper again. "Looks like you're out of luck on that score, Myra. They've got Anton Forbes and Kenny Colgate down as directors."

"Anton Forbes, really?" Nan leaned over to peer at the paper. "When did he join the show?"

"He came on about three months ago," supplied Myra, "when Benton

Griswold retired. I heard they wanted him bad. *People* magazine said they paid him a 'buttload' of money to do it." She gave Nan a baleful stare. "If you were a loyal follower, you'd know important facts like that."

I saw the color rise in Nan's cheeks and decided to head off a possible explosion. Aiming my most disarming smile at Nan I asked, "You're familiar with this Anton Forbes's work, then? He's done stuff other than television?"

"Oh, yes." Nan nodded. "He started out in movies. You know, those schlocky little horror films, and then he graduated to more artistic films." She named two films that I knew had been nominated for awards. "He's really come a long way these past few years, but I can't help but wonder. If it hadn't been for what happened with Dean Harriman . . ."

Whatever else Nan was about to say was drowned out by a loud *merow*. A second later a large black and white cat lofted onto the back counter and fixed all of us with a golden stare.

"Meower," he said again, and cocked his head.

Nan looked across the counter and giggled. "Looks like someone's not interested in our movie star gossip. Or maybe he is?"

The cat raised one black and white paw and waved it toward the ham on the counter. Then he started to purr loudly.

I chuckled. "I think Nick's just hungry." I broke off a piece of ham and walked over to the bowl in front of my refrigerator. I shredded the ham into several pieces and dropped it in. Nick jumped off the counter and padded over to the bowl, and a few minutes later the sound of contented slurping reached our ears.

Myra laughed. "He certainly likes to eat."

"Yes, it's hard to say which appeals to him more, food or a good mystery."

The tubby tuxedo cat formerly known as Sherlock, whom I'd renamed Nick (after Nick Charles—since my name is Nora Charles, it was sort of a no-brainer), had appeared on my doorstep one night and after some coaxing from my BFF Chantal, I'd adopted him—at least I think I did. It might have been the other way around, I still wasn't quite sure. Nick's former human, a PI who coincidentally was also named Nick, has been MIA for over a year now. I credit him with not only my kitty's flair for detective work, but his penchant for spelling out words with his favorite toy, Scrabble tiles.

"Yes, he's almost as talented as you in that area," Nan said with a chuckle. "Is he going to go along on the shoots?"

"That's a definite no," I said firmly. "Nick will stay here. Chantal, my sister Lacey, and Mollie are all going to rotate accompanying me and running Hot Bread, so there will always be someone around to keep an eye on him."

Nick looked up from his food bowl and bared his fangs. "Er-owl," he said, and then returned to his slurping.

Nan laughed. "I think he's trying to tell you he doesn't need a babysitter. Or maybe he wants to hear more about Dean Harriman." She laughed as Nick's head jerked up and he turned his golden gaze toward her. "I think you'd be interested too, Nora. Dean was Forbes's—"

Whatever information Nan was going to impart was interrupted as Myra gave her sleeve a hard tug and pointed to the television. "We're missing the best part of this show. There's an empty table right in front of the TV, too." She turned to me and peered over the rims of her glasses. "Well, good luck tomorrow, dear. If you get a chance, I'd love Preston's autograph, or a napkin of his, or a plate he ate off of. Really, anything he touched will do. Or better yet, if you can get your hands on something he wore, that would be even better." She closed one eye in a broad wink, then glanced over toward the door and let out a sharp breath. "Oh, great, here comes Doris Johnson. Come on, Nan. We've got to grab that table before she hogs it."

Myra snatched up her tray and gave Nan a push toward the table. As the two women hurried off, I found myself pondering just what I might find so interesting about this Dean Harriman. I felt a tug on my apron and looked down into Nick's furry black and white face.

5

"You're curious too, aren't you?" I glanced toward the register, where Mollie had Doris Johnson's order under control. "Let's take a little break."

Nick gave a loud *meow* and trotted off toward the back table and my laptop. I booted it up, clicked on the mouse, and a website selling designer shoes appeared, a sure sign that my sister Lacey had been on it earlier. I glanced longingly at a pair of to-die-for Louboutins in a plum color that cost almost an entire day's worth of Hot Bread receipts and then heard a soft *thunk* as Nick lifted his portly body onto the chair next to me.

"Let's see what Google has to say, shall we?" I typed "Dean Harriman" into the search engine and hit Enter. A few seconds later a plethora of articles popped up. I selected the one marked "Director Dies in Freak Accident," and a few seconds later a news article from the *LA Examiner* filled the screen:

> A director with a promising Hollywood career died yesterday in a freak accident on an LA movie set.
>
> Dean Harriman, 48, died Friday afternoon from a gunshot wound to the head. According to witnesses, Harriman was demonstrating how a suicide scene should be played. He took what was believed to be an empty prop, put it to his temple, and fired. The blank cartridge did not penetrate his head, but there was enough blunt force trauma to shatter a good-sized piece of his skull into his brain, causing massive hemorrhaging.
>
> Harriman was rushed to LA County Hospital, where emergency surgery was performed. He was pronounced dead at 9:25 Friday night. Police are investigating.

I clicked that article off and pulled up another one, dated a few weeks later:

Director's Death Ruled Horrible Accident

*Police have ruled the recent shooting death of director
Dean Harriman a "horrible accident."*

*Harriman, 48, was demonstrating to actors how to play
a scene when he put what he thought was an empty gun to
his head and pulled the trigger. According to eyewitness
reports, Harriman didn't wait for the prop master's
approval, just grabbed the gun to demonstrate. Apparently
there was one blank cartridge left in the chamber, which is
what killed Harriman. After a thorough investigation,
Detective Andrew Rizzoli of LA Homicide has officially
ruled Harriman's death "accidental." He was quoted as
saying, "There is no evidence to suggest any foul play. Mr.
Harriman's death was the result of his own carelessness."*

And yet another article entitled "Harriman Protégé Named as
Successor":

*Anton Forbes, Harriman's protégé, will assume
directorial duties on* The Mysteries of Maya, *effective
immediately, said Michael Parkerton, head of LightOne
Studios. "It is a terrible tragedy, but in the best show
business tradition, the show must go on. We have every
confidence in Anton turning out a quality product."*

The photo that accompanied all three articles depicted a smiling
brown-haired man who looked to be in his late forties. The last article
also had a photograph of another man with dark hair and eyes, looking
extremely serious as he bent over a young girl, ostensibly giving her
direction. I assumed that was Forbes.

I clicked on a few more articles. Some were interviews of other
actors Harriman had worked with, and some were the comments of

family members. All attested to the fact that Harriman sometimes acted rashly and without thinking. The general consensus was that Harriman had indeed acted rashly, as he had many other times before in his life. In this instance, however, it had cost him dearly.

"On the surface, it seems like a case of accidental suicide . . . but suicides aren't always what they seem, right, Nick?"

Nick cocked his head and let out a loud *merow*.

I leaned over to give him a scratch on the white streak behind his ear. "Let's think. Who stood to profit the most from Harriman's death?"

Nick's paw snaked out, tapped the screen where the article on Forbes taking over directorial duties was still on display. "Forbes is the logical choice, I agree." I typed his name into the search engine, and stifled a gasp at the number of pages that came up. There were easily over a hundred. I narrowed it down a bit by typing in "Anton Forbes– Dean Harriman" and got considerably fewer. I clicked on a handful and found them all to say mostly the same thing: Harriman was considered an eccentric genius, and though Forbes was talented, many felt he lacked Harriman's drive. Harriman had plucked him from doing horror movies and taken him under his wing. They'd worked together on two prior projects, both of which had been commercial successes. Every article ended with the same sentiment: Harriman's untimely death had given Forbes's fledgling career a much-needed boost. I started to close the computer, but Nick's paw shot out, covering my hand.

"Merow."

"You think I should search a bit more? Okay."

Finally at the bottom of the ninth page of results I found an article entitled "Dean Harriman, Casualty or Calculation?" It had been written two weeks after the director's death by a reporter named Millicent Martin. The gist of the article was that Harriman, although brilliant, had made many enemies in his life. Had someone decided to end it prematurely? There was a reference near the end to Forbes's good fortune at his mentor's demise. A veiled reference, perhaps, to a motive? The last line of the article was particularly interesting:

Rumor has it Harriman was set to reveal something stunning about one of his coworkers. Unfortunately—or is it conveniently?—his lips are now forever sealed.

I leaned back in the chair and rubbed my temples. Nick, sprawled next to the laptop, looked over at me, his golden eyes wide.

"Well, there was a police investigation, and they couldn't find any evidence to indicate it was anything other than an accident caused by Harriman's carelessness and ego. Aside from this Millicent Martin, everyone else seems to agree. That last line of her article is particularly interesting, right? I wonder what Harriman was going to reveal, and about who? I bet this Millicent Martin thought it was Forbes."

Nick cocked his head and the corners of his lips turned down. Then he jumped off the table and disappeared underneath. A few minutes later I heard the familiar sound of Scrabble tiles being batted around. I lifted up the edge of the tablecloth just as the tiles came flying out. I picked them up, laid them on the table and started to move them around. A few minutes later I stood back and surveyed the word I'd spelled out.

Bogus. A word that meant something not genuine. A phony, a sham.

I heard a loud *merow* from underneath the table. It seemed my kitty definitely thought there was something off about Harriman's death. "Fine, Nick." If I had to be perfectly honest, something didn't strike me right either. It was almost as if the death had been a bit too pat and terribly convenient for Anton Forbes, particularly if he'd been the object of Harriman's big reveal.

I'd been an investigative reporter for too long to just turn my back on what seemed to be a good mystery.

I heard a loud *tap tap tap* and shifted my gaze to the rear counter. Nick had wriggled out from underneath the table and had leapt onto the counter. He stretched up on his haunches, tapping his claws at the frame that held my newly acquired PI license.

"Okay, fine," I muttered and punched a number into my cell, that of Hank Prince, my former informant from my Chicago reporting days. If there was anyone who could dig up dirt buried deep, Hank was the man.

"This is Hank Prince. I'm not available to take your call right now, but leave a message and I'll return your call as soon as I can."

"Hey, Hank," I said. "Nora here. Can you do me a quick favor when you get some time? No rush, but I need some information about the death of a director named Dean Harriman. Also, anything you can find on a director named Anton Forbes, and any suspicious deaths he might have been associated with. It's, ah, for a possible *Noir* story. Thanks."

Well, I wasn't lying. *Noir* was the online true crime magazine I wrote for part-time. Since acquiring my license I'd written a few articles on becoming a PI, which had proven to be a big hit with the readers, but I'd no doubt that an article on an actual investigation into a mysterious death by a fledgling PI would have both readers and my editor salivating. I hung up and glanced down. Nick squatted by my feet. He lifted his head and I swear his kitty lips parted in a smile.

"Happy now?" I asked him. "We'll see what, if anything, Hank can scare up. And if he doesn't turn up anything suspicious on either front, it's a dead issue. Okay?"

"Merow," said Nick. Then he turned around, tail straight up, walked over to the refrigerator, turned around twice and lay down.

I sighed. It couldn't do any harm to see what, if anything, Hank might turn up. If there was one thing I knew from experience it was that when it came to crime, Nick's premonitions were nothing to sneeze at.

Chapter Two

I woke the Tuesday morning to a rough tongue licking my cheek. I winked one eye open and saw Nick sprawled across my chest. I turned my head and opened my other eye to look at my clock, then sat bolt upright, a motion that caused him to slide off my chest and onto his back across my comforter. "Three forty-five," I groaned. I'd set the alarm for three thirty, but it hadn't gone off. I scrubbed both hands across my face then glanced over at Nick, who'd righted himself and was now washing one black and white paw. "Thanks, buddy," I said, swinging my feet over the edge of the bed. "It wouldn't do to be late on the first day."

"Merow," said Nick, his tail straight up in the air, his kitty equivalent of *You're welcome*. He shifted his position slightly and raised one paw toward the end table, where my cell phone lay. I reached over, picked it up and checked it. I let out a long sigh.

"No messages, Nick. None from Hank, and none from you know who, either."

Nick padded over to me and butted his head against my arm, a sympathetic gesture for a cat. He knew I was talking about Daniel Corleone, the handsome FBI agent I'd been dating. A few weeks ago Daniel had sprung on me the news that he was being sent on a top secret assignment to London. The mission, if handled successfully, could result in a big promotion for him. The downside was he'd be virtually incommunicado for at least six months, possibly longer. Before he left he told me that he didn't want me to feel tied down, and if I wanted to date anyone else while he was away, he'd understand. I had the feeling, however, that he'd made that offer because he didn't think he had any competition. I myself wasn't sure if he did or not.

Damn that Leroy Samms.

I'd first met Samms in college. We'd worked on the college paper our senior year, and even back then our personalities clashed. We were the quintessential oil and water mix. Fast-forward eighteen years to last year, when my sister Lacey was accused of the murder of her art professor. Samms was her arresting officer, and we'd butted heads on that case too, although in the end I was convinced he had a sort of grudging admiration for my detective skills. Samms had since left Homicide for the FBI, and he now had Daniel's former job, as head of the Special Task Force based out of nearby Carmel. I'd be lying if I said there wasn't a spark of . . . something between us, only I had yet to ascertain just what that spark was, or how deep it went. And since Daniel was temporarily out of the picture, both my sister and Chantal had been egging me on to find out.

But did I want to open that Pandora's box? I might, except for another minor complication. Our current head of Homicide, Detective Dale Anderson. She and Samms shared a past, and I got the impression Dale would have liked to share a future with him too. How did Samms feel about either of us? Your guess is as good as mine.

I jumped off the bed so abruptly I startled Nick, who let out a sharp *merow*. I gave him a lopsided grin. "Sorry, pal. I shouldn't sit here and agonize over the state of my love life, or to be more accurate, my lack of one. It's best to concentrate on what pays the bills, right?"

Nick narrowed his eyes at me; then, with a soft *murp*, began the tedious process of washing every inch of his sleek black fur. It was hard to tell just what sort of a statement that action was supposed to make. I stumbled into the bathroom, washed my face, brushed my teeth and ran a comb through my auburn locks. Then I walked over to my sister's bedroom door, knocked briskly, pushed the door open and stuck my head in.

"Rise and shine. You've got the morning shift at Hot Bread today. Be ready to open at six a.m."

Lacey lifted her blonde head from the pillow, stretched and yawned. "I still think Chantal rigged that coin toss," she grumbled, her eyes still closed. "I wanted to go to the location shoot the first day."

"Really?" I cocked my brow at her. "Then you should have gotten up an hour ago."

She opened one eye to stare at me. "You only just got up," she accused.

"Yes, but that was only because my alarm didn't go off."

The eye closed again. "Whatever."

I leaned against the doorjamb. "I've got the ingredients for today's special in the fridge and I made up the signs last night. Jeff Peckham will probably be right outside the door when you open, so make sure he gets his extra-bold decaf and raisin bagel. And Steve Hockensmith will probably be early today, too, and he likes—"

"Oh, gosh. Stop. Stop." Lacey sat up, rubbed her eyes and then tucked an errant curl behind one ear. "I get it, Nors. I know all your regulars and what they like. Everything will be fine."

"I know that," I said, but my tone lacked conviction and we both knew it.

"Look. Even you have to admit my work ethic's undergone a dramatic change the past few weeks. Finding out the guy you've always thought would be there won't be will do that to a gal."

I knew she was talking about Lance Reynolds. He was actually my old flame from our school days and was now the owner of Cruz's premier and only tavern, the Poker Face. Lance had always maintained a gigundo crush on my sister—up until a few months ago, when he'd developed an interest in another woman. Suffice it to say that although my sister was definitely not the type to want to settle down, she hadn't taken the news well. She seemed to be adjusting now, but quite honestly I was waiting for the other shoe to drop.

Lacey must have sensed my misgivings, because she shot me a mischievous grin. "Hey, I'm moving on, okay? I'll take a page from your book. You've got the right idea. The next man in my life is going to be a lovable fur ball, like Nick. Say, I've got an idea! Nick can help me wait on your customers."

"Good luck with that," I said and laughed. "Oh, and about Nick. He likes the yellowfin tuna, unless you've got some lobster salad special left over, then you can give him a small bowlful of that. Be sure you keep an eye on the doors, front and back. Nick's pretty quick, and he doesn't like being left behind on anything."

She put her fingers to her lips and simulated a yawn. "Nora, I know how Nick is. Don't worry, I'll keep an eye on him."

"Mmm. Like you kept an eye on Mr. Chips."

Lacey's face darkened. "For God's sake, I was fourteen."

"Yes, and Mrs. Crandall trusted you with her pedigreed poodle, which you left tied up in the yard in the middle of a rainstorm. If I hadn't happened along, that dog might have gotten pneumonia."

"Geez," she grumbled. "I screw up one time and you never let me forget."

I folded my arms across my chest and put what I hoped was a stern expression on my face. "Just make sure you keep an eye on Nick. I'm not kidding. He can slip out the door like that." I snapped my fingers.

"Yes, I've seen him in action. We'll keep him occupied so he won't be missing you and want to chase after you, okay?" She glanced at the clock, groaned, and then slapped her palm down on the snooze button. "Don't worry," she said, pulling the sheet up to her chin. "Everything will be fine. Hot Bread will be fine. Nick will be fine. I'd like to say you'll be fine, too, but since you don't seem to be able to make a decision . . ."

"Oh, please don't start in on my having to choose between Daniel and Samms again," I murmured. Between her and Chantal I was hard pressed to decide who bugged me the most about it.

My sister's expression was one of wide-eyed innocence. "How do you know that was the decision I was talking about?"

"Because it's the only one you and Chantal ever talk about."

Lacey shrugged. "Have fun today. Who knows, maybe your dream man is neither of them. Maybe you haven't met him yet. Maybe he's on that set." And with those words of wisdom, she buried her head in the pillow and motioned me with one hand to shut the door.

I pulled her door shut with a confidence I didn't really feel. Dependability was never one of my sister's strong suits, but right now I had no choice but to trust she'd get through the morning rush okay. Comforted by the fact Mollie would arrive around six thirty, I returned to my room to finish getting ready. Twenty minutes later I was dressed in jeans, T-shirt and white smock and went downstairs to Hot Bread to admit my BFF and co-caterer for the day, Chantal Gillard. She was dressed in an outfit similar to mine, except her smock was pink and she wore a scarf in pink, fuchsia and violet tones wound through her cap of black curls. She stepped through the door and threw her arms around me in a giant bear hug.

"*Chérie!* This is *très excitant,* no?"

Chantal loved affecting a French accent, maintaining the attitude that it lent her an air of sophistication. Her brother Remy also spoke with a slight accent, but his was the result of attending college in France. He'd originally started out wanting to be a chef but ended up switching his major many times before finally getting a degree in plant biology and returning to the U.S. to go into the family flower business with their parents. Said parents had since retired to France, and Remy now ran Poppies. "*Oui,*" I answered. "But it is also *une tâche difficile*–especially with my sister in charge today."

She choked back a laugh at my attempt at "putting on the French." "*Touché.* Do not worry, Lacey will be fine. She still thinks I rigged that coin toss, right?"

I chuckled. "Well, you did, didn't you?"

Chantal's blue eyes sparkled and she held up both hands. "Guilty. But she would have done the same, and she knows it."

I had to laugh. "You're probably right."

Nick sauntered into the back room and gave us a look of gold-eyed kitty innocence. His left ear was turned partly inside out.

"Nicky," Chantal squealed. She hurried over to the cat and reached down to give him a chuck under his chin. "You look a bit tired. Late night?"

"He was hanging with me while I finished prepping. Plus, I think he's a bit disappointed that Hank didn't call me back."

Chantal's eyebrow rose. "Hank Prince? Did you call him?" At my nod, she let out another squeal. "Ooh, *chérie,* are you involved in another mystery? Did someone hire you for an investigation?"

"Hardly." I explained about Nan's remark, my subsequent search on the Internet, and the article by Millicent Martin that hinted at Forbes's involvement. "I tried Googling this Millicent Martin," I said, "and I came up with nada. So then I called the paper she wrote the article for, and they told me she was a freelancer. She wrote that article, got her paycheck, and then they never heard from her again. I tried contacting a few other papers in the area, but they never heard of her."

Chantal frowned. "That is unusual, no?"

I shrugged. "Not really. Lots of freelance writers move around a lot."

"Did you ask Louis? He has a lot of contacts, perhaps he can find out something." Louis was my editor as *Noir*.

"I started to and then I remembered he's on vacation. He made a point of telling me the deadline for my next article because he'll be off the grid. No cell, no tablet, nothing. He and his brother went hunting in Alaska. He'll be gone until the end of the month."

"Alaska, huh? *Noir* must be doing pretty good." Chantal wrinkled her nose. "Somehow, though, I cannot picture Louis as a hunter."

"Neither can Louis." I laughed. "His brother is footing most of the bill. I think he just did it to get away. He told me he hasn't had a real vacation in five years."

"That is because he is so cheap his shoes squeak."

"Louis would say he's frugal," I pointed out. "Anyway, I'll ask Hank to look into it when he calls me back."

"Well, if foul play was involved in Harriman's death, the killer seems to have covered his or her tracks pretty nicely," Chantal observed. "I can see why you would be interested." She hesitated and then said, "Oh, did I mention to you that Remy knows Anton Forbes."

I almost dropped the tray of eggs Benedict I'd picked up. "What?"

She nodded. "Apparently they were in a class together in college." The corners of her lips turned downward. "Once he found out Anton Forbes was part of the show he tried to forbid me to help you, can you imagine that?" She fisted a hand on one slender hip. "My brother does not tell me what to do, where to go, or who to date. And I certainly cannot accuse him of being overprotective all these years. Besides, if he thinks I'm missing a chance to see Mark Emerson in person . . . he is *fou*—crazy!" She waved her other hand emphatically. "He even wanted to call you and try to convince you to turn down the job. To quote him, 'no good can come of anyone being around that man.'" She threw up both hands. "I told him if he tried to stop us I would move out and take my two businesses with me."

I laughed. That was no idle threat. Chantal's two businesses, Lady C Creations, a line of homemade jewelry and pet collars, and her New Age Shop, had really flourished lately. Even though my friend was all of five two and ninety pounds soaking wet, get her mad and she had all the fury of a sumo wrestler. "Either something really hinky went down between them, or maybe Remy's in a mood because business has been slow lately."

Chantal shrugged. "Who knows? It could be anything. I tried doing a reading on him, but all that kept coming up were the Six and Eight of Swords, and Judgement, all cards that indicate unresolved issues, and a period of regretful but necessary transition." She slid a sly glance my way. "I did a reading for you too, *chérie*. Aren't you curious as to what the cards had to say about your romantic dilemma?"

Uh-oh. I waved my hand casually and said, "Not really. We're going to be too busy to worry about anything except food, especially today. We've got to get the crew's breakfasts and lunches ready, and my regular customers apparently think I'll be able to get them little souvenirs or mementos too. I've already got Myra on my back for 'anything Mark Emerson touches,' and even Ollie left me a message about getting him Casey Martell's autograph."

"Hard to imagine Ollie with a crush on a soap star." Chantal chuckled. I was a little taken aback myself that the two-hundred-plus-pound Black PI had a crush on the petite actress who played a policewoman on the show. "At least he didn't ask me to try and set up a date for him, unlike someone else I know."

Chantal clapped a hand over her mouth. "Oh, no. Lacey?"

"I found this in my tote bag." I opened said bag, whipped out a sheet of pink notepaper and read: "'Nors—if you can get me Mark Emerson's autograph or Bailey Norris's, that would be SO cool.' So is in all caps and underlined—twice. 'Better yet, see if either one of them would like to join me and some of my friends for a drink tonight! My treat! Love, L.'" I rolled my eyes. "Geez."

"She is obviously kidding," Chantal said and giggled.

I eyed my friend. "Wanna bet?"

She held up her hand. "No. Although I confess I wouldn't mind having a drink with either of those men myself. The McLintock brothers make many feminine hearts swoon, mine included."

I gave her a look of mock horror. "Not you too? It must be me. I just don't get the attraction."

"Good. The last thing you need in your life right now is another man."

I made a face at her. "That's not what Lacey said. She thinks I'll find my dream man on the set."

Chantal laughed. "Well, who knows. You were not interested in the cards' outcome, but I will tell you anyway. They said if you do not make a decision soon, the universe will choose for you."

"It will, huh? I hope it chooses someone rich."

Chantal shook her head. "Go ahead, laugh. You know how accurate my readings can be."

I did know, and I had to admit it scared me sometimes. "I would much rather you did a reading on how successful this catering venture will be."

"You do not need a reading for that. You know they will love your food."

I held up crossed fingers. "Here's hoping they do, and that things go smoothly. Although I imagine we've nothing to worry about as long as a dead body doesn't turn up, and what are the odds of that happening?"

Shows how much I know.

Chapter Three

I t was a little after five a.m. when we pulled into Sweeney Park, the site for the first location shoot. *"Mon dieu,"* exclaimed Chantal as I rounded the bend leading to the large clearing. "It looks like every RV in the state of California is here."

I nodded. There were easily two dozen vans and trailers scattered around. As we pulled closer, I could see there were signs above each one. There were separate trailers for props and for wardrobe, hair and makeup, one marked *PR* and another marked *Production*. I parked next to a large tent with the sign *Commissary* above it. Before either Chantal or I could alight from the van, a tall man dressed all in black—leather jacket, jeans and T-shirt—emerged, hand outstretched.

"You must be Nora Charles," he said. I detected a slight French accent that sounded authentic, not affected like Chantal's. "I am so pleased to finally meet you. I am Anton Forbes, the director."

I hopped down from the van and clasped the proffered hand. "I'm happy to meet you, too, Mr. Forbes. I've heard a lot about you."

His dark eyes twinkled. "Good, I hope, yes? I have heard much about you, too. I read the reviews on your shop, and on the museum gala you catered. Very fine reviews, indeed." His gaze shifted to Chantal. "I take it this charming young lady is one of your helpers?"

"Yes, this is Chantal Gillard."

"Gillard, you said?" I thought I saw Forbes's expression darken slightly as he turned toward Chantal, but it was gone in an instant, replaced with a dazzling smile. *"Je suis enchanté de vous rencontrer. Parlez vouz français?"*

"Oui." Chantal gave him her full grille smile—and when Chantal turns on the charm, she really lights up. "It is such a pleasure to meet you, Mr. Forbes. I am a big fan of the show."

"Are you? That is so nice to hear." He lifted Chantal's hand to his lips and kissed its back. "A sincere pleasure, mademoiselle." He held her hand a few seconds longer than necessary before releasing it, and I noticed that my friend's cheeks had turned a bright rose shade.

I cleared my throat. "The schedule that was sent to me said you wanted breakfast served promptly at six." I gestured toward the back of the truck. "It will take us a bit to set up."

His eyebrow rose. "You did not receive a revised schedule?" As I shook my head he went on, "My apologies. We amended the breakfast start to six thirty, in order to accommodate those cast members who arrived late last night." His lips twitched into a grimace. "Inconvenient for my shooting schedule, but it works out better for yours, no?"

The flap of the tent opened and another man stepped out. He was shorter than Forbes, and his brown hair grew longish at the sides. There was a smattering of gray both at his temples and in his goatee. He pushed the wire-rimmed glasses he wore high up on his beak-shaped nose and stood there, hands on his hips, and cleared his throat loudly.

"Oh, excuse my manners," Forbes murmured. "This is our assistant director, Kenny Colgate. Kenny, this is Ms. Nora Charles, our caterer, and her assistant, Chantal Gillard."

Kenny made no move to shake either of our hands, he just stood there and inclined his head. "Hello." He glanced pointedly at his watch, then pinned me with a stare. "The actors and crew will be arriving soon, and there are several who suffer from various ailments. I assume you received the memo?"

"Absolutely. I've taken everyone's dietary restrictions into account, as you'll see from the breakfast selection, and the lunch as well."

His brows drew together in a deep frown. "My blood pressure gets very high. I hope you have low-sodium items on those menus."

I swallowed. Forbes might have a reputation for being difficult, but it was pretty clear that Kenny Colgate was a real PITA. "Absolutely."

Forbes cleared his throat. "Kenny, we have a few scenes to discuss. Let us leave the ladies to their work." He turned and gave us a low bow. "We had the kitchen stocked with all the items you requested. If you should need anything, my trailer is over there." He pointed to a massive Winnebago sitting on the crest of the hill, just beyond a thick patch of trees.

Kenny leaned over and whispered something to Forbes, who nodded. Forbes flashed me a quick smile. "We shall talk more later," he murmured, and then the two men walked off, leaving us alone.

"Well," I said as we watched them go. "That was certainly interesting."

"Yes, it was," my friend agreed. Her smooth brow creased in a frown. "Do you think I should mention Remy is my brother? I would not want to poke *l'ours*."

"No, sometimes it's best not to poke the bear," I agreed. I recalled the shadow that had crossed the director's face when I'd introduced Chantal. It was possible he remembered Remy and his memories of him were less than fond as well. "Come on, let's get these trays unloaded and get breakfast started."

I opened the double doors and pulled out the collapsible cart. Even though the *Days of Tomorrow* people were providing the food, I preferred to work with my own pots, pans, and spices. As I reached for the first tray, a soft *merow* sounded from the depths of the van. I almost dropped the tray and I swiveled my head toward Chantal. "Did you hear that?"

Chantal's arms were loaded with the bags containing condiments. "What, *chérie*? I did not hear anything."

"Merow."

I glanced over at Chantal again, and I could tell from the expression on her face that this time she'd heard it too. I craned my neck into the van's depths. "Is someone back there?" I asked in a stern tone. "And by someone I mean you, Nick."

Soft purring reached our ears.

"So much for Lacey's watchful eye." I raised my voice slightly. "You're busted, so you might as well come out, Nick."

A few seconds later a black and white face popped up from behind the mound of trays. "Merow."

I wagged my finger at him. "Don't give me that. You're not lonely. You just thought you might get an opportunity to snoop around."

The cat drew himself up straight, wrapped his tail around his forepaws, and glared at me. But was I intimidated? Not in the least. I cocked my brow and gave Nick my best "you are the animal, I am the human" stare, which he matched. We stood there for what must have been a full minute.

Ever try to outstare a cat? It's not easy.

Finally I threw up both hands. "It's too far of a ride to take you back now, so you'll have to stay here. And by here I mean inside this van. Got me?"

Nick blinked twice and then stretched out lengthwise on his back, paws in the air. I grabbed a small bowl from one of the utility bags and reached into one of the trays. I pulled out another bowl containing a fluffy scrambled egg and two sausage links. I spooned some into the bowl and shoved it forward on the van floor. "Look, Nick. Your favorite, scrambled eggs and sausage," I said. "Just be a good kitty and stay in here. I've got the windows cracked so you'll have air."

Silence. I said a quick prayer and shut the van door.

"How smart of you," Chantal said, "to prepare some food in case Nicky decided to join us."

I grinned. "Well, it's not the first time he's managed to sneak in where he doesn't belong."

Chantal cast a dubious eye toward the van. "Do you think he will stay put?" she asked.

"You've met Nick, right? Heck, no."

• • •

Chantal and I worked for the next half hour in comparative silence, intent on meeting our six thirty deadline. I had a wide range of dishes in mind to prepare, taking into account the various dietary restrictions listed on the sheet I'd been sent, and all were quick and fairly easy to prepare. For the people who were lactose-intolerant, I planned a turkey breakfast sausage patty, milk- and egg-free pancakes, cinnamon applesauce pancakes, and pumpkin oatmeal. Diabetics could eat most of the same things as the lactose-intolerant, plus I'd added in some extras: muffins filled with shredded carrot, pineapple and raisins, whole-wheat pancakes, and an herbed egg white and spinach omelet. I'd also ordered two different types of oatmeal plus a tray of low-sodium bacon and ham for those with high blood pressure. Then there were the old standbys: French toast, buttermilk pancakes, eggs Benedict, and an assortment of fruit and warm bagels and cream cheese toppings. We'd barely set everything out when the hungry hoard started to file in. The area was set up as self-serve, and I'd placed little placards in front of each tray describing the dish. I'd also put little stars around the dishes that were specifically for lactose-intolerant people and for those with high blood pressure or sugar problems. It probably wasn't even necessary for me to hang around once everything was set up, but I wanted to be certain that everything went off without a hitch, and also to be available in case there were any problems or questions. As it turned out, there were questions, lots of them. Chantal and I answered each one, and everyone seemed to be pleased with the food.

Midway through, Chantal gripped my arm so hard I thought she might pull it off. "Look," she whispered. "There's Mark Emerson!"

I glanced toward the tent entrance and saw a handsome blonde man with perfect features, wearing a cream-colored sweatshirt and tight jeans, picking up a tray. He walked up and down the line, and I could see that he was reading each of the placards. He paused before one of the lactose-intolerant entrées and I saw him take a stack of whole-wheat pancakes, followed by the herbed egg white omelet. As he stepped up to the coffee urn he extended his hand toward me, lips split in a dazzling smile.

"You're Nora Charles, right? The caterer?" At my nod, the smile widened. "I have to confess, I'm a bit of a foodie, and I saw the reviews on your shop, Hot Bread. Not many sandwich shops get five-star reviews."

"I've worked hard building up the shop's reputation, and branching out into catering," I said. "It's gratifying to know it's paying off."

He nodded. "We haven't done location shoots in a while. Budget constraints, but Forbes was pretty insistent on us doing this, and the producers seem to bend over backward where he's concerned. Forbes convinced the producers it would be cheaper in the long run to feed us on the premises so we could stick to his rigid shoot schedule." He let out a tight laugh and made a motion of brushing sweat off his brow. "He'll work us like dogs, make no mistake. At least there's a light at the end of the tunnel. We'll be well-fed."

I returned his smile; it was hard not to. "Thanks, Mr. Emerson."

He waved his hand. "None of that Mr. Emerson stuff. I'm Mark. We're all pretty informal here." He glanced over toward the tent entrance and saw Anton Forbes enter. "Most of us, anyway," he muttered under his breath.

"Great. And I'm Nora." I felt a tug on my apron and saw Chantal out of the corner of my eye. I reached over and gave her a little push forward. "Mr.—I mean Mark," I corrected hastily, "this is my assistant, Chantal Gillard. She's a big fan of the show."

Chantal beamed at the actor. "Oh, I am so happy to meet you. We are simply thrilled to be catering your shoot."

Mark beamed right back at her. "We're happy to have you here."

Chantal giggled like a schoolgirl. "If you get a chance you should really stop by Nora's shop. The special this week is the Preston McLintock sandwich."

His lips curved into a pleased smile. "Really? I'm honored. I'd love to stop by, but with this rigorous shoot schedule, I doubt I'll be able to."

"Oh, that's okay," Chantal said quickly. "We can make you up a sample, can't we, Nora?"

"Sure." A vision of Myra's eager face and Lacey's note rose in my mind's eye, and I looked over at the actor. "I'm sure you get asked for your autograph a lot," I said, "and I really hate to act like a starstruck fan . . ."

His lips screwed themselves into a pout. "You mean you aren't?"

He sounded so disappointed I immediately regretted my words. "Not exactly. I mean, of course I've seen your show, I just don't get a chance to watch it very often. The cable station here airs them either during the day or real late at night, and even though it's usually on the TV in the shop, it's usually a busy time and . . ."

Mark let out a loud laugh. "Oh, Ms. Charles, let me put you out of your misery. I'm only busting you."

I sucked in a breath. "You are?" I waved my hand carelessly. "Sure you are. I knew that."

He grinned and motioned to a man sitting at a nearby table. The man rose rather reluctantly and approached us. Mark clapped him on the back. "This is Ned Reilly. He's one of our PR gurus. Ned, we've got eight-by-tens in the PR trailer, right?"

The shorter man nodded. "Yes, of course. We always have a supply on hand."

"Well, get a dozen or so ready for me to sign for Ms. Charles, here." He slid me a glance. "How does ten at the PR trailer work for you?"

"Oh, f-fine," I stammered. "Thank you so much."

Mark waved his hand carelessly. "No need. It's all part of the job, right, Ned?"

I couldn't see Ned's eyes behind the dark glasses he wore, but I was almost certain he was rolling his eyes. His thin lips twitched upward in what he probably thought to be a smile. "Of course." Then with a curt nod in my direction, he shuffled back to his table and sat down, his back to us.

"Friendly fellow," Chantal murmured. "Aren't PR guys supposed to have peppy personalities?"

"Ned's sort of an acquired taste," Mark said. "He doesn't seem to fit the conventional mold, but then again he's only been on board a few weeks. Takes a bit of time to adjust to this crew." He turned his dazzling smile on me. "If you want to get a list together, I'll sign each photo right to the person who'll be getting it." He closed one eye in a wink. "Even though you didn't ask for one, I'll inscribe one of those photos to you, Ms. Charles, and you can hang it in your shop. It'll be good publicity for both of us."

Before I could thank him again, Forbes, his own tray loaded, came up behind Mark and tapped him on the shoulder. "Enough chitchat, Emerson," he growled. "You've got a couple of big scenes coming up this morning, with lots of heavy dialogue. I hope you've got your lines memorized. I don't want to go through another episode like last week."

Mark's face clouded and his lips slashed into a thin line. "My lines are always memorized, Anton. You know, it's not always the actor's fault when a scene doesn't come together."

"It is when you need six takes for two lines," shot back Forbes. "You just be ready to go at nine."

"Hold on," Mark said with a frown. "The schedule said my first take isn't until eleven."

"Well, the schedule's wrong."

Mark's jaw set and his blue eyes took on a steely glint. "This isn't the first time you've pulled this. You tell me to be there at a certain time and I end up standing around, waiting and waiting for hours."

Forbes offered the actor a frosty smile. "Great art sometimes takes a good deal of time, Emerson. I would have thought you'd know that."

"Great art? This? Then again, I suppose it is . . . coming from one whose greatest accomplishment in life was *Werewolf Zombies from Planet Hedron.*"

Forbes's eyes flashed, but the smile remained perfectly in place. "Don't knock it, Emerson. There's a big audience for werewolves and zombies. Triple what there are for nighttime soaps."

"Yeah? If that's the case, one has to wonder just why you gave all that up."

"I believe that it's called creative challenge. Taking a bunch of second-rate actors and molding them into a network hit."

"Second-rate?" Mark set his tray down and balled his hands into fists. "I'll show you who's second-rate."

"What's the problem here?"

Kenny Colgate, holding a tray loaded with eggs Benedict, sausage, fresh fruit and coffee, appeared behind us. For someone who'd been so insistent about my low-sodium entrées, it appeared he'd opted for none of them. Forbes turned and gave him a smile that seemed more like a self-satisfied smirk. "Kenny, I was just telling Emerson his first call is at nine, not eleven."

Colgate raised an eyebrow. "Actually, Anton, Mark is correct. He's not needed today until eleven, although he is scheduled for nine the rest of the week."

Forbes's expression darkened. "Who made that change? You?" He towered over the smaller man. "I was not consulted."

"I didn't think it was necessary," Colgate said calmly. "As assistant director, the schedule is in my bailiwick. I don't have to run every change I make past you."

"That is what you think," muttered Forbes.

"No," Colgate said calmly. "That is what I know. The producers were all in agreement on this, or don't you recall the last meeting we had before we left LA?"

"I recall it quite well. Apparently the one with the faulty memory is you. We discussed this yesterday before we left to come here. We agreed to get his scene over with early."

"At first. Then we spoke later that afternoon." Colgate made a tsking sound. "You're slipping, Anton. First thing to go is the memory."

A muscle twitched in Forbes's lower jaw. "There is nothing wrong with my memory," he rasped. "We don't need to have this discussion now."

"No? Then when do we?" Colgate gripped the sides of his own tray so hard the knuckles of his hands were bled white. "You know, Anton, you aren't in as tight as you think you are. I've heard the producers are becoming rather disenchanted with your prima donna ways and your demands. One day you will be out on your ass, and I will be in charge."

"Hah! You are a dreamer. That will happen over my dead body," Forbes said calmly.

"If I were you, I'd be careful what I wished for," Colgate muttered. He turned his back on Forbes and stalked over to an empty table near the left side of the tent. Forbes shot him a scathing look, turned on his heel, and headed for the exit. As he marched down the center aisle, I noticed two women, one a brunette, the other with hair just a shade darker than mine, staring at him. Forbes started to walk past, then made a sharp turn and veered back toward their table. He leaned over and whispered something to the redhead. She laughed lightly and nodded. Forbes gave her arm a quick squeeze, then turned on his heel and left the tent.

I stole a quick glance at Mark Emerson, who still stood beside me. He was watching them, his jaw clenched. Then he let out a long, slow breath, picked up his tray, and turned to me. "Well, well. Sorry, ladies, it appears the drama's starting early today. As you can see, it's not all on the set." He stole another quick glance toward where the two women sat and then he murmured, "Don't forget to stop by for those autographs."

I smiled at him. "I won't, and thanks."

Emerson walked up to the front of the tent to the table where the two women sat. He leaned over and said something to the redhead. She shook her head, rose, and hurried out of the tent. Mark stood looking after her for a minute, then slid onto the bench and started to eat.

Chantal nudged my elbow. "Talk about drama!" She inclined her head toward the table. "The girl who just left is Emily Van Horn, the girl who plays Mark's ex on the show. They were rumored to be a real-life item, but from that chilly reception, it would appear the gossip columnists are right." She lowered her voice to a half whisper. "They say that Mark and Emily have hit a rocky patch, because Emily has become involved with someone else."

I looked thoughtfully back at the table and at the same time I couldn't help but recall the angry words Mark Emerson had spoken. Was it possible the new man in Emily Van Horn's life was . . .

"Yep. I know what you're thinking, and you're right. Emily's mystery man is Anton Forbes," said a voice behind me.

Chapter Four

I whirled around and found myself staring into a pair of wide brown eyes behind massive tortoiseshell glasses. The tall, thin woman they belonged to had hair the color of Raggedy Anne's swept off her thin, pinched face and tied into a messy topknot held in place by a large jeweled barrette in the shape of a ladybug. She grinned broadly, displaying teeth that were nicotine-stained and slightly uneven. "Yep, what you're thinking is true," she said. "If you think the drama's all on-screen, you're wrong. The best drama is off-screen, right here on this set." The smile widened. "Pardon me, I should have introduced myself. Mamie Monroe, no relation to Marilyn. I work in wardrobe and makeup, or as it's more commonly known, gossip central."

"Really?" Chantal leaned forward, her lips parted. "So what I read in *Star* magazine last week is true. Mark and Emily are putting off getting engaged because she's fallen in love with another man? And it's Forbes?"

Mamie sniffed. "I don't know how much love has to do with it, but Emily has been seeing him." She closed one eye in a broad wink. "You didn't hear that from me, though. The management frowns upon gossip, even though that's what the entertainment industry thrives on. They're frantic to keep this entanglement a secret, although if you ask me, it won't be one much longer. The lovebirds are getting sloppy." She leaned in close to us and whispered, "Last week I happened to be passing Ms. Van Horn's dressing room and the door was open a crack. I dropped my pen and as I stooped to pick it up, I caught a glimpse through the crack. Let's just say a postage stamp wouldn't fit through the cinch she and Forbes were in."

I recalled the look on Mark Emerson's face when he'd seen Forbes and Emily together. "Poor Mark Emerson. Does he know?"

"If he doesn't at least suspect, he's a damn fool." She glanced at her watch and gave a little cry. "Oops, I've gotta get goin'. Still got a few outfits to repair. Forbes doesn't like it if the actors have to wait for anything. See ya around. Oh, and great food!"

With that, Mamie Monroe took her tray and practically flew out of the tent.

"Oh, my God." Chantal made a motion of fanning herself with her hand. "I had a feeling something was up between Emily and Mark. You can even see it in their scenes together. There was always this spark between them. In recent episodes, though, it's faded."

"They play a divorced couple, right? So wouldn't it be natural for any sort of spark between them to be missing?"

Chantal shook her head. "You do not understand, *chérie*. Even after they divorced, you could still catch a glimpse of the love between them. It hasn't been there for the past few weeks and now I know why. It's because the spark is gone between Emily and Mark."

"You don't know that for sure. Maybe Emily and Mark are better actors than you give them credit for." I paused as my cell phone buzzed. I pulled it out and saw Hank Prince's number. "I've got to take this. Can you hold down the fort?" At her nod, I stepped into the kitchen at the back of the tent. "Well, hello there, Mr. Prince. Long time no hear."

"Hello yourself. How's my favorite redhead doing? Flexing your PI muscle, now that you've got a license?"

It always warmed me to hear Hank's jovial tone. "Getting that license was more the fulfillment of a goal than anything else, aside from being fodder for some *Noir* articles. Right now I'm in the middle of catering breakfast and lunch for a tribe of hungry actors." I laughed, then sobered. "You got my message, right?"

"Yes, ma'am, I did. Why all the interest in Dean Harriman and Anton Forbes?"

"Anton Forbes is here in Cruz, on a location shoot, and Nan Webb clued me in on the Dean Harriman angle. You can chalk it up to my reporter's curiosity. I know the death was ruled accidental, but I confess it's got me wondering."

"I remember reading about it and thinking pretty much the same thing at the time," Hank admitted. "My contact down at the LAPD said Rizzoli, the detective in charge at the time, thought at first the gun had been switched, and his suspect numero uno was Forbes, mainly because he was the one who appeared to benefit the most from Harriman's death. Forbes had an ironclad alibi for the time between when the gun was locked in the drawer and when Harriman removed it, as did the other cast and crew members. The prop master verified that he'd forgotten to double-check the gun once the shooting had finished. The desk didn't appear to be tampered with, the only key was accounted for, there was no sign of anyone going near the desk on the security tape. Long story short, they had no choice but to close it as an accidental death, particularly in light of the fact the movie's producer made a big stink with the commissioner."

I reached up to rub at my forehead. "You do know keys can be duplicated and tapes tampered with?"

"Yep, but they found no evidence of anyone doing that. And before you ask, they looked at Forbes particularly hard, in light of his association with Harriman."

"Great." My gut was still telling me things weren't as neat and tidy as they appeared. "What do you know about some big reveal Harriman had planned? This Millicent Martin hinted at it in her article."

"Nothing, but I can check into that angle, if you want."

"Might as well. No chance you can get in touch with Rizzoli? Maybe he knows something?"

"Not unless I want to make a trip to Alaska. Guy retired last year and moved up there. According to my contact, he became so disenchanted with law enforcement he didn't leave any forwarding information, and he doesn't even have a phone."

"Great. Too bad Louis left his phone at home. He's vacationing with his brother in Alaska, and I bet if I asked him to try and track Rizzoli down he'd be all over it."

"No doubt," Hank said and chuckled. I could hear papers riffling in the background and then Hank added, "Well, I'd better get to work. You be careful, hear me? You and that cat of yours always seem to attract the bad guys, and I want you in one piece when I get out to California to visit you."

His last comment elicited an excited squeal from me. "You're coming out here? Really? When?"

He laughed. "As soon as people stop giving me work. Now, I've really got to go. See you, Nora."

By nine thirty the last remaining crew member had departed and Chantal and I began our cleanup and preparation for the lunch portion. For those who preferred a heartier lunch, there was beef Stroganoff, veggie burgers and regular burgers, and a good old mac and cheese, one version regular, another made with lactose-free cheese. For those with simpler tastes, I had a tray piled high with sandwiches I'd prepared last night: turkey and Swiss, ham and cheddar, roast beef, and tuna salad. As I headed toward the refrigerator for it I paused. Was that a scratching sound I heard, just outside the tent?

It wasn't repeated, so I went back to my work. I lifted a tray of sandwiches out of the fridge and out of the corner of my eye caught a flash of black and white.

"Merow."

I let out a gasp and looked down at Nick, who was squatted next to the cart, his tail waving like a metronome. He raised one paw and pointed toward the tray that held what was left of the scrambled eggs and sausage. "Merow."

"So much for you staying in the van," I grumbled. "I could swear I locked that door, but that doesn't matter, does it, Nick? You always find some way out."

Nick cocked his head and waved his paw imperiously at the tray. "Merow."

I bent over and hefted the cat into my arms, pretending to stagger as I did so. "You're not getting any more food right now. If anything, you should go on a diet."

Nick reared his head back and glared.

Chantal came into the kitchen, caught sight of Nick and me in a Mexican standoff and started laughing. "He is amazing," she said, and then sobered. "Do you think you should call Lacey, so she doesn't go crazy thinking she lost Nicky? Or do you want me to call her?"

"No, she's still mad at you. Besides, I greatly doubt that she even knows Nick is missing." I shifted Nick in my arms, pulled out my phone, checked for messages. "She hasn't called. No doubt she thinks Nick's asleep somewhere."

"But what if she does know?" Chantal's tone was reproachful. "You would play such a mean trick on your sister?"

"I sure would. I'd—hey, Nick! What the heck!"

Nick, tired of being held, squirmed in my arms. I tried to hold on to him, but for a twenty-plus-pound cat he's surprisingly wiry. He slid out of my grasp and down the aisle and out of the tent he went, a black and white streak of pure cattitude.

"Great," I muttered.

Chantal waved me toward the exit as Nick streaked out. "I can take care of the lunch trays," she said. "You go get Nicky and lock him in the van."

"Easier said than done," I grumbled as I grabbed a piece of sausage and hurried outside after the runaway. "Nick!" I called. "Where are you? Come on, Nick, I've got something for you. A nice piece of sausage." I turned in a circle, waving the sausage aloft and scanning the area, and then a distant *owrr* reached my ears. I paused in my turning and listened carefully. A second *owrr* came, from over by the thicket of shrubbery and trees off to my left. I trotted over, keeping one eye out for my furry escapee. "Nick?" I called again. Out of the corner of my eye I caught sight of Nick's black plume of a tail disappearing behind a large elm. I approached the tree cautiously, hoping for the element of surprise. I reached the tree and looked around.

No Nick.

I peered around the side of the tree and saw that we'd wandered further than I thought. I could make out the outline of a large trailer— no, make that a *gigundo* trailer—and realized with a start that it had to be Anton Forbes's. I stepped into the clearing and looked around. There sat Nick, next to a tree about six feet away. He hadn't seen me yet. Right now his attention was occupied grooming his white paws. I approached slowly, and when I was about two feet away Nick raised his head and looked straight at me. I took another step forward and extended my hand.

"Here, Nick," I crooned. "See this nice bit of sausage? You can have it, but you have to come and get it."

Nick cocked his head and looked first at the sausage in my hand and then at me, apparently debating his options. Finally he hopped off the stump and trotted over to where I stood and paused, his eyes fixed expectantly on the bit of meat in my hand.

"Good boy," I said. "But you can't have it until we go back to the commissary tent."

Nick's upper lip peeled back to reveal a generous amount of fang . . . and then he was off again, like a shot, through the trees, headed straight for . . . Forbes's trailer.

"Oh, heck," I muttered. I quickened my pace, straining to see his black and white form through the trees. A few minutes later I saw him, sitting on a large rock a few yards from the trailer. As I drew closer, I saw that it was a Winnebago. There were two sets of steps. One set was in the rear and the other, at the side near the front of the vehicle, had a wooden sign that read *Entrance–Ring bell*. I'd seen a few trailers like this one—they were more like massive upscale homes on wheels. No wonder Forbes had said it was like a mini-hotel. I turned my attention from Forbes's mobile palace back to my cat. Mindful of his hearing, I tried my best to be quiet, but his head still swiveled in my direction as I approached. I shook my finger at him. "Nick," I hissed, "Don't you dare move."

Surprisingly, he made no attempt to get away. He sat there, his tail wrapped around his forepaws, his head cocked as if he were listening. As I approached, I understood what had captured his attention.

Voices, and rather loud ones, emanated from the rear of Forbes's trailer.

I got up behind Nick and bent over, laid my hand on his back, and cast a wary eye at the trailer. "Come on, Nick," I whispered. "We shouldn't be here. I'll take you back to the van and give you some sausage."

Nick's eyes widened at the word *sausage*, but my attention was momentarily arrested as I caught a glimpse of red among the shrubbery that surrounded the rear of the trailer. A blonde head popped up, looked right, then left, then vanished again. I frowned and rubbed at my eyes, unsure of what I'd just seen. The person was a good distance away, and I'd had only a quick glance, but I could swear that had been Chantal's brother, Remy Gillard. And if it were . . . what the heck was he doing out here, sneaking around Forbes's trailer? Was this his way of reassuring himself that Chantal was nowhere near Forbes?

I frowned. That seemed a trifle obsessive, even for Remy. If that were him, there had to be some other explanation. But what could it be?

I reached again for Nick, but my hand stopped in midair as one of the voices within the trailer let out a loud shriek. A minute later the front trailer door was flung open and Emily Van Horn stumbled out and down the steps. She didn't glance in my direction, but I could tell from the set of her jaw that she seemed very upset. She turned her head and flung over her shoulder, "You're crazy. I can't do that. I won't."

Another slightly accented voice growled from the depths of the trailer. Forbes, no doubt. "Don't be a fool, Emily. You have no choice. Come back inside so we can finish talking."

"There is nothing to talk about. How could you ever think . . ." Emily wavered on the step for a moment. "I'd rather die first," she shot back. "Or better yet, I'd rather see *you* dead."

With that dramatic statement, Emily reached out and slammed the trailer door shut, then hurried off at a brisk pace back toward the spot where the film crew was setting up.

It didn't take a genius to see getting caught right here, right now, was so *not* a good idea. I reached down and grabbed Nick, who surprisingly offered no resistance this time, and was just about to head back to the commissary through the protecting shelter of trees when the trailer door banged open again and Forbes, his face pale, his expression dark, emerged. His startled gaze rested right on me and he raised his arm dramatically and pointed.

"Ms. Charles," he growled, "what are you doing here?"

Chapter Five

For a moment I was rendered speechless, and then I squeaked out, "Nothing. I was looking for Nick."

His brows drew together and he shot me a puzzled look. "Nick?"

"Yes. My cat." I shifted Nick in my arms. Oddly enough, he didn't squirm this time, just lay there, complacent, a benign kitty expression on his furry face.

Forbes's tense expression relaxed a bit. "You brought your cat to a location shoot?"

"Yes. No. I mean, it wasn't intentional," I stammered. "He snuck into the van this morning and got out somehow. I was just trying to catch him."

Forbes came all the way down the steps and walked over to where Nick and I stood. Nick looked up at the director and blinked his big golden eyes. Much to my surprise, Anton Forbes let out a laugh, then reached out and gave Nick a chuck under his chin. "I like cats," the director admitted. "My family had several cats. Two of 'em were tuxedos, just like your Nick here. Most people don't like black cats, and tuxes are thought to be in that family by default, but a finer pet I've never had. I've always thought cats to be amazingly intelligent animals, tuxes especially so."

Nick's lips tipped up. "Merow."

I scratched at my head. Forbes a cat lover? Who would have guessed?

"He seems quite the adventurous type. Curious, you know, like the old saying," Forbes murmured, his thick brows drawing together.

"I've been known to be overly curious myself at times," I admitted. "A leftover trait from my former career."

"Oh? You weren't always a caterer?"

"No. I was a true crime reporter in Chicago. I took over Hot Bread after my mother passed away."

"A crime reporter?" Forbes stroked at his chin. "I'd certainly never have guessed that about you. Most of the reporters I've met aren't half as attractive, or intelligent, for that matter. Nick, here, has most of them beat." He reached up to scratch behind his ear as he added, "Forgive my attitude, Ms. Charles. I tend to be a bit paranoid when it comes to the press. A few years ago a zealous reporter did a hatchet job on me. I'm still trying to refute much of what was written. The person who wrote the article pulled a disappearing act, but, who knows? Things have a way of evening out. Perhaps soon I'll finally have my chance at vindication. Anyway, how did we get on that depressing subject?" His expression softened a bit as he reached out to give Nick another chuck under his chin. "Your little fellow here seems to have a good temperament. Think he'd like to be on the show?"

I was so startled by this abrupt change in topic I almost dropped Nick. "What do you mean, on the show? You mean this show? *All the Days of Tomorrow?*"

"Since I'm not involved with another project at this time, the answer would be yes," he said and laughed. "We have a scene coming up later this afternoon where Rachel's beloved pet, her cat Spunky, sits on her lap and offers her comfort after an argument with Preston. We were going to use a cat from the local shelter, but I think Nick here would be perfect for the role."

Nick's head swiveled toward me, and there was no mistaking the gleam in those golden eyes. "Er-Ow!"

"Your cat certainly seems to want to," Forbes coaxed. As I hesitated, he added, "Oh, and I wouldn't expect him to offer his services without remuneration. We'll pay him scale. Two hundred fifty a day."

I almost dropped Nick again. "Two hundred fifty? Dollars?"

Forbes barked out a laugh. "Unless Nick here prefers catnip? I anticipate needing him not more than two, three days at the most. I can make three days a guaranteed minimum, if you like?" He glanced at his watch. "If you meet me at the PR tent in about an hour, I can have a contract drawn up before lunch. What do you say?"

Nick reached up to stroke my cheek with one velvet paw. The ham. I looked over at Forbes. Seven hundred and fifty dollars would be a good sum I could put toward that commercial smoothie machine.

"Okay, fine, he'll do it."

• • •

"Woo-hoo, imagine that. You were always special, Nicky, but now you're going to be a celebrity! What do you think about that?"

Chantal leaned over to rub Nick's belly. True to his word, when I stopped by the PR trailer to pick up the photographs Mark had signed, Forbes had Nick's contract all ready. It specified a minimum three-day shoot at two hundred fifty dollars per day. Forbes had even had a clause added in that specified Nick was to have the "meals of his choice" for the duration of his appearance.

"Forbes was super accommodating with the terms, I must say," I said. "If I didn't know better I'd think he was trying to get on my good side."

Chantal managed to tear her gaze away from her signed photograph of Mark to grin at me. "Or he just recognizes feline talent."

"Please don't make his head any bigger than it is right now," I begged my friend. "Once I signed, Forbes took me onto the set and made the announcement, and you should have seen them all come up to ooh and ah over him. Soon his head will be too big to fit through Hot Bread's front door."

"No offense," Chantal chuckled, "but his head has always been pretty big. Like the rest of him."

I looked at Nick. No argument there.

Chantal ran her fingers down Nick's plump white belly, and he closed both eyes and let out a loud purr. I rolled my eyes. "Come back down to earth, Nick. You're going to be in one scene. I hardly think that qualifies you for superstardom."

Chantal laughed. "Around here it does. Myra will be wanting his autograph next. Or is it *paw*-tograph?"

Nick rolled back onto his stomach, stood up, and held out his front paw.

"Oh, look at him. He's a natural. Our Nicky loves the limelight," cooed Chantal. "Remember when he did that video to promote my line of cat collars? He was full of himself for a week. Ooh, wait!" She jumped up, her eyes bright. "Maybe he can wear one of my collars in his scene! I could call Remy, have him drop one off, what do you think?"

Chantal had her back to Nick, so she didn't see him bare his teeth.

"Maybe. We'll see." Mention of Chantal's brother reminded me of what I'd seen earlier. "Speaking of Remy, did your brother happen to mention what he was doing today?"

"He had some morning deliveries, and then he was going to be at the shop the rest of the day. Why?"

"When I went looking for Nick, I thought I saw him hiding in the shrubbery, behind Forbes's trailer."

Chantal's eyes popped, and then she started to laugh. "Oh, Nora. What a kidder you are."

I compressed my lips into a thin line. "I'm not kidding, Chantal. I wish I were. If that wasn't Remy I saw, it was some blonde guy who looks a lot like him."

The smile faded, replaced by a slightly worried expression. "You must be mistaken, chérie. That does not sound like something Remy would do. He is not the type to slink around in bushes. And he most certainly would not go anywhere near that set."

"True, but you said he was very upset when he learned about Forbes, and he tried to talk you out of coming with me. You said he even wanted to talk me out of taking the job. It definitely sounds to me like there's some unresolved issues there."

Chantal reached into her pocket and whipped out her cell phone. "There is one way to find out. I will call my brother and find out where he is. And it had better be either in the delivery truck or in the shop," she added grimly.

She dialed the number and a few minutes later I heard her say, "Remy! Où êtes-vous? She listened a minute and then said, "Bien. No, nothing is wrong. I just wondered how your day was going." Another moment and then, *"Non.* Everything is fine here. We will not have this conversation again." She hung up and tossed me a sheepish grin. "He just got back from making some deliveries. He asked if Forbes had made a fool out of himself yet, and if you'd come to your senses and quit."

Chantal looked relieved, so I decided not to press the issue, which was probably a good decision, since Mamie Monroe barreled into the tent about five minutes later. She ambled over to us and said, "Just thought I should tell you it looks like they're going to finish that love scene early, which means they'll probably be back here looking for food in, oh, about forty minutes or so. Think you can have something ready before twelve?"

I grinned at her. "We're nothing if not flexible, right, Chantal?"

My friend grinned also. *"Absolument!"*

Mamie walked over to me and said in a confidential tone, "I hear Forbes took a shine to your cat."

"Yes, he hired Nick to play a scene with Ardis Malone. I believe he wanted to try and shoot it today."

Mamie consulted a sheet of paper on the clipboard she carried. "Yep, he's got it down for the last one, six thirty."

"So late?" I cried. Mamie gave me a sharp look and I sighed. "Sorry. I wasn't figuring on that. I thought it would be earlier, like right after lunch, maybe."

"The schedule's booked from right after lunch up to your cat's shoot." She made a little face. "You can ask Forbes to change it, but take it from me, His Highness doesn't adapt to change too easily, unless he's the one making it. But if it's a real problem, you can ask."

I gave my head a quick shake. "No, not at all. Actually, it'll give me time to go home, get changed, and decompress a bit. I still can't quite wrap my head around the fact my cat is going to be on television."

Mamie inclined her head toward Nick, who was sitting up by Chantal, licking his coat into an ebony sheen. "What about him?"

"Oh, Nick's head is fully wrapped around the situation," I said and laughed. "Maybe a bit too much so."

Mamie grinned. "He's a cute cat, all right. Got a personality. It's easy to see why Forbes liked him." She glanced at her watch and gave a little cry. "I'd best get going. I've got an alteration to make on Emily Van Horn's dress for this afternoon's scene, and I don't want to miss lunch. Trust me, your food is the highlight of everyone's day." With a broad wink and a wave, she sauntered out of the tent.

Chantal let out a low chuckle. "That one is a real piece of work. But I bet if you really want to get some inside gossip, she's your gal."

"She does seem to have her finger right on the pulse of everything going on here," I agreed. "I wonder just how much she knows about Forbes?"

Kenny Colgate and Ardis Malone sauntered in, talking in low tones. Ardis looked up and saw me and immediately detached herself from Colgate and walked right over. "You're Nora Charles," she said, extending a perfectly manicured hand. "I'm Ardis Malone." Up close, I could see that she was somewhere in her twenties, and much prettier in person than on-screen. There was a decided coolness both in her gaze and her tone as she looked at me. "I understand you are the owner of my new costar. Nick, right?"

Upon hearing his name, Nick stopped licking his coat. His gaze settled on Ardis, and his tail went straight up. He got up and padded over to her, twining his furry body around her ankles. Ardis's whole body went rigid. She glanced quickly at me. "He's friendly, right? No biting?"

"Not unless there's a gun pointed at my head. Bad joke," I added quickly when I saw her startled expression.

"For goodness sakes, Ardis, he's a cat, not a panther," hissed Kenny. "Just give him a pat on the head."

Ardis reached down and tentatively stroked Nick's head. The big ham nudged his head into her hand, then started to purr like a race car. Ardis gave him a quick scratch behind his ear and then pulled her hand away as if she'd been stung. Nick swiveled his head around to look at her, his eyes widening as if to say, *What's your problem, human?*

Kenny Colgate stepped forward and took Ardis's arm. "Well, we'll get out of your way now, Ms. Charles," he said. "Ardis just wanted to get acquainted with her new costar. We know you've got to start getting lunch ready."

"It was nice to meet you, Ms. Malone," I said. Ardis mumbled something that sounded like "Thanks" and then she and Colgate hurried out of the tent. I looked at Nick. "So? What do you think of her?"

Nick rolled over on his back, exposing his privates and his white belly, and let out a large yawn.

I couldn't help but laugh. "Yep, Nick, that just about says it all."

I stepped inside the kitchen and saw Chantal frowning at the trays. "What's the matter?"

"We are short a sandwich tray. One of the ham and Swiss is missing."

I did a quick count and saw my friend was right. "I hope it's still in the van," I murmured. I snatched up the keys and decided that the rear flap of the tent was nearer to where I'd parked. As I exited, I caught sight of Ardis Malone and Kenny Colgate standing a bit to the left. They seemed to be deep in earnest conversation. I didn't mean to eavesdrop, but their voices carried clearly to where I stood.

"It's not fair," Ardis was saying. "He mentioned the gazebo as a possibility for filming, yet he knows it gets chilly out here when the sun goes down, and how susceptible I am to catching a cold. Does he care? Hell, no." She let out a loud sneeze. "See! It's starting already!"

Kenny Colgate laughed mirthlessly. "Maybe you're just having a delayed reaction to touching that cat. Anyway, you still haven't learned, have you? Anton Forbes cares about no one but himself. He'll stop at nothing to get whatever he wants, trust me."

"Oh, he's ruthless all right. Anyone can see it, except Emily. I can't believe she fell for his phony charm. Why, if I had a hunk like Mark Emerson crazy over me, I wouldn't look anywhere else."

"Don't blame her too much. Forbes is a master at getting what he wants. The man's a menace. Then again, he is an expert at getting away with murder. Literally."

Ardis sniffed. "One day he'll push someone too far. It'll be no loss, I can tell you that. Ah-*choo!*" She sneezed again. "Drat! Do you think I might be allergic to cats?"

Their voices faded as they walked away. I stood for a moment, looking after them. One thing was pretty clear. There were an awful lot of people on this set who wouldn't mind seeing something fatal happen to Forbes.

Chapter Six

It was a little after two thirty when I pulled the van into the garage. As Chantal and I alighted the rear shop door opened and Lacey hurried out. "Where is he?" she gushed. "Where's our little celebrity?"

I'd phoned her once the lunch rush had quieted down to check in and to tell her the news about Nick. As I'd thought, she'd had absolutely no clue Nick wasn't snoozing peacefully somewhere on the Hot Bread premises.

Nick hopped out of the van and padded toward Lacey. She scooped him up and gave him a hug, planting a kiss on the white streak behind his ear. "I can't believe it. Our Nick is going to do a scene with Ardis Malone." She gave me a hopeful glance. "Is Mark Emerson going to be in it too?"

"No, unfortunately," Chantal said. "It's just Ardis and Nick."

"I'm not sure I'm talking to you yet," Lacey informed Chantal with a toss of her head. "Not after the stunt you pulled."

Chantal widened her eyes. "What? Me?"

"Yes, you. You cheated."

"And you've already admitted you wished you had thought of it first." I looked pointedly at my sister, who still clutched Nick in her arms. "You might put him down and give us a hand with these trays. And I'll need help with the setup for tomorrow, since I have to take Nick back to film his scene later."

Lacey set Nick down and said hopefully, "You know, Nors, if you're busy with all the food stuff, I could run Nick to his taping for you."

I cut her an eye roll. "Thanks but no thanks. I'm not trusting you alone with Nick. You didn't even know he was missing today."

Lacey sniffed. "Oh, come on, Nors. I would have noticed. Eventually." Her tone turned wheedling. "Give me a chance to make it up to you."

"And, of course, this offer has nothing to do with the fact that you're dying to see the TV crew in action, right?"

Her cheeks colored. "Well, maybe a little bit."

I shook my head. "I appreciate the offer, I do, but I'm not sure where they're going to be filming the scene. Mamie Monroe said Forbes would let me know. I hope I get more than twenty minutes' notice."

"Er-owl!" Nick glanced up from grooming himself. Obviously he agreed with that statement.

We spent the next several minutes carrying in pots and trays from the van. When the last one had been unloaded my sister turned to me. "Did you get to see Mark Emerson? Is he as dreamy off screen as he is on?"

"Yes and yes," Chantal said. She dipped her hand into her tote bag and whipped out the eight-by-ten. "He signed a photograph for me."

I saw my sister's eyebrow start to twitch and her lower lip start to quiver, and before she could respond, I grabbed my tote bag and thrust it into her hands. "Before you start whining, there's one for you in there, too."

Her face brightened immediately. "Oh, cool!" She took the tote over to the counter and started rummaging through it. "Did you see Emily Van Horn? Could you tell if the rumors are true? Are they having trouble?"

Chantal opened her mouth to answer, but I shook my head quickly and put a finger to my lips. Turning to my sister I said, "We really didn't have time for chit-chat. We were, um, you know, kinda busy serving food."

"You are such a killjoy, sis." She pounced on the photo inscribed to her and pretended to swoon. "I'm gonna have to get a real nice frame for this. Larson's Department Store is having a big sale tomorrow."

I blessed her with my sternest look. "Sorry, but you'll be unavailable. You do realize that it's your turn to go with me tomorrow, right? Unless, of course, you'd rather go to the sale than the shoot?"

"Ooh, you are such a meanie!" Lacey stuck her tongue out at me. "You know I want to go to the shoot."

"Good. Then you won't mind helping get the food ready."

"We're going to cook now?" My sister's lower lip thrust forward in a pout. "I thought you prepared the food on the premises?"

"I prepare the hot food there. The sandwiches I make ahead of time. They seemed to go over real well, too. I think people enjoyed them more than the entrées."

"Of course they did. You're the Sandwich Queen of Cruz, dontcha know?" Lacey ducked as I mimed throwing something at her. "What kind of sandwiches are we doing?"

"I was thinking of subs. Those always go over well with large groups. I've got lots of turkey, ham and cheese, and I bought extra sopressata and capocollo." I moved over toward the bread box as I spoke. "We can put it together first thing in the morning, and add the seasonings before we serve. Oh, darn." I slammed down the lid on the box. "No more six-inch rolls! How did that happen?" I slid my glance toward my sister. "You did put the order in at Reed's, right?"

She hung her head. "Don't get mad. I forgot. But they're still open," she said quickly. "I'll just call them now."

"See if they have any twenty-four-inch breads," I called after her. "A giant sub might be a nice idea, I think."

As my sister leapt to the phone, I gave Chantal a nudge. "She hasn't moved this fast since she started working here. It's amazing what a dose of show business can do to a person."

Chantal chuckled. "My, my. How much do you want to bet she will be telling everyone tomorrow that the sub was her idea, and that she made it."

"Which won't be too far off from the truth, as I fully intend to have her make it," I said.

Lacey covered the receiver with her hand and said, "They have the twenty-four-inch bread. Someone needs to pick it up right away, though."

Chantal held out her hand. "I will go. I want to check up on Remy, and the bakery is near my friend Sylvie's shop, and I promised her I'd stop by and give her the scoop on the *Days of Tomorrow* stars." Sylvie was another friend of Chantal's who also possessed a certain amount of psychic ability. Sylvie was extremely talented with knitting, and ran a small shop at the other end of town where she sold her throws and scarves, and for a small fee also told fortunes.

"Thanks." I handed her the van keys and she gave me a brisk wave as she headed out. I turned to my sister. "We can start getting the ingredients ready for the subs. The cold cuts need to be sliced, and we'll need oil and vinegar, some onions need to be chopped up, tomatoes, lettuce . . ."

"Sure." Lacey walked over to the fridge, knelt down and gave Nick's behind a swift pat. "Sorry, Mr. Star. You'll have to move."

Nick rose, stretched, and waddled over to his other favorite spot next to the table. He laid down, placed his head on his forepaws, and closed both eyes. A few seconds later we heard soft snoring.

"Oh, yes, Nick, rest up for later. Sitting in a beautiful actress's lap can be very tiring." I took the tomatoes Lacey handed me over to the sink and started to wash them off. "Although how tired can you get? All you have to do is look, now how did Forbes put it? Oh, yeah. Catly."

"Well, since he's a cat, Nick ought to be able to manage that," Lacey said and chuckled. She brought lettuce and onions over to the counter and set them on the chopping board. As she reached for a knife she asked, "So, why did Chantal say she wanted to check up on Remy?"

"Apparently Remy went to school with the director, Anton Forbes, and there's bad blood, at least on Remy's part. He didn't want either of us to go to the shoot today."

"Wow. Remy's usually so cool about things. I wonder what happened between them to make him so adamant?" She gave a wise nod. "I'll bet it's got something to do with a woman. They say Forbes is quite the ladies' man."

"He certainly was turning on the charm to us."

"Sure, you're feeding him," Lacey said. "He's got a rep, though. If you believe all the gossip magazines, he's not well-liked at all."

I thought of all the people who'd made a comment on Forbes today and had to agree. I picked up a tomato and started to slice it, glancing casually out the large picture window as I did so. Suddenly I froze. "What's he doing out there?" I muttered.

"Who?" Lacey peered over my shoulder. Leroy Samms, his hands jammed in his pants pockets, was pacing back and forth in front of Hot Bread. He stopped, looked at his watch, then jammed his hands back in his pockets and resumed pacing. "Looks like he's waiting for someone. Oh, he's coming inside."

No sooner had Lacey uttered those words than the bell above my shop door tinkled and the man himself entered. I tried not to notice how the khaki pants he wore seemed molded to his muscular legs, or how his muscles rippled beneath his crisp white shirt. He made his way over to the counter and leaned both elbows on it.

Lacey turned to him with a super-bright, super-wide smile. "Hey there, Special Agent Samms. What brings you here so late in the day?" Her gaze swept him up and down, and a mischievous grin ticked the corners of her lips. "You're cleaned up nice. Going somewhere special?"

I took the knife and made a deep incision into the tomato.

My sister let out a squeal. "You've even shined your shoes! You must have a hot date!"

Samms cleared his throat and called over to me, "Hey, Nora. How did it go at the location shoot today?"

I paused in my dissection of the tomato and turned my face slightly toward him. "It went fine," I said in a tight voice. "Everyone seemed to like the food."

"Of course they did," he said easily. "Because you're an excellent cook."

I swatted at my ear. "Did I hear right? Was that an actual compliment?"

"I always compliment you, when you earn it." He let out a soft chuckle. "I take it there were no set-crashing incidents? Dale had extra officers guarding the park's perimeter but you never know."

"None as far as I know. Of course, Chantal and I were pretty busy in the kitchen, but I'm sure if any fans had crashed onto the shoot, we'd have heard something, especially from Forbes."

He reached up to flick an errant inky curl off his forehead. "Yeah, how'd you like that guy? I hear he's a real handful."

"He likes cats," Lacey blurted out. "Or at least he liked Nick. Nick's going to be on the show."

Samms's eyes widened a bit and he glanced over at where Nick lay. "Why? Are they filming a murder scene? Do they need someone to sniff out the body?"

I whirled, still brandishing the knife. "No, smarty. Nick's going to be in a scene with Ardis Malone, playing her cat Spunky, or maybe it's Sparky, I don't remember. Anyway, they're supposed to film it later today."

"Well, Ardis Malone, eh?" He leaned over the counter and grinned at Nick. "I hope she's wearing more than a towel when you sit in her lap. You're certainly coming up in the world, buddy."

Nick lifted his head and let out a sharp merow.

I glanced over at Samms. "You watch the show?"

His teeth flashed white against his tanned skin. "Hell, no. But my sister loves it, and when she heard they were coming here to Cruz to film she gave me a crash course, you know, in case I ran into any of them. Let's just say she wouldn't be averse to my getting an autograph or two for her."

I frowned. "I didn't know you had a sister."

There was an odd gleam in his eyes as he leaned a bit further across the counter. "There's a lot you don't know about me, Nora Charles."

The room grew silent as we both stared into each other's eyes for what seemed like an eternity. The spell was broken as my sister cleared her throat loudly and announced, "Well, I have to give Aunt Prudence a call. She and Irene will be thrilled about the photographs. Nice to see you again, Lee. I'll be back in a bit to help finish the subs, Nora." My sister gave a jaunty wave and clattered up the stairs to our apartment, photos clutched to her bosom. Samms watched her go, shaking his head, then eased one hip against the counter and switched his gaze to me. "Okay, now that your sister's gone, what did you really think of

Anton Forbes?"

I pulled another onion onto the chopping board. "He's definitely an acquired taste. I can see why people would refer to him as a prima donna." I slid him a glance out of the corner of my eye. "You certainly seem very interested in what went on there today."

"Do I?" He lifted his shoulders in a casual shrug. "I'm just making conversation."

"Uh-huh. Are you sure that's all it is? I thought perhaps you'd heard all the rumors about Forbes and the mysterious circumstances surrounding his mentor's death."

He chuckled. "I might have heard something about that. Dean Harriman's death appears to be one of those great unsolved Hollywood mysteries, right up there with George Reeves and Marilyn Monroe."

I set down my knife. "I can understand why it piques my interest, but you? You're an FBI guy now. I wouldn't think it's the type of thing that would interest you anymore."

"I was Homicide first, remember? Murder always interests me, same as it does you. You're thinking of looking into that case, aren't you?" When I didn't answer, he pinned me with one of what I called his "cop face" stares. "I knew it. You just can't resist snooping, can you?"

"You needn't sound so disapproving," I replied. "At least Daniel knew enough to refrain from making remarks about my so-called snooping."

"Probably because he realized he was beating a dead horse. I don't give up that easily." He jammed his hands into his pockets. "Have you heard from Daniel?"

I shook my head. "No. Have you?"

"Briefly. Fleming called him on a case of his, and I happened to answer the phone. We only talked for a few minutes."

I set my jaw. "It was a few minutes longer than I've talked to him."

"Come on, don't be like that, Nora. You know if he could have squeezed in a call to you, he would have." He paused and then added, "He asked me to look out for you while he's gone."

The knife I was holding clattered to the counter. I turned around, hands on hips. "What?"

He took a step back and held up his hands. "Now, don't get mad."

"Mad? What makes you think I'm mad?" I saw him glance at my hands, balled into fists at my sides, and I bit out, "What I am is insulted. I'm not a child, after all. You can tell Daniel I can look out for myself just fine, I don't need a babysitter. Heck, I'll tell him myself, if he ever finds the time to call me, that is."

Samms scratched at the back of his neck. "That might be a while. This is a rough mission he's on, Nora. But if anyone can pull it off, it's him." He coughed lightly and then added, "He cares about you, Nora. He wants the best for you. And what he doesn't need is to be distracted on this mission, worrying about you."

I hesitated. This was my opportunity to tell Samms that Daniel had told me the same thing before he'd gotten on that plane to London, that he cared about me too much to want to stand in my way or hold me back. He had, in essence, given me his blessing to date other men while he was away. This was my opportunity to ask Samms out for coffee, or dinner, or a drink at the Poker Face, or . . . something.

It was our opportunity to maybe find out where things might have gone between us . . . and then I remembered seeing him with Dale Anderson, her hand possessively on his arm. Who was I kidding? I looked at him and forced myself to nod. "I know he does. I care about him too, and I certainly wouldn't want to contribute to his getting into danger."

Another moment of awkward silence, broken as Samms's cell phone buzzed. His hand dipped into his pocket and he pulled it out and glanced at the screen. "I've got to get going." His gaze bored into mine. "Chin up, okay, Nora? Watch the snooping. And for goodness sakes, don't get involved with Forbes."

With a two-fingered salute, he was gone. I looked down at Nick and prodded his rotund bottom with the toe of my shoe. "C'mon, buddy. We've a lot to get done before you make your television debut. We've got no time to sit here and wonder about people who are best left alone."

Nick struggled to a sitting position. "Er-owl," he said, and he raised one paw and pointed toward the window. I looked in that direction. Samms was standing outside on the corner, his arms wrapped around a female wearing a black dress in a tight clinch. She lifted her head and I saw it was none other than Dale Anderson. Well, if I'd ever needed proof they were in a relationship, this cinched it. My cell phone buzzed just then, and I dragged my eyes away from the tableaux on the street and reached for it. "Nora Charles."

"Ms. Charles. Anton Forbes." He didn't wait for me to answer, just went on. "I've had to make a scheduling adjustment. We'll need to shoot Nick's scene a bit earlier than originally planned."

"That's fine," I said. Actually I was a bit relieved. The earlier I got done with Nick's close-up, the sooner I could get back and finish what needed to be done for tomorrow's food service. I glanced out the window and noticed that Samms and Dale had gone "When do you need him?"

"It's three thirty now. Can—pardon me one second." He put his hand over the receiver and I could hear some sort of muffled conversation in the background, and then Forbes was back on the line. "Sorry. Can you get here by quarter to five?"

"It shouldn't be a problem."

"Good. I'll see you then."

"Wait, where is here?" I bit my lip in frustration at the sound of dead air. So now I had a summons to appear, but no location. Great. A good thing I had Forbes's number stored in my phone directory, just in case of a problem. I found it and hit Dial, then groaned aloud as it continued to ring. I ended the call, waited a few minutes, then tried again. Still nothing.

Nick walked over, swishing his tail impatiently. "Hang tight. I've got another number," I told him. I'd also been given a general information number when I'd accepted the catering gig. I dialed that and let it ring fifteen times before I finally disconnected. I ran my hand through my hair, and then my expression brightened as I remembered what I'd overheard Ardis Malone tell Colgate earlier. "The gazebo," I said to Nick. "Ardis said Forbes wanted to film at the gazebo. He might have changed his mind, but it's worth a shot, right? If no one's there, then we'll just head over to Sweeney Park."

Nick waved his plumelike tail. "Er-owl?"

"Yeah, well, he'd better not get uppity. It's his own fault, after all, for hanging up so fast." I grinned at him. "Come on, buddy. You've got to get ready. It's time for your close-up and we can't be late."

• • •

The gazebo was located about a mile away from where the *All the Days of Tomorrow* crew had set up shop. I knew a back road that led to it along the river and I decided to take that. The water shimmered in the late afternoon sun, which glinted off three sailboats that bobbed in the water. The gazebo was on a little hill that overlooked the river, surrounded on both sides by dense shrubbery. It was definitely a secluded area, but it was also very beautiful, particularly in the fall with all the leaves changing colors. I parked my SUV near the flight of steps that led upward into the gazebo and looked around. Oddly, the parking lot was empty. There wasn't a sign of a film crew, or any actors, or Forbes himself for that matter.

"Hello?" I called out. "Anyone here? Mr. Forbes?"

Silence.

I looked down at Nick. "Well, strike one. It doesn't look as if this is where they plan to film your big scene."

Nick started to turn away, then stopped and cocked his head. His ears flicked forward, then flattened against his skull. Not a good sign. Cats have extremely sensitive hearing. They can hear sounds that humans can't. My heart did a little flip-flop.

"What is it?" I cried. "What do you hear, Nick?"

With a low growl, he wiggled his bottom and then launched himself forward and up the steps.

"Nick, wait."

I took the stairs after him two at a time, thankful that I'd decided to wear my good sneakers. Nick was a black and white streak, a blur before me. As I reached the top step, my foot stumbled as it came in contact with something slick. My hand instinctively reached out to grasp the railing; I looked down and saw a splotch of red.

No. It couldn't be. Blood?

My hand slid off the railing and my foot slipped again, sending me forward. Instinctively I put out my hands to break my fall and a gasp left my throat as, instead of the wood I expected to touch, I felt something else instead. Something soft and springy. Something barely warm.

I pushed myself upward and struggled to my feet. Nick was there, perched on the railing, and his eyes were bright as we both stared down at what I'd fallen over.

A body, and not just anyone's.

It was the body of Anton Forbes.

Chapter Seven

Forbes was half sitting, slumped sideways against the railing at the top of the stairs. His eyes were closed and I could see what appeared to be blood on the collar of his shirt. I leaned over for a closer look. There were ragged scratches circling his neck, deep wounds in a sort of lattice-like pattern. I frowned. Was that what had killed him? If so, what could have possibly caused it? I glanced quickly at his hands. No defensive marks that I could discern. If he'd been strangled, it didn't appear he'd put up a fight when he felt pressure against his throat, unless someone had approached him from behind without his being aware of it, which seemed unlikely.

I gave the body another quick once-over, looking for a more obvious wound, like a knife or a bullet hole, but saw nothing else. My stomach clenched and I could taste something sour in the back of my throat.

The body was still warm. Rigor hadn't yet set in. He couldn't have been dead too long. Nick watched me from his perch on the railing. "Er-owl," he said.

"I know," I said to him. "We didn't miss the killer by much." I glanced around cautiously. Was he or she still out there, watching? I pulled out my cell and punched in 9-1-1. A few seconds later the operator came on the line. "Your location, please."

"I'm calling from the gazebo just outside of Sweeney Park," I said. "I want to report a murder."

Fifteen minutes later a police cruiser pulled up and I was more than a little surprised to see Dale Anderson alight. I looked at her closely as she walked up the gazebo steps. With that form-fitting black dress, hair caught up in a chignon, and wearing blush, lipstick and eye shadow, she didn't look at all like the capable homicide detective I knew she was. Nope, she just looked like an attractive woman whose evening plans had been disrupted. My pang of guilt, however, barely lasted a moment as Dale caught sight of me. She stopped and put one hand on her hip, inclined her head. "Nora."

I inclined my head. "Detective Anderson."

"Mrrr."

Dale flicked her gaze to the railing where Nick perched. "And your cat. I presume one or both of you found the body?"

"We both did," I said.

"Well, why am I not surprised?" said a voice behind me. I glanced up and saw Samms, hovering about two steps behind Dale. Ah, I should have figured. A murder scene was probably Samms's idea of the ideal date.

I glared at him. "No jokes, please. Although Nick did sense something was wrong before I did. He ran up the steps and I followed him and found the body."

Dale pulled a small ring-bound notebook out of the tiny bag slung over one shoulder. I wondered if she had a small automatic tucked in there as well. She looked at me. "Did either of you touch anything?"

I nodded. "When I came up the steps I almost fell over the body. My hand touched the top of his head. And I touched his shirt collar, too."

Dale's eyebrow went up. "You touched his shirt? Why?"

I pointed to his neck. "He's got several deep welts along the throat line. You can see the flecks of dried blood on the collar. I didn't see any knife wound or bullet hole." I paused. "He *might* have died of natural causes."

Dale's lips slashed into a thin line. "Are you adding medical examiner to your list of talents?"

I flushed. "Hardly. I'm an ex-reporter. You know how that goes."

Her lips thinned out even more. "I sure do. You're an ex-reporter with a newly minted PI license. That's a dangerous combination."

"Why, thanks for the compliment," I remarked, flashing a wide smile. "He might have known whoever did this. I didn't notice any defensive wounds on his hands indicating he fought off an attacker."

Dale, eyes flashing, started to say something but Samms neatly stepped in between us. "What were you doing here, Nora?"

I turned to him. "Well, you remember I told you that Nick was supposed to shoot his scene with Ardis Malone tonight. After you left Hot Bread, I got a call from Forbes. He said I should bring Nick to film his scene, only he didn't mention where. I remembered Ardis Malone mentioning the gazebo as a possible location earlier, so I thought I'd try here first."

Dale, who'd been bent over the body, jerked her head up. "What time was that?"

"Three thirty. He wanted us here by quarter to five."

"He hasn't been dead too long," she muttered. She made another notation in her notebook. "Did you see anyone when you arrived here?"

"No. I called out for Forbes, and then Nick took off up the stairs."

Dale straightened and snapped her notebook shut. "The coroner will be along any minute. You and your cat can go. I'll need you to be available for questioning, though."

"Of course." I reached out and took Nick into my arms. Dale flipped open her phone and moved over into a corner of the gazebo. As I passed Samms, I swallowed and said, "I'm sorry that Nick and I ruined your evening."

"My evening?" He seemed puzzled, then his expression cleared. "Oh, right. My evening." He lifted an eyebrow. "I would think you'd be sorrier that your cat's shot at stardom has been derailed."

I frowned. That hadn't occurred to me. Anton Forbes was the one who was so hot on Nick being in the scene. Now that he was dead, I had the idea things were going to be vastly different on the *All the Days of Tomorrow* set.

And maybe not for the better, either.

• • •

My apartment was dark when I returned home. There was a note on the refrigerator:

Chantal brought the bread back; it's in the bin for tomorrow morning. Gone out with Marcia. Be back by ten. Can't wait to hear how Nick made out with Ardis!
—Lacey

I crumpled the note and tossed it into the wastebasket, then looked down at Nick. "Well, Lacey will be disappointed, and she's not the only one, huh, Nick?"

Nick lay down on the floor and put his paws over his ears.

"Well, tomorrow we'll find out what's what. Who knows, maybe they will still want you for that scene. At any rate, you've got a contract, Nick. They have to pay you for three days no matter what."

Nick lifted his head. "Merow?"

"Yes, I'm sure. Are you hungry?"

He meowed softly and stretched, Nick-speak for "I could eat."

I looked in my refrigerator and sighed. Hot Bread's was well stocked, but Nora Charles's left a lot to be desired. Apparently my sister had forgotten to do the weekly food shopping for our apartment, no doubt because she'd been so excited about the television stars' appearance in Cruz. I reached for the staples that always seemed to be around: eggs and cheese. I felt Nick rub against my leg, so I grabbed the bowl of sardines as well.

I scrambled a couple of eggs with cheddar cheese and a few of Lance's home-grown peppers thrown in for good measure. As the bread toasted, I mashed up some sardines and put them in Nick's bowl. While he slurped contentedly away, I spooned my omelet onto a plate and sat down at my kitchen table. I propped my feet up on the empty chair across from me as I ate. I knew I should have been thinking about my menus for tomorrow's shoot, but instead I found myself replaying the day's events in my head, ending with the grisly discovery Nick and I had made at the gazebo.

"Lots of questions about this," I murmured. "Suspects? Too many to count. Motives? Probably too many of them too."

What I really found myself wondering was a long shot: Could Anton Forbes's death in any way be connected to Dean Harriman's?

The cause of death was what really puzzled me. What could have made those funny welts on his neck? I pushed my plate back and walked into my den and booted up the laptop. I typed in "red welts on skin" and got a ton of results, mostly connected to allergies. I frowned.

It hadn't looked like an allergic reaction to me; still, one never knew.

I went downstairs into Hot Bread's kitchen, walked over to my middle drawer and pulled out the list I'd been faxed from the studio, the one that listed everyone's dietary restrictions. I ran my finger down the list of names.

As I'd thought, Anton Forbes wasn't on it.

"Not an allergic reaction, most likely. What then, I wonder?"

I closed my eyes. I was visualizing a crime scene I'd been at several years before in Chicago. The victim had been a woman; her husband had killed her. Her throat had been mottled with bright red lines.

"Strangulation?" I murmured. It was certainly possible, but Forbes had impressed me as a strong man. If that were the case, either his assailant had been stronger or had had the element of surprise on his or her side. I visualized the marks on Forbes's neck. They had formed a sort of checkered pattern. What weapon would make those types of marks?

"Whoa," I said aloud. "Hold on. Not every death is suspicious. Lots of things might have caused those marks. It could be medication, or a blood disorder."

Even as I said those words, I didn't believe them. In my gut, I knew Anton Forbes had been murdered, but how and by whom was a mystery.

Difficult as it was, I put the event from my mind and spent the next hour and a half fixing up the trays for tomorrow's breakfast and lunch. I sliced the hero bread and put it back in the bin, deciding that I'd let Lacey add the cold cuts and season it tomorrow. If she were going to claim credit, she might as well actually do the work. I was just about to head back upstairs and hit the trusty Google search engine again before retiring at a decent hour when I happened to glance up and see Nick standing in the entryway.

"Nick. You finished your dinner? Come on, we're going back upstairs. I bet you'd like a nice saucer of milk for dessert, hm?"

Instead of turning toward the stairway, Nick stared at me for a minute, then padded over to the back door. He sat down and looked over his shoulder at me, then back at the door.

A second passed, and then I heard a knock.

"How on earth do you do this, Nick?"

I bent over to give him a quick scratch behind his ear. All I got in return was a flick of his white whiskers, and then he moved to one side as the knock was repeated.

"Coming," I called. "Is that you, Lacey? Did you forget your key again?"

I rolled my head from one shoulder to the other and flung open the door. But it wasn't my sister who stood expectantly on my stoop.

It was Leroy Samms.

Chapter Eight

For a minute all we did was stare at each other. Then I brushed an errant curl off my cheek. "Oh, hi. I wasn't expecting you," I said stupidly.

Samms's lips twitched. "That's obvious. I know it's a bit late, but mind if I come in? I was going to try your apartment, but then I saw the shop light on." As I hesitated he added, "It's police business. I'm helping Dale out. She had some follow-up questions for you, but she needed to see the coroner, so I told her I'd take care of it."

Well, wasn't that nice of him, to help his girlfriend out? I tamped down the burst of annoyance I felt and stepped to one side. "Sure," I said through gritted teeth. "Come on in."

He followed me into Hot Bread's kitchen. Nick had moved away from the door and now squatted in his usual place, in front of the refrigerator. I gestured at the table. "Have a seat. Would you like some coffee? Or hot chocolate? Could I make you a sandwich?"

"No, thanks. Like I said, it's a business call, not a social one." He stopped as he noted the expression on my face. "Ah, that was supposed to be sarcastic, right?"

I just gave him my sweetest smile. "So the FBI must be slow right now, huh? Or do you just miss working homicide?"

"My caseload is a bit slow right now." He shrugged. "That's how I got permission to help Dale out. I'm sure you're aware she's a bit short on manpower right now."

"That is so nice of you," I said with exaggerated sweetness. "To help your good friend Dale out like that. It's even nicer for the FBI to let you."

His brows knit together. "Am I missing something?"

I ignored his question and leaned against the counter as Samms eased himself into a chair. "You said you have follow-up questions?"

"Routine, mostly." He pulled a notebook similar to the one Dale had from his pocket. "Tell me again how you found Anton Forbes's body."

I sighed and repeated the story. Samms listened, his expression impassive. When I finished, he remarked, "And you didn't see anybody around, anyone at all?" I shook my head and he scribbled something in the notebook. "What about the parking lot when you pulled in?"

I closed my eyes as I thought. "I saw two trucks that I know belong to the marina in the far corner. That was it. No sign of any other vehicle, which I thought was odd. No camera trucks, no sign of anyone. Oh, wait!" I paused as a sudden thought occurred to me. "There were no other cars, no vehicles at all, so how did Forbes get to the gazebo?"

Samms pointed to his legs. "He could have walked it."

I wrinkled my nose. "He could have but it's a pretty good walk, at least twenty minutes, and frankly he didn't strike me as the type of guy who'd enjoy a good walk. He'd want to get where he was going the fastest way possible. Besides, his shoes were all wrong."

Samms looked at me. "Come again?"

"His shoes. He had on a pair of pretty expensive-looking loafers, and they were spit-shined and polished to perfection. If he'd walked, there would have been evidence of it, dirt or dried mud on the soles."

He reached up to scratch at his forehead. "The things you notice never cease to amaze me," he said. "I bet you topped your PI class in observation."

"Actually . . . I did."

Samms ignored my remark and scribbled in his notebook. "Now, you said you touched the body, right?"

"The top of his head, when I tripped and tried to steady myself. And I touched his neck when I pulled down his collar, trying to figure out what could have made those marks." I let out a breath. "They could be ligatures. Or they could be petechiae from natural causes."

"They could." He tapped his pen against the notebook. "Did you see anything lying around, anything that might have been used as a weapon, perhaps?"

I shook my head. "Not a damn thing, and certainly nothing that could have made those odd marks." I gave him a shrewd look. "Did the coroner venture an opinion on the cause of death? If it could be attributed to natural causes or not?"

Nick chose that moment to launch himself upward and onto Samms's lap. Samms looked startled for a moment, then laughed and ran his hand down Nick's sleek black fur.

"I bet you're disappointed you didn't get to do that scene with Ardis Malone, aren't you?" he said to Nick. "I know I would be."

I stood, my hands crossed over my chest. "Am I going nuts, or did you just talk to my cat?"

Samms looked over at me. "I never said I didn't like animals. As a matter of fact, I had a golden retriever when I was growing up."

Was I imagining it, or was his tone a bit defensive? "You're a dog person. Most men are."

"I don't mind cats." He glanced at Nick. "When I refer to your cat as a 'body sniffer,' it's mostly meant in a humorous vein."

Nick let out a loud *merow* and then his tongue darted out and swiped against the tip of Samms's chin. Samms let out a loud chuckle.

All I could do was stand and stare at this unexpected display of male bonding. Nick had never jumped on Daniel's lap, or any other male's except Ollie's. And the chin licking? What was going on here? Nick couldn't possibly prefer Samms to Daniel, could he? My stomach roiled as a thought occurred to me. Was this what Chantal had meant by the universe making up my mind for me?

"Seems your cat isn't the type to hold a grudge, unlike his owner," commented Samms.

"I'm sorry. What is that supposed to mean?" I sputtered.

Samms grabbed Nick firmly around his middle, set him down on the floor, and then turned back to me. "I'm talking about our college days, back when we worked on the paper. You always resented me."

I goggled at him. "I didn't resent you. I just thought you were unnecessarily bossy."

His lips twitched. "With that crew, I had to be. They were a pretty undependable bunch, even you, at times. You hated the fact I rode you harder than the others."

I let out a sharp laugh. "I didn't hate the fact you worked me harder, I hated the fact you refused to listen to my point of view."

"I listened, when I thought it had some relevance."

"Yeah, and that was about one percent of the time," I said dryly. "You never seemed to have any respect for my writing ability. Plus, you gave me crummy nicknames."

He ran a hand through his hair, mussing up the ends. "If I gave you that impression, I apologize. I always had plenty of respect for your writing ability. And FYI, those nicknames weren't crummy."

"Really? You consider 'Sweetie,' 'Legs,' and my all-time favorite, 'Red,' the cream of the crop?"

He chuckled. "Well, I guess you could say they're a tad chauvinistic."

"A tad?" I shook my head. "If your aim was to inflame me into doing a stellar job, then you succeeded."

"So I'm found out after all these years." He reached up, rubbed at the bridge of his nose. "You didn't like me back then, did you?"

"I'm not sure I like you now," I answered.

He dropped his hand to his side and stared full into my eyes. "That's because you never took the time to get to know me."

"Because there's a lot I don't know about you, right?"

"Right. Actually, I think there's a lot we don't know about each other."

I'd felt uncomfortable the first time he'd said that, and now was no different. I turned my face away, hoping he hadn't noticed the heat that was searing my cheeks, and murmured, "If you have a point, please make it."

He reached up to rub at the nape of his neck. "You have a naturally rebellious nature, and it seems to come out especially strong whenever we're together. You and that darn cat of yours have gotten lucky and solved a few mysteries, and now you've gotten a PI license. It makes it hard."

I narrowed my eyes. "Makes what hard? Watching out for me?" I drummed the tips of my fingers on the counter. "I don't need a guardian angel, Samms."

"You think you don't, but you seem to be on the scene whenever there's a murder. Has anyone ever told you you're a natural-born snoop?"

"My editor on the *Chicago Tribune* told me that all the time. Snooping is part of the job when you're a true crime reporter."

"Which you aren't, anymore. I think you tend to forget that at times. One day this curiosity of yours is going to land you in real hot water." He raked one hand through his hair, and an inky curl carelessly caressed his forehead. "I know how you get when you're faced with a puzzle. You plunge ahead and don't think of the consequences. Are you forgetting those last few times when you almost got yourself killed? If Daniel and I hadn't gotten there in time . . ."

A loud yowl came from the corner.

I couldn't stifle a grin. "Nick is telling you that he had a hand in those rescues as well, like the time on the *Lady L*, when he sat on that hit man Wyatt's face. You weren't around for that one."

Samms looked over at Nick and grinned at the cat. "Yeah, sorry I missed it. I bet that was some sight."

Nick rose, let out a little yowl, turned around twice and then sat back on his haunches. If a kitty could wear a proud expression, he did.

I cleared my throat. "Look, I'm a big girl, and I don't take unnecessary chances, or at least I try not to." I glanced over toward Nick. "Anyway, I've already got a guardian. A black, furry one."

Samms muttered something under his breath that sounded like "stubborn female" and scraped his chair back. He walked over to stand in front of me. His hand shot out, cupped my chin, and turned my face up to his. "You really don't get it, do you?" he said softly.

We both stood there for a moment, an awkward silence stretching between us. He took a couple of steps closer to me, and I could feel the warmth emanating from his body. I caught a whiff of aftershave—Calvin

Klein—at around the same time I saw a flush of pink appear on the tops of his cheekbones. His lips were poised above mine, and for a brief second I imagined myself backing him up against the counter and giving him a thorough kissing, the kind you read about in romance novels. For a second I was tempted to shuck all my doubts and do just that, but before I could decide whether to act on my impulse or not, the loud sound of throat-clearing reached our ears. We broth broke apart instantly, like two guilty teenagers, and turned to stare at Lacey, standing in the rear doorway.

"I'm sorry. Did I interrupt something?" she asked.

I frowned at my sister, who didn't look one bit sorry. What she looked was smug. I wanted to slap that grin right off her face, the grin that was loudly saying, *See, I told you that you had feelings for Samms, and that he does for you, too.*

She stepped all the way into the kitchen. "Sorry," she said again. "I forgot my credit card. Can't treat my friends to drinks if I don't have my credit card."

"Oh, I don't know about that," I said tightly. "I'm sure Lance would be happy to start a tab for you, or put them on my account."

"You have an account there?" She gave a careless wave. "It's okay, it doesn't matter. We weren't going to the Poker Face. We thought we'd try that new karaoke bar over at Simms Landing."

"I heard that place wasn't that good," I said. "Why don't you want to go to the Poker Face? You like the drinks there."

"Yeah, but Lance is on tonight." She made a show of examining the toe of her shoe. "I feel funny about accepting favors from Lance since, well, you know, since he dumped me."

I let out an exasperated cry. "Since *he* dumped *you?*"

"Poor choice of words. I meant to say, since he no longer feels the same way about me. It's awkward." She slid me a curious glance. "Say, shouldn't Nick be filming his scene now?"

My hand shot up and rubbed at the back of my neck. "We got a little sidetracked when we found Anton Forbes's body at the gazebo."

"Oh, *God!*" My sister let out a squeal I was certain could be heard in nearby Carmel. "Anton Forbes is *dead!*"

"Yep." It was Samms who answered. He flicked his gaze in my direction. "And Nora and her cat found the body." He avoided my stony stare and glanced at his watch. "I've got to get to the station. In addition to curious fans, the press has been camping out since the actors came to town, and it won't be long before they get wind of this. Dale will need my help." He threw me a look I couldn't fathom and then said tightly, "Thank you for your cooperation, Nora. Nice to see you, Lacey." He nodded as he eased past my sister and then he was out the door.

Lacey looked at me. "Anton Forbes is dead, huh? Was it murder? Who in the world would want to murder Anton Forbes? Wait"—she held up her hand—"dumb question. Don't answer that."

"I won't." Now that Samms was gone, I felt breathing a bit easier. "Samms wouldn't comment on whether it was a murder, but I've got the feeling it is. As I told them earlier, there's no shortage of suspects. I must have heard at least half a dozen people wish him dead today. Chantal can tell you."

"Speaking of Chantal, I saw a police cruiser pull up in front of Poppies when I was coming here. I wonder why?"

As if on cue, my cell phone rang. Seeing *Poppies* on the screen, I answered quickly. "Chantal? Is that you?"

"Oh, *chérie*," my friend wailed, "you will not believe this! Anton Forbes is dead, and Dale Anderson is here. She's questioning Remy."

Oh, swell. "Sit tight," I told my friend. "I'm on my way."

Nick twined his furry body between my ankles. I sighed. "And yes, you can come too."

Chapter Nine

We hopped into my SUV and arrived at Poppies within ten minutes. I saw the police cruiser parked at the curb as I pulled into the driveway. I parked and Nick and I got out and went around to the back entrance. Chantal was there waiting for me, her face pale. She leaned down to give Nick a pat on the head and then turned her anxious stare on me.

"Can you believe Forbes is dead?" she cried. "*Sacrebleu*, we only just saw him this afternoon."

"Yes, I can believe it," I responded. "Nick and I found the body."

Chantal's eyes popped and she looked from me to the cat and back again. "You and Nicky did? When?"

I quickly hit the highlights for her, leaving out the part about my close encounter with Samms. "I have a gut feeling he didn't die from natural causes, either." I glanced over Chantal's shoulder at the closed office door. "Remy's in there?"

"Yes, with Detective Anderson." She let out a long, slow breath. "You were right when you said you saw him, Nora. The PR guy reported seeing a figure that matched Remy's description lurking in the bushes and talking to Forbes, and when Anderson's men combed the area they found one of his business cards stuck to a bush." She cast an anxious glance toward the door. "Detective Anderson was quite insistent on speaking to Remy in private. Do you think she somehow found out that Remy went to college with Forbes? And that he didn't exactly like him?"

I was spared commenting as the office door opened and Remy and Dale Anderson walked out. Remy looked very tired. His shoulders sagged and his chin drooped. Chantal immediately went over to him and enveloped him in a hug. Anderson glanced up, saw me, and then her gaze fell on Nick. "Well, well, two for the price of one. It's nice of you to come by, Nora," she said, walking over to where I stood. "I have a few more questions for you."

I held up my hand. "Yes, Special Agent Samms came by Hot Bread and interrogated me." The devil on my shoulder whispered in my ear and I couldn't resist adding, "It's very nice of him to help you out like this."

Did I imagine the surprised look that crossed her face? "Yes, Lee's been a big help to me. However, I do have a few more questions." She whipped her notebook and pen out of her pocket. "Did you notice any specific incidents of friction today between Forbes and any of the crew members?"

"Gee, which one would you like?" I asked dryly. "There were so many."

Dale's smile was frosty. "Pick one."

I hesitated and then repeated the argument I'd heard between Forbes and Colgate. Dale scribbled down everything I said and when I'd finished asked, "So you witnessed his famous temperament firsthand, eh?"

"I did." I gestured toward Nick, sprawled at my feet. "Nick got out of the van and I chased him over to Forbes's trailer. He was a bit angry when he saw me, but it seemed to dissipate the moment he caught sight of Nick."

"Um-hum. Have any idea why he was angry?"

"No. Well, maybe." I hesitated and then said, "Emily Van Horn had left his trailer only a few minutes before. He probably thought I might have overheard their exchange."

"And did you?"

"Not the whole thing, just enough to know they'd had some sort of misunderstanding." I hesitated, and then said, "I overheard Emily Van Horn say she'd rather die first, and then she said she'd rather see Forbes dead, but," I added quickly, "she wasn't the only person I overheard wishing Forbes harm today. He wasn't well-liked."

Dale scribbled in her notebook. "You're certain you didn't touch anything at the crime scene, other than what you've already mentioned?"

"Positive."

Dale inclined her head toward Nick. "What about him? He get his paws on anything there?"

Nick sat up straight and his lip curled back, baring his fangs. "Er-owl!"

I bit back a chuckle at Dale's startled look. "He's telling you he knows better than to touch anything at a crime scene. And so do I."

Dale smacked at the side of her head with her palm. "Of course. What was I thinking?" With a dubious look at Nick, Dale snapped her notebook shut and slipped it back in her pocket. "Thanks for your cooperation."

"Sure." I jammed my hands in my pockets. "I guess I should try and get in touch with Kenny Colgate to see if they plan on suspending work for tomorrow in light of what's happened."

"Somehow I wouldn't count on it," Dale said dryly. "When I spoke to him, Colgate was muttering something about the show having to go on despite personal tragedy." She barked out a laugh. "I'm not sure just how tragic he thought the death of his coworker was, though."

I nodded. "Sad but true."

"You seem pretty interested in this case." Her eyes narrowed as they rested on me. "This is the sort of thing Louis Blondell eats up. You're not thinking of investigating on your own for a story for *Noir*, are you?"

"I honestly hadn't given that a thought, but it's not a bad idea. A murder investigation as seen from the eyes of a fledgling PI. Louis would love that."

"You might have a PI license, Nora," Dale huffed, "but you have no practical experience in investigation."

My chin jutted forward. "Oh, I don't know about that. I've gotten a lot of experience in solving crimes over the past year. Who knows, I might be able to help."

Dale took a step closer to me. "Don't take this the wrong way, but there's a murderer out there. I can't be worrying that a civilian's interference could put them in danger."

"So it's official then? Forbes didn't die of natural causes?"

She shrugged. "It'll be in the papers anyway, so I'm not saying anything you can't find out on your own. The cause of death appears to be strangulation." When I remained silent, she cocked her head at me. "You don't seem too surprised."

"It was one of the things I considered after seeing the marks on his neck," I admitted. "Although I can't imagine what could have made them. Have you found the murder weapon?"

"Not yet. That's all I'm at liberty to say right now." Her head jerked in Remy's direction. "Gillard, do you want to reconsider your 'no comment' position?"

Remy gave the detective a stony stare. "Not at all."

Dale abruptly swung her gaze to Chantal. "How about you, Chantal? You were at the shoot today too. Did you notice any friction between Forbes and the rest of the cast and crew?"

"I did not see or hear anything specific, but there were definite bad vibes," Chantal answered.

"Uh-huh. Got any idea why your brother might have been hanging around Forbes's trailer today?"

Remy stepped forward, his hands clenched at his sides. "I asked you to leave her out of this. She doesn't know anything."

"I can answer on my own," Chantal said briskly. She turned to Dale. "As far as I knew, Remy was making a few deliveries and then tending the store. I had no idea he wasn't where he said he'd be."

"I see. How about your brother's whereabouts between three thirty and five thirty today? Can you vouch for him?"

She hesitated and then shook her head. "No. I went to pick up some bread for Nora for tomorrow's lunch, and then I stopped by my friend Sylvie's shop. I dropped the bread off at Hot Bread and then I got back here a little after five thirty. But Remy was in the store then," she added quickly.

Dale nodded. "Okay, that'll do for now. Remember, Gillard, don't leave town." She glanced at me. "And you, stick to your cooking. I mean it." With that, she turned and swept out of the shop.

Once the door had closed behind her, Chantal turned to her brother. "Remy! *Que se passe-t-il?*"

Remy's lips slashed into a thin line, and he reached up to run a hand through his shock of unruly blonde hair. "She wanted to know why I was snooping behind his trailer. I told her it was none of her business. She asked me where I was this afternoon, and I told her I was here, albeit with no witnesses. Then she asked me if I knew Forbes, if I had any sort of relationship with him. So I asked her if I were being charged with anything, and she said no, so I said I was within my rights to refuse to answer."

Chantal let out a gasp. "Why did you do that? Why did you not tell her?"

"My reasons are personal and none of her business. I did not kill him, so it should not matter."

Chantal shot her brother an exasperated look. "I doubt Detective Anderson will see it that way."

"Than that is her problem," he sniffed.

Chantal fisted both hands on her slender hips. "Well, I would like to know. Why did you go there? Why did you lie to me? When I called you, you said you were making deliveries and minding the shop."

"I had the shop phone forwarded to my cell," Remy said sullenly. "After you left this morning, I called Gaston and asked him if he could do the deliveries today, and then watch the shop until I got back. As to why I lied to you, well, it was to protect you."

"Protect me!" Chantal shook her head. "I do not like the sound of all this."

"I can't help that. You have to trust me. What I'm doing is for your own good." He reached up to pinch the bridge of his nose. "It's over now, she's gone. I don't want to talk about it, so can we please drop the subject."

"Yes, it is over, for now. But didn't you hear the determination in her voice? She will be back."

I looked at Remy. "Did Anderson happen to mention if they'd determined the time of death?"

He pursed his lips as he thought. "Somewhere between three forty-five and four thirty, I believe," he said finally.

"And he called me at three thirty and asked me to bring Nick by at quarter to five." I did a quick calculation. "He had to be at the gazebo when he called. There was no car in the parking lot, and there's no way he could have walked from his trailer to the gazebo in fifteen minutes."

"Unless he got a ride from someone," suggested Chantal.

"He did excuse himself for a minute when we were on the phone, and he covered the receiver. I could hear him mumbling. He could have been talking to his killer." A shudder ripped through me at that thought. I looked at Chantal. "When you look at it from Dale's point of view, Remy is an ideal suspect. He has a history with the deceased that he's reluctant to talk about, and then someone spots him snooping around the guy's trailer. Forbes turns up dead hours later and there are no witnesses who can corroborate his whereabouts at the TOD."

"All very well and good, but this is all supposition," Remy cut in, his tone annoyed. "What they call circumstantial evidence. There is no proof."

I looked Remy straight in the eye. "Remy, did you see or speak to Anton Forbes at all today?"

Remy's head jerked up, and his eyes narrowed as he averted his gaze away from me. "What? No, of course not. Why would you ask such a thing?"

"I'm just trying to figure things out. Get them straight in my mind."

"Anderson is right, eh?" His lips compressed into a thin line. "Now that you have a PI license, you feel you must act like one?"

"Remy!" Chantal cried. "Apologize this instant. Nora is only trying to help."

"It's all right," I began, but Remy let out a huge sigh.

"I'm sorry," he muttered. "I know you think you are helping, but really, it isn't necessary. There is no cause for alarm. I did not kill Anton Forbes, you must believe me."

"Of course Nora believes you, *mon frère*," Chantal said soothingly. She placed her hand on Remy's arm. "Let me take you upstairs so you can lie down."

Remy shrugged off Chantal's hand. "I can go upstairs on my own." He glanced quickly at me. "Again, Nora, I am sorry." He turned and walked out of the room.

Chantal sighed. "I'm sorry too, *chérie*, for my brother acting like such a huge . . . horse's patoot."

"No problem. It's understandable, considering the circumstances."

Chantal walked Nick and me to the door. "Let me know what's on for tomorrow with the food service. I might be a little late getting to Hot Bread. Even though he says he is fine, I know my brother. He is very troubled by all this."

"Of course he is. Don't worry about it," I said. "You do what you have to do with Remy. Maybe they'll cancel the shoot tomorrow. I'll let you know if I hear anything."

Chantal smiled. "Thank you, Nora. You are such a good friend." She squeezed my arm in return. "Thank you for believing in Remy."

I gave her a reassuring smile, but it faded once Nick and I were back in my SUV. As I strapped on my seat belt, I gave my kitty a sidelong glance.

"I don't want to alarm Chantal," I said, "but Remy's actions do seem more than a little suspicious. I mean, if I were Dale, I'd have lots of questions too. And for her to specifically ask him if he had a relationship with the deceased? That indicates to me that she already knows he did."

Nick leaned backward on the seat to stretch out his front legs.

"Remy said he never spoke to Forbes," I murmured. "What do you think?"

Nick leaned over and butted my elbow with his head.

I sighed. "Yeah, that's what I was afraid of. He's lying. Why?"

I eased the SUV away from the curb. The main question, as I saw it, was just what had happened between Forbes and Remy? And was it serious enough to give Remy a motive for murder?

For Chantal's sake, if nothing else, I sincerely hoped not.

Chapter Ten

When Nick and I walked in the back door of Hot Bread about an hour later, I was treated to the sight of my sister, munching on a sandwich, seated on a stool right in front of the television, her eyes glued to the screen. Nick immediately ambled over and sprawled at her feet, his gaze fixed firmly on the sandwich.

I pulled off my light jacket, tossed it over the back of one of the chairs, and went over to stand next to her. "What are you watching?"

Her eyes never left the screen, even as she pulled a bit of ham out of her sandwich and tossed it to Nick, who pounced on it. "The evening news. Do you believe they have a story about Anton Forbes's death coming up?"

"What?" I pulled up a stool next to my sister. "How on earth did they find out so quickly?"

She shot me a sly glance. "I cannot believe that you even asked that question. There's been press hanging around Cruz all day."

"Yeah? Then Anderson's men did a good job of keeping them at bay, because we didn't see a hint of one near the shoot site."

"Or maybe you just didn't notice, what with all those TV stars around," Lacey said with a chuckle. She put a finger to her lips. "Ssh. The report's coming on now."

I flinched slightly as the image of a good-looking man appeared on the screen. I recognized him instantly—the jet-black hair, graying slightly at the temples, deep brown eyes and even, perfect teeth. The man looked like a movie star himself, and he was certainly conceited enough to be one.

"Blaine Carmichael has this story," I muttered. "Great. I can just imagine the circus he'll turn it into."

"Ssh," my sister hissed. She reached for the remote and turned the volume up, then tossed Nick another bit of ham.

"We have breaking news from Cruz, the site of the location shoot of the popular nighttime soap *All the Days of Tomorrow*. This reporter learned earlier tonight that tragedy has struck the set. Director Anton Forbes is dead." He paused, his face suffused with an expression of sadness. The camera pulled back a bit, showing Carmichael standing in front of the gazebo steps. He flung his arm backward as he continued, "Details are sketchy at this point, but my sources revealed that Forbes's body was discovered just hours ago in this very spot." He waved his arm at the gazebo again. "When asked for a statement, Detective Dale Anderson of Cruz Homicide had this to say."

The screen switched to show Dale, a microphone shoved under her nose, looking more than a bit harried and definitely annoyed. "Yes, the body of Anton Forbes was discovered in the gazebo shortly after five p.m. tonight. No, I have no comment right now as to the cause of death."

Carmichael, undaunted, asked in a concerned tone, "Since you are the head of Homicide, might we assume foul play is involved."

"I would not assume anything until our investigation is concluded," Dale said. She made a shooing motion at the microphone with her hand. "Now get this damn thing out of my face."

The screen switched back to Carmichael, who still wore a hangdog expression. "Detective Anderson declined further comment, but it is this newsman's belief that Anton Forbes was murdered. Rest assured I and Channel KLBY News will follow this story to its conclusion."

Lacey picked up the remote, muted the TV, and turned to me. "He certainly seems persistent, in a pain-in-the-butt kinda way. I guess that's what makes him a top entertainment reporter. He's always first with all the gossip, and nine times out of ten he's right."

"Oh, he's persistent, all right, and definitely a pain in the butt. There's no doubt in my mind he will play this for all it is worth, and I bet Dale Anderson will be real happy about that," I muttered.

Blaine Carmichael had gotten his start in Chicago, on my old newspaper, the *Tribune*, in fact. He'd been a smarmy ass-kisser back then, and had gotten promotions by leap-frogging on the backs of others, one of whom had been yours truly. He'd gone from reporting on local sports to a small column on a rival paper before being snapped up by a local station as one of their roving reporters. Shortly thereafter he'd left Chicago for California, and had landed the job as entertainment reporter for KLBY, one of California's larger stations. It was certainly a change from photographing crime scenes, for sure. Aloud I said, "Blaine was always adept at digging up dirt on people. It's what makes him a good entertainment reporter. So, if they want dirt dug up on Forbes, he's the man for the job."

My sister shoved a potato chip into her mouth, chewed and then asked, "What happened at Poppies? Did you find out why they wanted to question Remy?"

"Someone saw a man hanging around Forbes's trailer earlier, and they found Remy's business card stuck to a bush. Dale was questioning him as to why he was there."

Lacey washed down her chip with a sip of Coke. "No kidding! Why on earth would Remy do something like that? Don't tell me he was worried that Anton Forbes might try to put the moves on Chantal?"

"Maybe. Who knows?" I figured it was best if I didn't mention Remy's past with Forbes to my sister, who is not well known for either her tact or her ability to keep a secret.

"I think that's sweet, that Remy was that worried about his sister," Lacey said. "But why on earth was Anderson wasting her time? I mean, Remy, of all people, a murderer?"

"It's her job. She has to follow up every lead."

"Even the dead-end ones, huh?" She reached in the bag and grabbed another handful of chips. "At least one good thing came out of all this."

I eyed Lacey as I reached for the bag of chips. "Yeah? What's that?"

She shot me a mischievous grin. "Why, it interrupted Anderson's big date with Lee, of course."

I popped a chip into my mouth. "You saw them hugging on the corner too, huh?"

She nodded. "It's so disgusting. I thought Lee had better taste.

Although I guess I can't blame him, what with the way Anderson's always throwing herself at him."

I almost choked on the potato chip. "She throws herself at him?"

"Not in the literal sense, but her tongue practically drops down to her chin whenever they're in a room together. Come on, Nors, you have to have noticed those little intimate gestures she makes to him, running her fingertips up his arm, squeezing his shoulder." She leaned back and let out a giant sigh. "I swear, I don't know what he sees in her. She's like a man."

"Actually she's like a female Samms."

"Say, you're right. So you know their romance is doomed from the start."

I looked at her curiously. "Why do you say that?"

"Everyone knows opposites attract. Samms and Dale are too much alike to ever make it work." Lacey reached in the bag, pulled out the last potato chip, then crumpled it and tossed it into the wastebasket. "I'm sorry I interrupted you before. It looked like the two of you were finally getting cozy."

I got up and went over to the refrigerator, pulled out a bottle of water. "Not exactly," I said. "We were just reminiscing about our college days."

Lacey cut me an eye roll. "Oh, puh-leaze, Nors. You didn't see the expressions on your faces when I came in the door. You looked like two guilty high school seniors who were caught necking in a place they shouldn't have been. Or maybe like two kids caught with their hands in the cookie jar. I can't decide which."

"Then let me help you out. Neither."

My sister tapped her foot impatiently. "Look, Daniel's in London now, for God knows how long. I know you care about the guy, but have you even considered the possibility that he might never come back to the States? That they might base him permanently out of London?"

I frowned, the water bottle midway to my lips. The plain truth was, I hadn't even thought about anything like that happening. "I doubt it," I said finally. "Daniel said this was a temporary assignment."

"That might not be his call," Lacey pointed out. "Lots of temporary things turn permanent. He's a career FBI man, and if they want him there, he'll be there." She looked at me. "What would you do if that happened, Nors? Would you give up everything here, your family, your friends, Hot Bread, maybe even Nick, to move there to be with him? Maybe you should think about that."

Nick apparently sensed that I was upset because he ambled over and started butting his head against my legs. I reached down to give him a reassuring pat then straightened and looked at my sister. "It's silly to even talk about something like that," I said. "It'll never happen."

My sister pulled a face. "Never say never. Look, all I'm saying is don't cross Samms off your potential date list. He's probably only seeing Dale because he figures you're off-limits. If he thought he had a chance with you, I bet he'd dump her like that!" She snapped her fingers in the air.

Thankfully at that moment my cell rang. I gave my sister a dark look and snatched the phone up. "Nora Charles."

"Ms. Charles?" a clipped voice I didn't recognize came over the wire. "This is Kenny Colgate. We met at the shoot today."

"Oh, yes, Mr. Colgate." I pushed my hand through my hair and turned to avoid my sister's curious stare. "I'm sorry for your loss."

"Thanks. I understand it was you who found his body. I'm sorry you had to go through that experience." He cleared his throat. "I'm calling about the food service. By popular demand, we will be suspending work tomorrow. The studio suggested it might be in everyone's best interests to have a short memorial, you know, to put the horror behind us. I was wondering if you could perhaps put together a buffet for afterward." He paused, and I had a mental picture of him pinching the bridge of his beak-shaped nose. "We were going to hold it at Sweeney Park, but the mayor suggested Cruz High. There's a chapel right across from the high school, and the auditorium will be perfect for the buffet afterward."

I knew the kitchen at the high school had been recently remodeled, with state-of-the-art stainless steel appliances, and a smoothie maker to boot. "That should work."

"We don't want to turn this into a circus. I've been in touch with Detective Anderson about keeping curious onlookers at bay, and the press, of course. Although I imagine we'll have to admit some of them." I could almost see him wince as he said that. "It will start promptly at four fifteen, and we'll have the buffet immediately afterward. I'm going to try and limit it to cast and crew only, but in the interests of public relations, we might have to allow a few members of the press to be in attendance."

I said a silent prayer that Blaine Carmichael wouldn't be one of them. "I understand. If you'd like, I can prepare the food here and take it over to the high school."

"Thank you, that would be a big help. Of course, you and whomever you bring to assist you are welcome to attend the service, if you wish." He paused and then said, "I shall see that you receive extra compensation for preparing the buffet, Ms. Charles. Even though there will be one day less of regular food service, you won't be penalized. Oh, and yes, one other thing. It's about your cat."

I glanced down at the floor. Nick had finished his ham and now sat, head cocked to one side, one ear flapped over. The expression on his face was what my mother would have referred to as sour. Obviously Nick sensed he was about to be told his "catly" services would no longer be required.

I cleared my throat. "It was Mr. Forbes's idea to feature Nick, after all, so I completely understand if you want to cancel."

"Cancel?" There was no mistaking the note of surprise in his voice. "Not at all. We still intend to have Nick do the scene, that is, if it's still all right with you."

"What? Oh, yes, of course it is," I said. I looked down at Nick and made a thumbs-up gesture. He immediately began grooming his bib.

"I'm not certain exactly when we'll shoot it," Colgate went on. "The schedule is tighter than ever now. But I'll figure it out and let you know."

"Thanks, Mr. Colgate. I'll see you tomorrow."

I rang off and turned around to find my sister standing almost at my elbow. "What happened?" she cried. "Is Nicky still on the show?"

I set the phone back on the counter. "Surprisingly, yes. I guess they figured that since Nick has the contract and will get paid anyway, they might as well use him."

Lacey leaned over Nick and rubbed his head. "Hear that, Nick? You're still gonna be on the show! You're gonna be a star!"

Nick lifted his head and sniffed, undoubtedly expecting more ham. "Merow."

I reached up to pinch the bridge of my nose. "No breakfast or lunch service tomorrow. They're suspending shooting for one day."

Lacey's happy expression clouded. "Oh, sure, the day I'm supposed to go. That figures."

"Relax, little sis. Instead of the breakfast and lunch, Colgate wants us to prepare a small buffet supper. They're going to have a memorial service for Forbes and they want something to eat afterward. I'll ask Chantal if she wants to come too, although she might prefer to stay with Remy." My sister started for the stairway that led to our apartment and I stuck out my arm and grabbed her wrist. "Where are you going?"

"To make sure my black dress looks okay. Black's what you wear to a memorial, right?"

"Right. But it would be more practical for us to wear black slacks and a black top, since we'll be serving food immediately afterward."

"I'll bring black slacks and change." She gestured toward the television. "Don't think for a minute your old pal Blaine Carmichael is going to miss an opportunity like this! He'll be reporting on every bit of that memorial, you can be sure. And just in case I get on camera, I want to look my best. You never know who might be watching."

I made a face at her. "Lance usually doesn't watch the news."

She drew herself up straight. "I wasn't thinking of him."

"Uh-huh. Sure you were, and you were also thinking of Peter Dobbs, and maybe Hal Frey too." I named two other recent men in my sister's life. "Trust me, if Blaine Carmichael shoves a microphone in anyone's face, it'll be Kenny Colgate's, or Mark Emerson's, or Emily Van Horn's or Ardis Malone's. Not us."

Lacey sniffed. "Next you'll be telling me that if he could, he'd try to get a statement out of the corpse."

I couldn't resist a chuckle. "He would if he could."

My phone rang again and I picked it up. "Nora Charles."

"Nora!" The voice that boomed at me over the wire sounded vaguely familiar. "I'm glad I got you. It's Blaine Carmichael. I'm sure you remember me, from the *Trib*?" He didn't wait for my acknowledgment, but rushed on, "I'm in town, so we should get together and catch up. Oh, and by the way, I understand you found Anton Forbes's body? Any comments? Anything you'd like to share with my viewers?"

"Not a damn thing that you could repeat on the air," I hissed, and hung up.

Chapter Eleven

"I cannot believe he had the nerve to ask you that."

It was a little after nine Wednesday morning, and I was taking a short break during the lull in business. Chantal had dropped by to say that Remy seemed much better and none the worse for wear. I promptly filled her in on Colgate's call, the memorial service and the buffet, ending with Blaine Carmichael's call and subsequent request.

I laughed. "I can. Blaine always had more nerve than tact. He always seems to find a way to get what he wants, too, but not this time." I gave my head a little shake. "Let's change the subject, shall we?"

"Fine with me," said Chantal. She leaned forward and propped her chin in her hands. "So what are we going to serve for the buffet supper? Have you got anything planned?"

"I thought about it last night. Colgate said nothing too fancy, which usually means exactly the opposite." I whipped a sheet of paper out of the middle drawer. "How about some chicken breasts stuffed with artichokes and Parmesan, a vegetable lasagna, and a nice glazed ham for the entrées? We can put some sliced bread and rolls near the ham just in case some people might prefer to make sandwiches. For the sides I thought of a nice crudité platter with a sour cream/yogurt dip, roasted red potatoes, and a lettuce and pear salad with raspberry vinaigrette."

Chantal licked her lips. "It sounds delicious. I am hungry now!"

I laughed. "Great, because I already called Pott's and ordered the chicken breasts and ham. It should be delivered soon. Are you sure you want to go?"

Chantal waved her hand. "Remy said he does not want me fussing over him, and you know how he can get when he thinks I am acting like a mother hen."

"Well, in that case, maybe you and Lacey can get the prep work out of the way once the meat's delivered. Mollie and I should be able to handle the lunch crowd." I glanced over at my sister, who was leaning against the back counter, thumbing through the latest issue of the *Daily Enquirer*, a San Fran–based gossip rag. "That okay with you, Lace?"

She nodded, but I wasn't sure she'd been paying attention. She seemed completely absorbed in the magazine. I scraped my chair back, walked over, pulled down the magazine and snapped my fingers in front of her face. "Hey! Are you listening?"

"Yeah, I heard you. Chantal and I will do the grunt work." She snatched the magazine back and pointed to a page. "There's an article in here about Forbes and Emily Van Horn. It definitely outs Forbes as the 'mystery man' Emily was seeing."

"Yeah?" I peered over my sister's shoulder. "Does it say who wrote the article?"

"Brad Thatcher. He's a freelance reporter."

"Oh." I'd been hoping it might have been written by Millicent Martin. "What's it say?"

She riffled the pages. "Apparently Emily was ready to break it off, but Forbes wasn't. They had a very public argument outside the studio in LA just last week."

"Well, they were definitely arguing yesterday," I said. "Then again, Emily Van Horn wasn't the only person who wouldn't mind seeing Forbes dead."

"Really? Would you mind sharing exactly who else is on that list?"

We'd been so engrossed in our conversation we hadn't heard the bell above the door tinkle, or notice the man who'd entered and now stood at the front counter. My lips drooped downward as I recognized him.

"Blaine Carmichael."

His thick lips parted in a wide smile, revealing teeth so white and dazzling they just had to be caps. "Ah, you remember me. It's great to see you after all these years, Nora. You haven't changed one bit."

I took in the expensive haircut, the form-fitting, well-cut suit, the silk shirt and tie. "I can't say the same. You've changed, Blaine. A lot."

He spread his hands. "What can I say? Life's been good. So what was that you were saying? There were a lot of people who threatened Forbes's life?"

I bit down hard on my lower lip before I answered. "Now, now, Blaine. You should know better than to take a remark out of context. That's not exactly what I said."

With that he held up his right hand, and I saw a mini tape recorder lying in its palm. He depressed a button, and a few seconds later we all heard my voice saying: "Emily Van Horn wasn't the only person who wouldn't mind seeing Forbes dead."

Blaine shut off the recorder. "Now, if you know something, Nora, it's your sworn duty to tell all."

"I've already told Detective Anderson," I snapped. "I certainly don't need to go into it again, and certainly not with you."

"Why not? Don't you think the public, Forbes's fans, have a right to the truth?"

"Indeed they do, but there's a vast difference between the truth and sensationalistic reporting."

He smiled again, but this time the smile didn't reach his eyes, which were cold and hard as he stared at me. "I keep forgetting what a hotshot, holier-than-thou reporter you were, although that is the operative word, isn't it? *Were.* Now you're a"—he gave a quick glance around the shop—"businesswoman." He paused. "A *small*-business woman."

Count to ten, Nora, I told myself. When I reached nine, I twisted my lips into what I hoped was a pleasant expression. "What are you doing here, Blaine?"

"Can't I visit an old friend? I was just curious to see your shop."

"Bzzt," I said. "Wrong answer. Try again."

He eased an elbow onto my countertop. "Well, I confess I was a little upset when you hung up on me so abruptly last night. All I wanted was a brief comment."

"On my finding Forbes's body. Well, there's not much else to say other than yes, I was the one who found it, now is there?"

He made a clicking sound against the roof of his mouth and shoved his hands into his jacket pockets. "Come, come, Nora. We both know there's a lot more to it. For instance, what led you to find the body? Were you just out for a walk and happened to stumble across it?"

"No," I said evenly, "I suppose I may as well tell you, since it'll be public news anyway. Forbes wanted my cat for a scene with Ardis Malone, and they were going to film it at the gazebo. He asked me to bring the cat by, and when we got there he was dead."

His eyes widened. "Oh, yes, your cat. I didn't think you cared for animals?"

"I like animals just fine. Better than some humans I know."

With that, Nick crawled out from underneath the back table and launched himself onto the back counter. He sat, tail wrapped around his forepaws, his golden eyes gleaming as he stared at Blaine.

Blaine had jumped back when Nick landed with a thump on the counter. Now he peered at him. "That's the cat, huh? He's a big one."

Nick's lip curled back to expose his sharp fangs, and he let out a loud hiss.

Blaine took another step back and straightened his tie. "He's not too friendly, is he?"

"Nick is very discerning, and a good judge of character," I responded.

"The cat's name is Nick? Nick Charles, eh? What's his nickname? The Thin Cat?" Blaine barked out a laugh, even as he regarded Nick warily. For his part, Nick let out another hiss, louder than the first. Blaine cleared his throat. "So you and Nick here found the body?"

"I believe that's what I said, yes."

Blaine splayed his hands on my countertop. "It's not the first time either, is it, Nora? That you and your cat have found a body, right?"

I narrowed my eyes. Of course, Blaine would have done his research, particularly when he'd learned it was me who was catering the *Days of Tomorrow* location shoot. No point in denying it. "No, it's not."

"So, what's the deal? I heard you recently got a PI license. Are you helping the police investigate this case?"

I barked out a laugh. "Hardly."

"Well, then, I can't see why you can't give an old friend a quote or two," he said easily. "I realize there might be some bad feelings on your part toward me, but I'm sure you would never let your personal feelings stand in the way of my reporting the news."

"I certainly wouldn't," I said, "but you don't just want to report the news, Blaine. You want to sensationalize it. You enjoy blowing things up out of proportion, and in this case you might prove to be a hindrance to Detective Anderson doing her job and finding the killer."

He took a step back and shook his head. "I mean, after last night I figured you might be jealous, but I didn't realize until now just how much."

"Jealous?" I resisted the urge to laugh out loud. "From what I understand, you're the lead entertainment reporter. Why would I be jealous?"

He lowered his voice and continued, "It's not my fault you gave up on your career and went back to your hometown. I took advantage of the breaks that life threw my way."

"It seems you're trying to take advantage of this, too."

"You bet I am! This story could be my ticket out of Hollywood reporting and into the big time, maybe even an anchor slot."

"Really? I thought you liked Hollywood reporting?"

He shot me a look. "Oh, puh-leaze. I'd trade in my studio pass for an anchor slot any day of the week. I'd get to report on real news, not who's dating who or who threw a hissy fit on some movie set. So be a pal, Nora, and help me achieve my dream."

I shook my head. "Sorry."

His lip thrust forward in a pout. "Give me one good reason why not."

"Fine. Your intentions might be good, Blaine, but your stories smack of sensational journalism. You're not above blowing facts out of proportion in order to make a story more attractive to the public."

"Oh," he jeered, "and I suppose you've never done anything like that?"

"Not to the degree I've seen you do it," I answered.

"But you have done it," he persisted. "Back in Chicago you were unstoppable when you were on a story. I know what's really going on here. You just don't want to see me catch a break."

"That's not true."

"Hell it isn't."

"What's going on here?"

We all turned to face Leroy Samms, whose face was dark as a thundercloud. His six-foot-three frame easily towered over Blaine's five-foot-eight one, and Blaine instinctively took a step back.

Samms's gaze flicked from me to Blaine back to me again. "What's going on here?" he repeated. "Who is this guy?"

"I'm Blaine Carmichael," Blaine managed to squeak out. He fumbled in his pocket, removed his press badge, and held it up to show Samms. "And just who are you?"

"Leroy Samms." Samms flicked back the lapel of his jacket, where his FBI badge was pinned. "I'm a Special Agent with the FBI, formerly the head of Cruz Homicide. Just what are you doing here, Carmichael?"

Blaine tugged at his jacket lapels. "I'm just doing my job, Special Agent Samms," he said. "I'm reporting on the death of Anton Forbes, and since Ms. Charles here found the body, I wanted to get a quote from her."

Samms leaned over so that his nose was almost even with Blaine's. "It didn't sound like you were trying to get a quote. From where I stood, it sounded like you were badgering Ms. Charles."

Carmichael took a step backward. "Me? Badgering Ms. Charles? Oh, goodness, no, Special Agent Samms, certainly not. I was merely clarifying why she refused to comment."

Samms's lips slashed into a thin line. "Pardon me, but I fail to see how the words 'no comment' could possibly be made any more clear. If Ms. Charles declines to comment, then that's her right. You continuing to harangue her, on the other hand, can be construed as harassment." His gaze settled on Blaine's hand and he noticed the tiny tape recorder clutched in his palm. "Are you recording this without Ms. Charles's consent?" he snapped.

"I . . . I . . ." Blaine stammered.

Samms trained his gaze on me. "Did you consent to him recording you?"

I shook my head. "Absolutely not."

"Well, then." Samms fixed Blaine with a stony stare. "I'm assuming you're unfamiliar, Mr. Carmichael, with California Recording Law."

Blaine blinked. "With what?"

"California Recording Law. Penal Code Section 630-638 clearly states, 'If you are recording someone without their knowledge in a public or semi-public place like a street or restaurant, the person whom you're recording may or may not have "an objectively reasonable expectation that no one is listening in or overhearing the conversation," and the reasonableness of the expectation would depend on the particular factual circumstances.' In other words, both parties have to give consent, and Ms. Charles just said she didn't." Samms reached out and plucked the mini-recorder from Blaine's outstretched hand. "I'm afraid I'm going to have to confiscate this."

Blaine's jaw dropped open, then shut again. His cheeks turned a bright shade of pink. "I have other interviews on there," he said weakly. "And notes that I'll need for my broadcast later."

Samms crossed his arms over his chest. "Well, that's too bad. Guess you should have done your homework before you started browbeating innocent citizens."

Blaine licked at his lips. "I'll have to consult with my legal department. Where can I find you later?"

Samms twirled the tiny recorder in his hand. "I'm afraid I'll be unreachable most of today, but you and Legal can take the matter up with Detective Anderson at Cruz Homicide. She's well acquainted with the law, and I'll make sure she's apprised of the situation."

"Fine." Without a backward glance in my direction, Blaine turned and stalked out the front door, letting it slam behind him. Once he'd gone, Samms set the recorder on the counter and looked at me.

"Nice friends you've got."

I gave a mock shudder. "Oh, he's not my friend. I did work with him, though, in Chicago, a long time ago. He's only gotten worse with time."

Samms scratched at his ear. "He's that nosy reporter from LA, looking to make a big name for himself. Not that we haven't been overrun with the press since yesterday, but Carmichael seems a bit more zealous than most. I'd keep an eye on him if I were you."

"You don't have to tell me," I said with feeling. "Well, thanks for getting rid of him. Is it true, what you said about California Recording Law?"

"Sure is. Look it up." He chuckled. "Sonny didn't do his research thoroughly enough on that end. Besides, there was no way I was going to let him twist your words so he could garner high ratings on his broadcast." He grinned and slid the recorder into his pocket. "I sure would like to be a fly on the wall of Dale's office, though, when Carmichael finds out I really had no right to confiscate it without a warrant." As my jaw dropped, he gave me a two-fingered salute. "See you at the service."

Chapter Twelve

"I would have loved to see the expression on Blaine Carmichael's face when Samms took that recorder away. It must have been priceless."

Ollie Sampson put down his half-eaten turkey and Swiss and dabbed at his lips with the edge of his napkin, a dainty motion I found to be completely at odds with his linebacker look-alike appearance. Ollie was a PI, and a darned good one, although he was constantly belittling his abilities. In the short time I'd known him, I'd come to consider him a close friend, and I was pretty sure he felt the same way about me.

"It was," I said and laughed, "but what would be undoubtedly even more priceless would be his expression of outrage when he goes back for the recorder, no doubt armed with the information from his legal department that Samms really had no right to confiscate it in the first place."

Ollie broke off a tiny sliver of ham and dropped it on the floor for Nick, who was lying at his feet with a hopeful expression. "I'd keep my eyes open if I were you. From what I know of Carmichael, it's a sure bet he managed to wangle an invitation to that service, and he'll be on the prowl."

"True," I agreed. "I debated attending the service at all, but then I decided it might be a good opportunity to observe the suspects, of which there are legion. Chantal and Lacey will get everything ready and I'll leave a few minutes early to help them finish up."

"Your sister was okay with that? I know how starstruck she is over the actors on that show."

"Yes, she is, but she figured she'd have a better shot at getting an autograph at the buffet than the service." I cast a cautious glance over toward the rear counter, where Lacey and Chantal were busy prepping chicken breasts. "One thing I certainly don't want Blaine getting wind of is the fact that Dale Anderson questioned Remy Gillard in connection with the case. He would, no doubt, seek him out for an interview, and we all know what a disaster that would be." My lips settled into a grim line. "I called a friend of mine at the *Trib*. Seems Blaine has aspirations of moving on from reporting on who's cheating on who in Hollywood, and he's settled on this as his breakout story. He's got his eye on an anchor job, and to get it he'd waste no time in painting Remy as nothing short of Jack the Ripper. So we can definitely count on him to be a nuisance."

Ollie finished his sandwich, pushed his plate off to one side. "Why was Anderson questioning Remy, anyway?"

I stretched my legs out in front of me. "It seems Remy has a past with the deceased, one he's being extremely closemouthed about. I think Anderson got wind of it."

"A past, eh?" Ollie's eyes slitted. "That's never a good sign. Any idea what kind of past?"

"Nope. He hasn't elaborated on that. He was snooping around Forbes's trailer today, and he's adopted a 'no comment' attitude on that as well. He also has no alibi for the TOD. He says he was at Poppies, but there are no witnesses to prove it." I let out a sigh. "I've known Remy practically my whole life. He can be a bit eccentric, shall we say? But a murderer?"

"You never know what some people will do when they're backed into a corner. I imagine it depends on this mysterious past he and Forbes had, and on whatever it was that went down between them."

I wiggled my eyebrows. "That, my friend, is the million-dollar question. His truculent attitude is what's landed him on Anderson's short list of suspects, and there's no indication he'll change anytime soon. He even refuses to talk to Chantal about it."

Chantal and Lacey walked up toward the front of the shop just as I finished speaking. Chantal came right up to the table and cocked her head. "Hey, you two look so serious. What are you talking about?"

Ollie flashed me a quick wink and smiled benignly at my friend. "Nothing much. Nora was just filling me in on what happened with

Blaine Carmichael. The guy sounds like a real trip."

Lacey plucked an oversized spoon and fork out of one of the drawers. "If you ask me, the whole episode is another example of just how much Samms cares about Nora. After all, he broke a law so that she wouldn't get embarrassed by Blaine Carmichael's cavalier reporting style."

"He didn't break a law," I sputtered. "He just took some liberties with one."

Lacey grinned. "Same difference."

"And just to be clear, no one asked you."

She made a face and turned her back on me.

Chantal spoke up as she slid the chocolate mousse I'd prepared for dessert into the refrigerator. "I have to agree, *chérie*. Samms did not have to do that. He was trying to spare you embarrassment. Oh, yes." She bobbed her head up and down. "It is a definite sign."

"A sign from the universe?" I asked dryly. I turned to Ollie. "Chantal is convinced that if I don't choose between Samms and Daniel soon, the universe will make up my mind for me."

"It's true," Chantal said earnestly. "I saw it in the cards twice. But Nora refuses to listen."

"Hm," said Ollie. "One thing I wouldn't fool around with is the universe."

I cut Ollie an exasperated look. *"Et tu, Ollie? Et tu?"*

"Hey." He held up both hands in a gesture of surrender. "There are some things you just shouldn't fight, that's all I'm sayin'."

I cleared my throat. "We've got other things to think about. Can we please put my love life on the back burner and concentrate on getting this food ready?"

"Fine," Chantal said. "But you should listen to Ollie, Nora. Some things are just inevitable." She motioned to Lacey. "Come on, Lacey. You can help me put the glaze on the ham."

As the two of them moved off, I grinned at Ollie. "Just over a year ago Chantal couldn't even boil water, and look at her now. There's hope for Lacey yet." I ducked as my sister threw a dishrag at me. I snatched it up and snapped it between my fingers. "Would you like to come along? I can say you're one of my assistants, but don't worry, I won't make you cook or serve."

He grinned and pushed back his chair. "As much as I enjoy a good memorial, I have an appointment with a prospective client in Carmel."

"Another philandering husband?"

"No. A philandering cocker spaniel. Poor Roscoe is missing, and Mrs. James suspects her sister-in-law of dognapping. Apparently there's been a family dispute over the pooch going on for quite a while. What can I say?" He spread his hands. "It's a job. Someday, perhaps, when I acquire a new partner, then the caliber of my cases might improve."

I followed his gaze toward my PI license. "Is that a gentle hint?"

He grinned. "No, it's a flat-out offer. I've told you this before. Anytime you want to hang up your apron for a deerstalker cap and magnifying glass, you let me know."

I laughed. "You know the minute I did that, Nick Atkins would come back, right?"

Ollie shook his head. "I'd like to agree with you, but since it's been a while since either of us has heard anything from him, I rather doubt it."

I knew Ollie was referring to the postcards his former partner and Nick the cat's prior human had sent to both of us, often with cryptic messages. It had been a few months since either one of us had received one. The last one I'd gotten had said simply, *Good Job. N.* The postmark had been California, but Atkins, presumably a spy, could be anywhere. "I haven't heard from Daniel either," I said, "although he did warn me it might be a while. Maybe that's why I'm so fixated on Forbes. It keeps my mind off other things."

Ollie leaned back, his eyes slitted in concentration. "Want some advice?" Before I could answer he went on, "If I were you, I'd make a comprehensive list of suspects and any possible motives you can think of. It'll help you narrow down the field. Don't leave anyone out, no matter how big or small you think their motive for wanting Forbes dead might be. I also think it would be a good idea for you to revisit the crime scene. Your sharp eyes might find something the police have overlooked."

I frowned. "I don't think they've released the gazebo yet."

"Doesn't matter. You can form a plan, jot down areas that need to be worked. You went over the scientific method in your PI class, right?"

"Oh, yeah." I closed my eyes and recited, "State the problem, form the hypothesis, collect the data, interpret the data to test the hypothesis. If supported, collect additional data. If your hypothesis is disproved, go through the steps again. Then when your data and hypothesis match, draw conclusions and develop your theory."

"Excellent," Ollie said. "So, the problem is Anton Forbes, murdered in the gazebo with the, the what? We don't know what the murder weapon is, do we?"

I shook my head. "I didn't see any evidence of a gunshot or stab wound. He had odd, lattice-like marks on his neck, which might indicate strangulation, but I didn't see any defensive marks on his hands, either."

"Hm. You need to definitely determine the cause of death before you can work on narrowing down your suspect list." He reached out and patted my hand. "Just remember, trace evidence is always present, and nine times out of ten a valuable piece of it is often overlooked. Check out the gazebo first chance you get and take little Nick with you. He's got a nose for clues."

The cat in question let out a sharp merow of agreement.

I laughed. "You know, you're pretty smart, Ollie. I should ask for your input more often."

He laughed as he started for the door. "I'm always available to help you out on detection matters. When it comes to your love life, though . . . you're on your own."

"Because Dear Abby, you're not, right?"

"Right." He started out the door, then turned abruptly and came back. "I almost forgot. I looked through Nick's old case files. I found something on that case you asked me about, the one that involved a magic shop?" He reached into his breast pocket, pulled out a few sheets of paper and pressed them into my hand. "I have to warn you, the notes are pretty sketchy."

I unfolded the sheets and scanned them quickly. "You're right," I said at last. "From this it appears that he's not certain if the owner of Castorelli's Magic Shop, one Philip Castorelli, is involved in any illegal activity or not. He mentions following up on several dead-end leads, and then he mentions getting a tip, but he doesn't say from whom. Then on the last page he mentions a stakeout. That's probably the one that resulted in the shoot-out and his adopting Nick."

"Most likely," Ollie agreed. "I used to get very frustrated when I had to look through his notes. Nick was always very cagey with what information he'd consign to paper." He offered me a thin smile. "Nick wasn't exactly the most trusting of individuals, and he certainly wasn't the most eloquent. He did have a habit of separating what notes he did write into different sections, though. There might be more scattered in some of the other files. I'll keep looking."

"Thanks, Ollie. I really hate to bother you with this, but . . ."

"But the thought of Nick the cat being found behind a magic shop intrigues you," Ollie said. "I confess it's piqued my interest too." He barked out a laugh. "Nick being Harry Houdini reincarnated would explain a lot, wouldn't it?"

I smiled. "It certainly would, although we both know that's not possible."

Ollie glanced over at Nick. "Isn't it? Sometimes I wonder."

Ollie left and Nick lofted up onto the rear counter. He stuck out one paw toward the papers I held in my hand. "Merow?"

"Yes, they belonged to your former human. These are notes on the case he was working on when he found you." I tapped the papers against my chin. "I guess the question is, do I want to open up a can of worms? Heck, no, but I am curious to find out more about you, you rascal. Not that I really think you're Harry Houdini, or anything like that, but sometimes you have to admit, your abilities are a bit . . . uncanny? Otherworldly? Downright spooky? All of the above?"

Nick sat back on his haunches and puffed out his chest. "Merow."

I frowned. "I'd sure like to find out more about you, Nick, but . . . I wouldn't want to lose you in the process. I've always said that I'd fight Atkins for you if he ever came back, but . . . maybe Atkins wouldn't be the only one with a claim to you. What if that Philip Castorelli wanted you back?"

Nick blinked, then rolled over on his side. Apparently that possibility didn't bother him. I wished I could say the same. I walked over to the counter, jerked open the middle drawer, and shoved the papers inside. "I guess this can wait a while." I blew out a breath. "After all, one mystery at a time, right?"

Nick emitted a loud snore, and I grinned in spite of myself. "My thoughts exactly," I said.

• • •

By three o'clock the food was precooked, packed and ready to be trundled over to Cruz High. I had to confess to a bout of nostalgia as I parked the rented van in the back parking lot near the cafeteria service entrance.

"What's the matter, Nors?" Lacey, in the backseat, looked at me in the rearview mirror. "Missing the good, old, carefree days of Cruz High, or the times you and Lance got caught necking by that tree over there?" Her grin was wicked as she gestured toward a large elm with spreading branches at the far end of the lot.

"Maybe a little bit of both." I shut off the van and we all climbed out. Lacey started to open the van's double doors, but I held up my hand. "Let's take a look at the cafeteria setup first. I'm dying to see all the improvements they've made."

We all trooped through the rear service entrance into the cafeteria. I had to make a conscious effort to keep from drooling as I took in the remodeled floor, freshly painted walls, and state-of-the-art appliances, including a top-of-the-line smoothie maker that I knew cost a pretty penny. Lacey came up behind me and touched my shoulder. "Don't worry, Nors. With the money you'll make from this job you'll be able to get two of those."

"I hope so. I noticed the back burners on the stove weren't working properly the other day, and I know the freezer in the back is going to need to be replaced soon. Unfortunately, those take precedence over a smoothie maker."

There was a large cart in the corner. We commandeered that and used it to wheel in the trays of food, then we went across the hall to the auditorium. The maintenance crew had done a good job. They'd pulled in tables from the cafeteria and set them with white tablecloths. A long table had been set up right in front of the stage, also covered with a white tablecloth, and there were plates and cutlery already out.

"This is great," Chantal said. "All we have to do is heat the food, set up the trays with the Sterno, and then set out all the cold food and drinks."

"Colgate said the service would take about a half hour, so I'd start heating things up around four. Everyone should be back here by four forty-five at the latest."

"Hm. I wonder how many reporters will be in attendance, and how many will be on hand for a free meal?" mused Chantal.

"Well, if Blaine Carmichael is there, you can bet he'll be one of the first in line. Back when he was on the *Trib* we always used to kid that 'free' was his middle name." I glanced around. "Say, where's Lacey?"

"I'm right here."

Chantal and I glanced up at the stage and there was my sister, standing next to a large poster board that had photographs plastered all over it. She waved her hand. "Come see," she said. "It's a collage of photos of Forbes."

Chantal and I walked up the short flight of steps and over to where my sister stood next to an immense poster board covered with photographs. I recognized photos of Forbes with the *Days of Tomorrow* cast. Most of the actors were wearing large, phony smiles as they posed with their director. There were others that must have been culled from movies Forbes directed prior to joining the television show. One in particular caught my eye: Forbes, standing just off to the left of a good-looking man seated in a director's chair. The two men were surrounded by cast members, and I figured the guy in the chair was probably Dean Harriman. Forbes was smiling, but his eyes, fastened on the director, looked cold and hard. A well-endowed blonde stood just in back of Harriman. Her hand rested on the director's shoulder, but her head was turned slightly toward Forbes and there was no mistaking the worshipful look in her eyes. It seemed to me that I'd seen the woman somewhere before but couldn't place just where—an old movie, perhaps? I'd have to inquire who she was. I glanced at some of the other photos and recognized several of my favorite actors in shots where Forbes was in formal dress. They must have been taken at awards shows. I also noted the expressions on the actors' faces. No one seemed particularly thrilled to be with Forbes, although the man himself wore a wide, albeit probably phony, smile in every shot.

"They sure made it look like he had lots of friends, didn't they?"

We all whirled around at the same time. Mamie Monroe stood behind us, a wry look on her face. She gestured toward the board. "PR put this up. They're trying to perpetuate the myth that Forbes was well-liked. Hah! What a crock. No one could even stand being in the same room with Forbes for very long. Look around at all the faces when everyone starts coming in and you'll see what I mean. None of 'em are gonna look particularly sad, except for one or two."

Chantal arched a brow. "You mean Emily Van Horn?"

Mamie frowned. "Maybe. Jury's still out on that one. One thing's for sure, though. Morale on this set will improve a thousandfold, now the wicked witch is dead, or should I say wicked warlock?" She closed one eye in a broad wink. "Colgate's no angel, but at least he has some regard for humanity. He doesn't expect the impossible out of people, and from what I've heard, he hasn't sold his soul just to get a promotion, at least not yet."

I eyed her. "Is that what Forbes did? He sold his soul?"

"A long time ago." Her eyes took on a dreamy aspect. "He started out in the business directing horror movies, did you know that? He was good at it too, but then he started to think he was too big for his britches. He thought he was better than everyone, especially his mentor."

I raised an eyebrow. "His mentor? You mean Dan Harriman?"

Mamie leaned over and tapped the photo I'd been looking at. "Yep. Harriman was a genius, all right. Not to say he didn't have his faults, or at least, that's what I've heard," she added quickly. "On the other hand, there're very few people with anything nice to say about Forbes. Personally, I'm dying to hear the eulogy Colgate's prepared. Now there will be a quality piece of acting."

The auditorium door opened and Colgate walked in, Ned Reilly trailing behind him. Mamie Monroe gave me a nudge with her elbow and said, "Oops, there's my cue to scram. Let me know if I was right, okay?" She turned on her heel and tripped down the steps and over to the side door. As she opened it, Ned Reilly happened to look up. The two of them stared at each other for a moment, and then Mamie hurried out the door. For a split second I thought Reilly was going to go after her, but then Colgate glanced up and saw the rest of us standing on the stage. He nudged Ned and the two of them came over to us.

"Ah, there you are. I saw the van outside." He gave me a tight smile and then nodded briefly to Chantal and Lacey. "I trust the kitchen accoutrements are satisfactory?"

"Very much so. We were just taking a quick look around. The maintenance crew did a great job."

"Yes, well, they were paid enough," Colgate sniffed. "We'll be starting promptly at four fifteen. Ned and I just came in here for a quick moment to practice my speech." He patted his breast pocket, where a sliver of paper peeked out. "Will you be attending the service?"

"I will," I said. "My sister and Chantal will have everything ready for people to come in and start eating as soon as it ends."

"Perfect. Thank you again, Ms. Charles."

Ned Reilly also inclined his head. "Yes. Thank you."

The two men turned away, and we slipped quietly out the side door and back to the cafeteria kitchen. After giving a few more instructions, I left everything in Chantal's and my sister's capable hands (well, in Chantal's anyway), and made my way to the chapel, which was only about a five-minute walk from the high school. Once inside the building, I made my way up the staircase that led to the semicircular balcony that overlooked the chapel. The balcony was deserted, as I'd expected, and I took a seat in the first row and scooted over to the edge of the pew to peer over the railing. I had an excellent view of the wide, carpeted center aisle that separated the rows of dark wood benches. At the front was the pulpit on the cherrywood stage, a magnificent stained glass window in the background. A large photograph of Forbes rested on an easel just to the right of the podium, one that had apparently been taken in the director's younger days—his hair was darker, his face not as gaunt.

A few minutes later the doors to the chapel opened and people started to file in. I recognized many of the cast and crew as they shuffled in and took seats, most of them in the back. Ardis Malone came in, her trim figure accentuated by the tight black sheath she wore, and took a seat right in the front pew. A few minutes after that, Emily Van Horn came in. She had on a surplice wrap dress in a dark indigo color that was especially flattering with her dark red hair and fair complexion, and matching low-heeled shoes. Her hair was pulled back in a severe bun, and she looked definitely ill at ease. I noticed that she slid into a seat in the very last pew, slouched down, and then slipped on a pair of dark glasses, almost as if she wanted to become invisible.

I saw several other cast and crew members I'd met enter and take seats. I also recognized Ira Heff from the *Cruz Sun* as he sauntered to a seat in the middle. Right on his heels was Mamie Monroe. To my surprise, she walked right up to the front pew and seated herself next to

Ardis Malone. Ardis leaned over and whispered something to her, and I saw Mamie shake her head vigorously. Ned Reilly entered by a side door and headed toward the middle. He passed right in front of Mamie Monroe, and I saw his head turn slightly toward her. Mamie, for her part, fiddled with the hem of her skirt and didn't look up until Reilly had gone by. It seemed as if she were deliberately ignoring the PR guy.

A floorboard creaked somewhere behind me and I glanced up to meet Samms's surprised gaze. "What are you doing here?" we both said at once. After a second I couldn't resist adding, "Helping Dale out again?"

He nodded. "There are a lot of curious onlookers out there, not to mention those vultures called the press that have been swarming around ever since news of Forbes's death got out." He eased himself down next to me. "I thought this would be a good observation post. I see you thought the same thing."

I nodded as I glanced down at the chapel again and sucked in my breath as a familiar face came into my line of vision. "I see Blaine Carmichael managed to get himself invited."

Samms nodded. "His producer at the news station must have pull with someone," he muttered, then a slow grin spread over his face. "He sent some lackey down to the station to pick up his recorder. I guess he wasted no time contacting Legal."

"Probably not," I agreed. "Let's just hope that nothing happens today that raises his antennae."

"Don't worry. If nothing exciting happens, I'm sure he'll make something up."

I peered over the edge of the railing. "I don't see Mark Emerson anywhere," I said.

The chapel door opened again and the murmuring in the crowd ceased as Kenny Colgate strode purposefully toward the lectern. Samms leaned over and whispered, "I understand he's to be the only speaker, so this should be a very short service."

I watched Colgate take his place. "From what I observed, Colgate wasn't fond of him either. I imagine he was ordered to give this little speech. It's kind of sad when you think of it, isn't it, that someone could be disliked so much?"

Kenny Colgate adjusted the microphone and cleared his throat. "Good afternoon, everyone. As you know, we've recently suffered a tragedy here. We've lost a brilliant director in Anton Forbes. Forbes had an incredibly creative mind, and he only thought about the good of the show. It's a tremendous loss for both the show and for those who knew him . . ."

"Oh, puh-*leaze!*"

Everyone turned at once to the rear of the chapel at the sound of the double doors banging back. Mark Emerson stood framed in the doorway. From where I sat he bore no resemblance to the pleasant, affable man I'd met the day before. His face looked red and puffy, his eyes a bit glassy. Instead of a suit he wore a baggy sweatshirt and jeans with holes in the knees. He moved away from the door and began to walk down the center aisle, his movements jerky, his gait unsteady, almost as if he'd imbibed one too many.

Without thinking I reached out and gripped Samms's arm. "Look at him," I whispered. "Is he drunk?"

A muscle in Samms's jaw twitched. "Could be."

Mark had arrived at the podium. He made his way to stand next to Kenny, who was looking at him with a horrified expression on his face. "Mark, I don't think this is the right time," he began, but Emerson cut him off.

"Sure it ish," he said, his words slurring slightly. He leaned across the podium and opened his mouth to say something to Kenny. Colgate took a step back, a sour expression on his face.

"Good Lord, man," he said. "For pity's sake, step down."

Mark gave Kenny a push to the side and took his place at the podium, gripping its sides tightly. "We all knew Anton Forbes. Of course, some of us knew him better than others. Way better." His gaze darted around the chapel, finally coming to rest on Emily. "Forbes was a brilliant man, true. He was brilliant at hiding his true self from the world. Many thought he was a charming man, a successful man. They had no idea what a demon he truly was. Forbes was a man who wasn't above lying and cheating and taking what wasn't his to achieve his end goal." Emerson leaned almost all the way across the podium, his eyes overbright. "Some even think he was the type to take a life to get what he wanted." He jabbed a finger into the air. "Look at you all sitting here, feigning remorse for a man who we're all better off without. You know what you all are? Hypocrites! You'd rather sit here and pay homage to a man you all hated rather than admit the truth. There's not one person in here, not one, who's sorry he's dead. Wait, maybe there is one." He put his hand up to shield his eyes and looked out over the crowd. "Emily? Are you here?"

Kenny Colgate stepped forward. "I think that's quite enough, Emerson. Please leave the altar or I'll have you escorted off."

"I'd better get down there," Samms muttered. He rose and started toward the stairwell. I debated going with him, but my eyes were glued to the drama going on before me. It was like watching an episode of the nighttime drama unfold in real life.

Emerson whirled to face him. "Leave the altar, huh? Not before I say what I came to say." He passed a hand over his eyes, and a confused look appeared on his face. "Forbes was murdered, and for all I know, I could have done it. I could have killed Anton Forbes."

There was a loud, collective gasp from the audience, and then Ardis Malone jumped to her feet. "What!"

Kenny's arm shot out. "Mark! Not another word."

Blaine Carmichael was on his feet, with a cameraman directly behind him. He pushed his way to the front and jabbed a microphone up toward Mark. "What are you saying, Mr. Emerson? Are you confessing that you did it? That you murdered Forbes?"

"Why . . . I dunno. Maybe," Mark mumbled. And then the entire chapel was on their feet as the actor let out a long sigh and slid, unconscious, to the floor.

Chapter Thirteen

Kenny Colgate was the first to reach Mark. He bent over him and pressed his head to his chest, and after a few seconds shouted, "He's barely breathing. Someone call 911."

Several people scrambled for cell phones, while Ardis Malone and Mamie Monroe jumped up and hurried toward the altar stairs. Emily Van Horn, her knuckles pressed to her mouth, half rose from her seat. I thought for a brief second she was going to follow Ardis and Mamie up onto the altar, but instead she turned and headed toward the rear door. Out of the corner of my eye I noticed Blaine Carmichael shove his microphone under Ardis Malone's nose just as she was about to ascend the steps. "Miss Malone! Tell our viewers what you thought about Mark Emerson's confession?"

Ardis whirled on Carmichael, her lip curled back, teeth bared in a snarl. "You reporters are crazy," she burst out. She gestured with her arm wildly toward where Mark lay, Colgate and Mamie bent over him. "Can't you see there's something wrong with him?"

Blaine, unfazed by Ardis's reaction, pressed closer. "So, would you say that Mark Emerson's confession was nothing more than an act?"

Ardis let out a sharp gasp, then slapped at the microphone. "How can you say something like that! Get this out of my face."

"You didn't answer my question, Ms. Malone—ow!"

Carmichael winced as Samms grabbed him by the shoulder and pulled him away from Ardis, who scrambled up the steps. "Just what do you think you're doing, Carmichael?" Samms growled.

Blaine tried unsuccessfully to shake Samms's hand off. "Let go of me," he rasped. "I have a perfect right to be here and report this story."

Samms shook his head. "I swear, Carmichael, you've got more guts than brains."

"I beg your pardon. Didn't you hear him? Mark Emerson practically confessed to murder. Shouldn't the police look into that, or am I mistaken?"

"I heard him just fine, and I'm quite sure Detective Anderson will conduct a thorough investigation. What Mark Emerson needs most right now is a medic, not a reporter looking to make a name for himself jamming a microphone under his nose. Now take your cameraman and get the hell away."

Samms released Blaine's arm and the reporter staggered backward, narrowly missing his cameraman. Blaine drew himself up straight and tugged at the lapels of his expensive Brooks Brothers jacket. "Fine, I'll move. But you can't stop me from reporting this news. I assume you're familiar with the First Amendment, which guarantees freedom of the press? Shall I quote it?" He didn't wait for Samms to answer, but put his hand over his heart and recited in a clear voice: *"Congress shall make no law . . . abridging the freedom of speech, or of the press . . ."*

Samms waved him back, a look of disgust on his face. "I'm quite familiar with our Constitution. Now, do everyone a favor and go do your reporting elsewhere."

Blaine's jaw thrust out, then he turned to his cameraman. "Come on, Hugo. We'll get statements from some of the *cooperative* people."

Blaine stalked off, Hugo trailing behind. Two uniformed officers pushed through the crowd and a few minutes later they had the remaining onlookers pushed back and a path cleared for the EMT's arrival. When Blaine didn't reappear, I figured it was probably safe for me to come down from the balcony. I emerged onto the main floor just as the wail of an ambulance reached my ears. The front door of the chapel burst open and two EMTs hurried in, carrying a stretcher. They made their way to the stage and I heard Colgate say, "He's got a pulse, but it's very thready." They continued CPR, and after a few minutes got Mark onto a stretcher and out of the chapel and into the waiting ambulance. The crowd, who had been silent for the most part while all this was taking place, now buzzed with conversation. As I stood on the fringe, unsure of what to do next, Kenny Colgate came up to me. He pulled a handkerchief out of his vest pocket and swiped at his brow.

"Good Lord, what a mess," he said.

"What happened?" I asked. "Was Mark Emerson drunk?"

The director nodded. "That appears to be the case. His breath reeked of alcohol. I knew he'd been upset the last few weeks, but I didn't realize he'd lapsed." At my look he added in a low tone, "Mark is a recovering alcoholic. It's not something the studio advertises. I'm sure I can trust you to be discreet with this information?"

I nodded. "Of course." After a moment I added, "You said he'd been upset? With Forbes?"

"Yes, of course. You don't read the gossip columns much, do you? He's been upset over his broken relationship with Emily. She's been seeing another man for several weeks now. The producers warned him against getting involved with a costar, but did he listen? Hell, no."

"And Mark knew Forbes was the 'other man' Emily was involved with?"

Colgate sighed. "If he didn't know it before, he surely found out when some reporter's article hit the stands. We tried doing damage control, but . . ." He spread his hands. "It was hard to buck a man like Forbes. The studio turned a blind eye to his many faults because they were eager to latch on to his talent, they wanted him to make a raging success of the show. And now they all have to ask themselves, was it all worth it?" He swiped a hand over his chin. "For my money, Mark Emerson's a good kid and a fine actor. He's worth ten of Forbes."

"So you don't think there's anything to his confession?"

Colgate frowned. "I'm not sure. Not that there weren't many times I'm sure Mark could have cheerfully killed Forbes, but if he went on a binge and blanked out . . . well, who knows?"

Ned Reilly bustled up to us. Totally ignoring me, he said to Colgate, "The police want to speak to you, Kenny. They've advised us to send everyone on their way."

"Thanks, Ned." Colgate gave me an apologetic look. "Excuse me, Ms. Charles. Duty calls."

"The food is all set up in the high school auditorium," I offered. "If anyone feels like eating, that is."

Kenny glanced around. "It appears that the majority of the cast and crew have left," he said. "I'll tell whoever's left, but I'm afraid on the whole, the buffet is a bust."

He and the other man hurried off. I looked around for Samms, but he was nowhere to be found, so I made my way back over to the high school. As I entered the auditorium, Chantal rushed up to me.

"*Chérie*, is it true? Mark Emerson murdered Anton Forbes?"

I glanced around. There were a few people sitting at some of the tables, picking half-heartedly at the food. I noticed Mamie Monroe seated at one, so I had a pretty good idea who'd filled Chantal in.

"He's unsure. He thought he might have done it," I said. "But it appears to be more the product of a drunken stupor than an actual fact, at least, I hope that's the case." I rolled my head slowly from one shoulder to the other to work the kinks out of my neck. "He was in pretty bad shape. The EMTs took him out in an ambulance."

"And I suppose your friend Blaine Carmichael was there, reporting every step of the way."

"Actually, Samms got rid of him just before the EMTs got there. He was being his usual insufferable self, trying to get Ardis Malone to comment on Mark's remark that he might have murdered Forbes." I looked around the room. "I have a feeling this is all that's going to show up. Mark's appearance definitely put a damper on things."

"We'll start packing up as soon as these tables clear out." Chantal waved a hand toward the trays. "You will have lots of food for specials this week."

"Hmm," I murmured. My attention was focused on the activity outside the auditorium's big picture window. A police cruiser pulled up, and Dale Anderson alighted. She spoke rapidly into her cell phone, and a few minutes later I saw Samms run out of the chapel. Dale said something to him, and then the two of them got back into the sedan. Dale pealed out of there like her tires were on fire.

Chantal touched my arm. "Nora? Is everything all right?"

I smiled at my friend. "Sure, everything's fine. Let's start packing some of this food up."

I couldn't help but wonder what that little meeting had been all about, because unless my sense of direction was off, Dale and Samms were headed straight for the gazebo.

• • •

About an hour later, when I let myself in the back door of Hot Bread, I found Nick waiting just inside the door.

"Hey, buddy." I leaned down to him, rubbed the top of his head. Nick's golden eyes narrowed as he looked up at me and he began to purr. I chuckled. "Glad you're not upset that I locked you in the kitchen so you couldn't sneak in the van this time."

Lacey and Chantal followed me in, and both women promptly knelt down to make a fuss over Nick. I removed my jacket, tossed it over the back of a chair, and then walked over to the stove. I picked up the teakettle, filled it, and put it on a low flame. "This was some day," I said.

"Agreed." Chantal bent to give Nick a pat behind his white streak. "You should be glad you missed it, Nicky," she said to the cat.

Nick cocked his head and let out a resounding purr.

"I suppose we should bring in those trays from the van," mumbled Lacey. She walked over to the cake plate on the counter, lifted the lid, and selected a red velvet cupcake. She sat down, carefully peeling the paper liner away with the edge of one fingernail.

"It can wait a few minutes," I said. The kettle whistled, and I spooned cocoa mix into three mugs, added the hot water and some marshmallows. "I think we need a little pick-me-up first, and what better than cocoa?"

Chantal grinned. "Cocoa with a little something extra?"

I opened one of the bottom drawers and pulled out a bottle of Kahlúa. "Exactly."

We all sat around the table sipping cocoa laced with Kahlúa for a few minutes before anyone spoke. "Maybe I should turn on the TV," suggested Lacey. "The six o'clock news is just coming on. Maybe there will be some news on Mark."

"With Blaine Carmichael there, you can bet there will be," I said. "I only hope he doesn't blow it up too much out of proportion."

Lacey grabbed the remote and turned the TV on, then switched it to channel KLBY. The news was on, but it was a female newscaster reporting on a school fire, not Blaine.

"I wonder if the shoot is still on for tomorrow, and if our services will be required?" Chantal asked.

I sighed. "Good question. Unless I hear otherwise, I'm assuming it is. It was a close call for Colgate to agree to suspend it for a day in Forbes's memory, so I doubt he'll feel Mark's lapse is worthy. I've got plenty of bacon and sausage, so tomorrow I'll get up early, cook up some hash, prepare some scrambled and easy-over eggs and French toast. That should be plenty."

"It is Mollie's turn to go with you, right?"

"Yes, but she texted me earlier that she's got to study for a Spanish test, and she'd just rather work here at Hot Bread, so"—I gestured toward the two other women—"you two can duke it out."

"Lacey can go," Chantal said generously. "After all, she got cheated again today what with all the excitement."

Lacey's head snapped up. "Yeah, but now Mark Emerson won't be there, and he was the one I really wanted to meet." She let out a long sigh. "With my luck, Dale is probably reading him his rights right now, in a hospital bed."

Chantal clucked her tongue. "Detective Anderson is not that cruel. Surely she would wait for him to recover."

I recalled Dale and Samms hightailing it out of the parking lot and frowned. "Dale might have other things on her mind right now," I said.

Lacey suddenly pointed at the screen. "Look! There's Blaine Carmichael."

She jabbed at the remote, making the volume higher, and Blaine's nasal tones filled the room. "This is Blaine Carmichael reporting from Cruz, California, where I attended the hastily prepared memorial service for the fallen director of the nighttime drama *All the Days of Tomorrow*, Anton Forbes. Kenny Colgate's tribute to the slain director was dramatically interrupted by the appearance of Mark Emerson. Emerson, clearly in an inebriated state, made a dramatic confession."

We all watched as the tape of Mark staggering onto the altar played. Chantal and Lacey watched, mouths agape, and when we got to the part where Mark admitted he wasn't certain if he'd murdered the director, Lacey jumped up, waving her arms. "He filmed this? That guy has *no* scruples, Nors, none whatever! Not in a million years would you have done something like this."

"Of course she wouldn't," Chantal said, tugging at the hem of Lacey's tunic. "Now sit down."

"Sorry," Lacey mumbled, sinking back into her chair. "It's just I can't stand that guy."

"Who can?" I remarked. I glanced over at Chantal and pointed. "Your pocket is moving," I said.

Chantal looked down. "I had my phone on vibrate," she said as she pulled out her cell. She glanced at the number, frowned, murmured, "Excuse me," and moved off to the far corner of the kitchen. Lacey and I turned our attention back to the screen, where Blaine froze the frame as Mark collapsed to the floor. "Mark Emerson was taken to Cruz General, where he is now reported to be in stable condition. Onlookers were stunned by Emerson's declaration that he might have murdered the director; however, this reporter learned, just minutes ago, that new evidence has come to light that exonerates the actor. He is not under suspicion in Forbes's murder. According to an unnamed source, police already have a suspect in custody. Rest assured, I'll report more details as they become available. Back to you, Marlene."

Lacey grabbed the remote and muted the TV. "Did you hear that? They've cleared Mark! I wonder who this suspect is they have in custody?"

A feeling of apprehension started to inch its way along my spine. I glanced over at Chantal. She was just sliding her phone back into her pocket. Her face was pale, and I noticed her hand was trembling. I immediately jumped up and raced to her side, slid my arm around her shoulders.

"Chantal, what's wrong?"

"That was Remy. He needs me to get him a lawyer." Her voice broke and tears threatened to spill down her cheeks. "Dale Anderson has arrested him for the murder of Anton Forbes."

Chapter Fourteen

I wasted no time bundling Chantal into my SUV and heading out to the Cruz police station. The uniformed woman who sat at the front desk wasn't one I recognized. She wore a name tag that read *Officer Adams*, and both her thinly penciled eyebrows rose when Chantal said she was there to see Remy Gillard. She pulled a stack of fat folders in front of her, thumbed through them, and finally pulled a sheet of paper out of one.

"Remy Gillard was just brought in," she said. Her tone was hard, but there was a sympathetic gleam in her eye as she looked at Chantal. "You can wait in the lobby or come back later. It'll take a couple of hours to process the paperwork and get him in the system."

"Is Detective Anderson in? Or Leroy Samms?" I asked.

Officer Adams peered at me over the rims of her wire-framed glasses. "Detective Anderson is occupied. I'm not sure where Special Agent Samms is." The phone at her elbow rang, and she gave me a pointed look. "Excuse me."

I took that as a dismissal, and guided Chantal over to a bank of chairs on the left wall. She sank into one and looked up at me. "What do we do now?" she moaned, balling her hands into fists. "You know as well as I, Nora, that my brother would never kill anyone."

"Since Anderson and Samms are unavailable right now, the next step is to get Remy a good lawyer." I said. "I can give Peter Dobbs and Hal Frey a call, see which one is available to take Remy's case."

Chantal leaned back in the chair and closed her eyes. "Yes, please do that," she murmured.

Fortunately I had both numbers on speed dial on my phone. In both cases I got voicemail. I left a message for each to call me regarding an urgent matter and then looked at my friend again. "I read Remy's cards this morning," she said. "The Tower, reversed, kept popping up. That card usually foretells of impending disaster." Her lips parted in a

114

gigantic sigh. "What do we do next?" she asked.

"Well, once he's booked and we get him a lawyer, there will be a preliminary hearing as soon as they can get it scheduled, the sooner the better. I'm sure either Peter or Hal will try to get Remy out on bail." I paused. "In a murder case it can go pretty steep. Does Remy have any money socked away, any investments you know of?"

The corners of Chantal's lips twitched. "My brother? He is so frugal his shoes squeak, you know that, Nora. He has the first dollar he ever earned. And of course there is Poppies. Our parents put the business in both our names."

"You might have to put the business up. But don't panic yet. We'll see how things go. Damn, I wish Anderson or Samms was available. I want to know what they found at the gazebo."

"Maybe you should ask Blaine Carmichael," Chantal said tonelessly. "He must have an inside source. After all, he knew about the police arresting Remy."

I slapped my forehead with my palm. "Carmichael! I forgot about him." I could just see him now, camped out in front of Poppies, lying in wait for Chantal. "You'd better stay with me tonight," I said. "Unless you want a microphone shoved in your face too."

"Nora? I thought that was you."

I looked up and smiled at the familiar face. Bill Kelly was a longtime customer of Hot Bread and one of the more forthcoming detectives on the force. I reached out and clasped the proffered hand.

"Hey, Bill, good to see you. You haven't been in the shop lately."

"No, sorry. Anderson's been keeping me pretty busy." His eyes widened slightly as he noticed Chantal. "Hey, Chantal," he said softly. "I guess you're here to see Remy."

"Yes," Chantal said, "but the officer at the desk said he was being processed, and it would be a while. Processed," she spat out, "like he is a common criminal."

Kelly's eyebrow rose. "I know you're upset, Chantal, but Anderson didn't really have a choice."

I pounced on Bill's remark. "No choice? Why?"

Kelly shifted his weight from side to side uneasily and glanced toward the desk. "Now, Nora, you know I can't say anything."

He started to move away but I followed him. I had no intention of letting this go, not by a long shot. "I think you just did, Bill," I said. "They found something at the gazebo, didn't they?"

"Look, I can't—" Kelly began, but stopped as Adams looked up and saw him. She made a motion for him to approach the desk. "Sorry, kids. Good luck. Nora, I'll visit Hot Bread soon, I promise."

Bill moved off and Chantal slumped back miserably in the chair. "Now I am really worried," she said. "What on earth could they have found to make them arrest Remy?"

I mentally berated myself for not taking Ollie's advice and searching the gazebo sooner. At the very least, we'd have known what Remy was up against. My cell rang and I fished it out of my pocket. Seeing Hal Frey's number, I clicked the phone on and said, "Hal, thanks for getting back to me."

"Well, when Nora Charles calls, I can be certain it's got something to do with a murder," he said. "I'm not wrong, am I?"

"Nope," I said. I hit the highlights and when I finished said, "Do you think you can take the case?"

"Fortunately for you, my caseload's a bit light right now, so yeah, I'd be glad to help out Chantal and her brother," Hal said. "He's being processed now, you said?"

"Yes. The officer at the desk said it might take a few hours."

"Hm," Hal muttered. "That's because they'll try to grill him to get him to admit to the crime. Tell you what, I can be down there in about forty-five minutes. I'll also try to get an arraignment hearing set up as soon as possible. Tell Chantal to hang in there. Oh, and by the way, how's your sister doing?"

His question surprised me for a moment and then I replied, "Lacey? She's fine, thanks for asking."

"Great. Tell her I said hi, and I'll see you in a few."

I patted Chantal's hand as I slid my phone back in my pocket. "Keep a stiff upper lip. Reinforcements are coming. Hal's got good contacts. He might even be able to persuade a judge to hear the case tonight. Then if all goes well, you could take Remy home."

Chantal crossed her fingers. "Oh, I hope so."

The station door opened and Leroy Samms walked in. He paused as he caught sight of me and Chantal sitting there, and then he squared his shoulders and walked over to us. He nodded to me and then trained his gaze on Chantal. "Chantal, I'm sorry. I assume Remy called you?"

She gave Samms a tight nod. "Yes. Nora helped me find a lawyer for him. Agent Samms, this is all a horrible mistake."

"If it is, it'll all get sorted out," Samms said. "The processing takes a while, though, so you two might want to come back later."

I shook my head. "Hal Frey's meeting us here in about a half hour, so thanks but no thanks."

Samms nodded. "So you got him Frey, eh? Well, he's a good attorney."

We stood for a moment in awkward silence and then I cocked my head at Samms. "Were you there when Dale arrested Remy?" I asked.

Samms nodded. "Yes, I was. I have to say he had quite a belligerent attitude."

"One usually does when they are unjustly accused," Chantal piped up.

Samms's lips thinned. "No comment," he said brusquely. He started to turn away but I reached out and grabbed his arm. "Not so fast," I said. "Dale decided to charge Remy with the murder because of something they found at the gazebo, right?"

His eyes narrowed. "How do you know we found something there?" he asked. "Don't tell me that Carmichael had it on his broadcast?"

"No, but I'm sure it's only a matter of time, since he broadcast Emerson was off the hook because the police had a suspect in custody." I waited expectantly, and when Samms didn't answer, I asked, "You found something out there, didn't you, something that implicated Remy?"

"You know I can't answer that."

"Can't or won't?"

He looked me straight in the eye. "Both."

I fisted my hands on my hips and glared at him. "You are the most frustrating man," I growled.

"Right back at ya, kiddo. Really, Nora, you know I can't share information like that with members of the public."

"What about members of the public who are also private investigators?"

His eyebrow rose. "Nice try, but didn't they teach you police don't ordinarily share information with PIs, unless the PI's hired by someone to look into a matter."

"Really? That's the way it works?" Chantal cried. She waved her hand in my direction. "Fine, then. Nora, you're hired."

"What!" both Samms and I chorused in unison.

"He just said it. The only time he can share information is if you were hired. Well, I am hiring you to investigate this ridiculous charge of murder against him." She whipped her purse off the floor, fumbled in it, and held a dollar bill out to me. "Here, take this as your retainer. I will give you more later. Now, you have been officially hired." She sat back in her chair and crossed her legs at the ankles. "So, Agent Samms, please. Feel free to share what you know with my employee."

Samms ran his hands through his mass of hair and I shot him a triumphant look. "Okay, you heard her. I've been hired, so share."

He blew out a breath, ran a hand through his hair again. "Fine." Samms grabbed my arm and pulled me into the far corner of the station, away from Chantal and the front desk. He backed me up against the wall and hissed, "A van matching the description of Remy's was seen in the vicinity of the gazebo just a short time before you discovered Forbes's body."

I raised one eyebrow. If that were true, it would place Remy in the area at the time Forbes was murdered. "I know Dale wouldn't arrest Remy on such flimsy circumstantial evidence. There's more."

"Yes. The murder weapon's been found."

"I thought so," I cried triumphantly. "And what, Remy's prints were on it?"

Samms shook his head. "No prints, but there were traces of blood, and the blood was a match with both the deceased's type and with Remy's."

"Hm. Still pretty good, but one might argue that blood type alone isn't a determining factor." I looked him straight in the eye. "What was the murder weapon, anyway?"

Samms crossed his arms over his chest. "A length of mesh netting. The kind florists use to bind bouquets." At my startled gasp, he added, "And this particular netting was a special kind, ordered just a few days ago by one Remy Gillard."

Chapter Fifteen

"Apparently the netting was a special order, a blend of metallic yarn and mesh. It does account for those odd, lattice-shaped marks I saw on Forbes's neck, though. God, what a mess."

It was eight o'clock Thursday morning. Chantal had slept over, and she, Lacey and I had just finished cleaning up the trays from the film crew's breakfast serving when my cell vibrated and Ollie's number popped up. I immediately launched into a summary of the previous day's events, ending with what I'd been able to find out from Hal about the mesh.

"Hm, you're right. It doesn't sound good," Ollie said. "Did Gillard have any explanation as to how someone might have gotten hold of it?"

"He had no idea. All he'd tell Hal was that he was innocent. It's really a miracle Hal agreed to stay on the case. Remy's shut up tighter than a clam."

"Then he's a fool," Ollie declared. "Did Hal tell him that's the kind of attitude that will get him a permanent spot on Death Row?"

"He did, but Remy still wouldn't break his silence. Chantal is positively sick over it all. She's with Hal now. Remy's bail hearing is set for nine a.m. I'm going to be there, to show my support."

"Ah, then who's minding the store?"

"Believe it or not, Lance and Alexa Martin." I let out a soft chuckle. "Lance was upset as well. He's known Chantal and Remy almost as long as I have. Anyway, Alexa offered and Lance jumped right in and said he could help out until his shift at the Poker Face started at one."

"Think the judge'll let him out on bail?"

I sighed. "Not if he keeps pulling the silent treatment. We'll know soon enough. Both Hal and Peter Dobbs are known to be miracle workers when it comes to that sort of thing."

"And how's Little Nick? Up to his old tricks?"

"I left him in Alexa's capable hands this morning," I said and laughed. "Fortunately she brought her cat Valentina along, so Nick had a little female playmate to show off to. When we left they were engaged in a tug-of-war over a catnip carrot."

"Need I ask who won?"

"Valentina, of course. Nick's a gentleman."

"That he is." Ollie chuckled, then sobered. "Did you get a chance to look at those papers?"

"No, I put them away for now. Once Remy's cleared, I'll devote more attention to it."

"That's probably a good idea. And like I said, I'll have another look through Nick's old files, just in case."

We chatted a few more minute and then my call waiting beeped. I said goodbye to Ollie and clicked on my other call.

"Hey, sunshine," Hank Prince's deep voice boomed in my ear.

I let out a breath. "I was hoping you'd call. Have you found out anything?"

"I've got a thing or two that may interest you." I heard the sound of paper riffling. "I called in a few favors and I found out something very interesting about that reporter, Millicent Martin. That wasn't her real name."

"No? What is it?"

"Your guess is as good as mine. One of my contacts managed to find the guy who'd made up her phony ID and press credentials. The guy said she paid him a lot of money and specifically requested he keep his mouth shut. Said he hasn't heard from her since, but when my guy flashed a wad of cash in front of him, he caved."

"Interesting. I don't suppose this contact of yours could give us a description of Millicent Martin?"

"Better than that. He got her photo from the negative of the fake ID. I'll email you a copy of the photo." I heard the sound of paper riffling and then Hank added, "I did manage to contact the reporter who broke the story on Forbes and Emily Van Horn. He said he received a packet in the mail detailing their liaisons along with some pretty incriminating photos."

"Interesting," I muttered. "Sounds like someone squealed. I'm betting it was someone with a vendetta against Forbes. Emily didn't seem to have many enemies." I let out a sigh. "The big question mark for me is Remy's past with Forbes. I have to wonder if whatever happened between them was serious enough to warrant taking a life?"

"I've alerted some of my contacts over in Europe to start digging into Gillard and Forbes's past. I'll let you know when I find out something. Anything else you need?"

"Yeah, a break. A big one, because I'm afraid if we can't find the real killer, Chantal will be visiting her brother in prison for a long, long time."

• • •

I left Lacey with the rest of the cleanup and took the van back into Cruz for Remy's arraignment. As I put the van into Park, my phone pinged, and I saw I had an email from Hank. I opened it and looked at the photo of Millicent Martin. She was what I'd call nondescript. Mousy brown hair done in a pageboy hairdo, thick glasses that practically concealed the upper portion of her face, and full lips. I slipped my phone back into my pocket and went into the building. Hal Frey and Chantal sat on a wooden bench outside the courtroom. Chantal looked even paler than she had yesterday. She did manage to give me a wan smile as I approached.

"We might have a break," Hal announced. "Judge Grimshaw is hearing the case. She's known to be flexible on the issue of bail. I'm going to try and get Remy released on his own recognizance. I think he might have a good shot since this is his first offense. It would eliminate Chantal having to put Poppies up as bail. Even with Grimshaw, though, it's a long shot. Remy's going to have to appear a lot more cooperative if this is going to work." He shook his head. "I spoke to him about this, and tried to convince him of the importance of making a good impression, but I'm not certain I got through."

"They let me see him briefly as well," Chantal said. "I also tried talking to him, but my brother can be very *bête*—thickheaded."

We entered the courtroom and took seats in the rear. As we waited for Remy's case to be called, Judge Emily Grimshaw dispensed several others, banging the gavel down with a sharp crack as she set stiff amounts of bail and remanded prisoners back to jail. From what I observed she didn't appear to be a fan of low bond, or of letting people out on their own recognizance either. I wondered just what Hal had meant by saying we'd drawn a break. Judge Grimshaw seemed pretty formidable to me.

At last Remy was ushered into the courtroom. I glanced around and saw no one other than us. We were, apparently, the last case to be heard today. "The State of California versus Remedius Gillard. Accused is charged with murder in the first degree. How does your client plead, Mr. Frey?"

Hal stood up and said in a loud, clear voice, "My client pleads not guilty, Your Honor."

Judge Grimshaw shuffled through the papers before her. "I see you're asking for bail to be waived, and for Mr. Gillard to be released on his own recognizance?"

"Yes, Your Honor. This is Remedius Gillard's first offense, and he is innocent of the crime he's charged with. He and his sister have operated a successful business in Cruz for many years, and he's considered an upstanding citizen of the community. Remedius and his sister have participated in many charitable functions, and the defendant is more than willing to surrender his passport to prove he is not a flight risk. We would respectfully ask the Court to consider this."

Judge Grimshaw nodded and then turned to the prosecutor. "Does the prosecution have any comment?"

The prosecutor, a round, red-faced man in his late fifties, rose to his feet. He turned and pointed a finger dramatically in Remy's direction. "This is news to me, Your Honor," he said. "I, for one, do not believe the citizens of Cruz would sleep well at night knowing a potential murderer is running around loose in our fair city."

"What does he mean? While they waste time with my brother, the murderer is already running free," hissed Chantal. The court bailiff turned and glared in our direction. I squeezed my friend's arm and put a finger to my lips.

"Remedius Gillard's claim of not guilty is laughable," continued the prosecutor. "The state has irrefutable evidence that will prove him guilty. We balk at the idea of his being released on his own recognizance."

Judge Grimshaw picked up her gavel, and Hal spoke again. "Your Honor, we realize that asking for no bail for the defendant on a first-degree murder charge is unusual, but I ask you to take his impeccable record thus far into consideration. Remedius Gillard is a victim in all this, too, and we are prepared to prove it."

Judge Grimshaw adjusted her glasses, set down her gavel, and perused the papers in front of her. "No prior criminal history," she muttered. "He'll surrender his passport, you said?"

Hal reached down and picked up a square of blue. "We have it right here, Your Honor."

Judge Grimshaw folded her hands on the desk and peered over the rims of her glasses at Remy. "I would like to hear from the defendant himself. Remedius Gillard, please stand and address the court."

Chantal and I sucked in a breath as Remy stood. He adjusted his jacket, then folded his hands in front of him and looked straight at the judge before speaking in a loud, clear voice. "My name is Remedius Gillard. I am innocent of the charge of murder that has been placed on me. I was not born in Cruz, but I have lived here most of my life, as have my parents and my sister. Our parents worked hard to give us a good life and a good education, and they instilled values in us. My parents had a thriving business here, Poppies, which I and my sister have since taken over. Through the past years, we have worked hard for the good of the community. I consider myself a law-abiding citizen, and I have never received so much as a parking ticket. I am aware also of the value of a human life." Here Remy paused and turned his head slightly toward the prosecution bench. "I do not know what this 'irrefutable evidence' might be, but I swear that I am innocent. I beg the Court's indulgence in granting me my freedom until the trial, at which time my attorney will present evidence in my behalf."

And then he gave the judge a small nod and sat back down.

Chantal gripped my hand so hard I thought my fingers might break off. "Who was that and what has he done with my brother?" she whispered.

I squeezed her hand back. "I didn't know he could speak so eloquently. He sounded almost like a lawyer himself."

Grimshaw riffled the papers in front of her some more and then looked up. "The Court finds this a serious matter, not to be taken lightly. I will deliberate on this and I would ask defense and the prosecutor to meet me in my chambers in half an hour." She banged down the gavel. "Court dismissed."

The judge swept from the courtroom and Chantal and I hurried over to the defense bench. Chantal pulled her brother into a fierce hug and I took Hal aside. "What happens now?"

Hal gave me a tight smile. "We pray. Believe me, her taking a half hour to mull over the pros and cons is a good sign. I think she was impressed with Remy's forthright attitude. We've got a shot at least."

I looked over to where Chantal still had her brother trapped in a gigantic bear hug. "Yeah, who came in and took over his body? That's the most I've heard Remy speak in, well, in a very long time."

Hal chuckled. "I guess I was finally able to impress upon him that his cone of silence wasn't going to do him much good. I tried to tell him how all this was affecting his sister, and if he didn't care about himself, he should think of her."

"Well, let's hope whatever you said worked."

A half hour later Chantal and I paced in the hallway outside the judge's chambers. Not long afterward the door opened and the prosecutor marched out in a huff, a scowl on his ruddy face. I didn't need to see Hal's beaming face to know how things had gone.

"Released on his own recognizance, bail waived," he said. "He will have to wear an ankle monitor, but it's a large victory for us."

I made a motion of brushing sweat off my brow. "Now all we have to do is find the real killer."

Hal smiled. "That would certainly simplify matters."

"It would simplify them more if Remy would just come clean about his relationship with Forbes," I said.

"I agree," Hal said. "I told him to come to my office tomorrow. I might get him to open up about Forbes yet."

I nodded, but I knew that Remy could be very taciturn and stubborn. Although I couldn't imagine what could make him choose to spend the rest of his life in prison rather than reveal what went on between him and Forbes. I rose and started to follow Hal and Chantal down the hall when a door across the hall opened and Ned Reilly walked out, nearly running into me. "Why, hello. Ms. Charles, right?" He barked out a nervous laugh. "Fancy running into you here. Don't tell me you had to appear in court?"

I smiled back. "No, I just came to show support for a friend."

He glanced at the closed courtroom door. "For the man they arrested for Forbes's murder?"

"Yes. He's the brother of my best friend."

His lips clamped into a thin line. "This must be pretty awkward for you. From your demeanor, I guess I can assume the hearing went well?"

"Better than expected. The judge released Remy on his own recognizance and waived bail."

Ned's eyebrows rose. "That was fortunate. They don't usually do that with first-degree murder charges." He glanced quickly at his watch. "I'm sorry, I've got to get going." He turned abruptly on his heel and practically sprinted down the corridor.

I watched him go through narrowed eyes. Something about his manner gave me the impression Ned Reilly knew more about Forbes's murder than he was letting on.

But what could it be?

Chapter Sixteen

I left Chantal and Remy in Hal's capable hands and drove back to Sweeney Park. I arrived a few minutes before eleven, switched my skirt and jacket for jeans and a smock, hurried inside the tent and gave a quick look around.

No Lacey.

I gritted my teeth and started setting out the sandwich trays. Fortunately, the hot entrées I'd prepared earlier—a baked ziti and spinach casserole, chicken stir-fry and salmon patties—didn't require a long amount of time to heat up. The sandwiches were a no-brainer, accompanied by a squash soup that was quick also. I'd unwrapped all the sandwich trays, set them out, and just turned on the oven to heat up the rest when the tent flap opened and Lacey walked in, her hands full of eight-by-ten photographs of the cast members of the show. She flushed guiltily as she saw me.

"Hey, back so soon?" She saw me looking at the photographs and added, "There was a whole box of signed ones on a table. No one was looking, so I just grabbed a bunch. I know a lot of people who will love getting one."

Knowing it was useless to chastise her, I tapped at the face of my watch instead. "It's almost eleven thirty. When did you intend to start putting out this food?"

"Oh, relax. Kenny Colgate told me that they might be delayed a bit for lunch and not to start anything until at least a quarter after twelve. Honestly, I thought I'd have it all under control before you got back." She set the photographs down on a clean part of the table. "Man, Aunt Prudence will be thrilled when I send her one of these. I guess I'd better add one for Irene too, although she likes Captain Christie better."

"Remy was released on his own recognizance, thanks for asking. Chantal didn't have to sign over Poppies."

At least my sister had the grace to look ashamed. "Sorry. I should have asked you straight out. But that's reassuring, right? The fact that the judge let Remy out on bail? I think if anyone can get him off, it's Hal."

I crossed my arms over my chest. "Peter Dobbs was no slouch when he defended you, you know."

"No, but I didn't get out on bail." Her expression turned wistful. "It's a good sign, right?"

"It could be," I said. "At this point, though, I think the only thing that will help Remy is finding the real killer."

The tent flap opened again and Kenny Colgate came in. Without any preamble he said, "We wrapped those scenes up early, so lunch can be served at twelve. I'm assuming that's no problem?"

"Oh, no," I said quickly. "The sandwiches are ready now, and I just have to heat up the soups and entrées. We'll be ready."

"Excellent." He paused and then said, "I might as well tell you now. Saturday will be our last day here in Cruz. The producers want us to wrap everything up and get back to LA as fast as we can, in light of recent events. We'll be filming at the Inn tomorrow, and Cruz High Friday and Saturday. But you'll be compensated for the entire two weeks," he added quickly.

Lacey pushed forward and gave the director an anxious look. "How is Mark Emerson doing?"

"He's resting comfortably, from what I understand." He flicked a piece of lint from his sleeve and added, "Mark's part of the reason we have to finish by Saturday. He's going to have to be written out for a while, and since we tape several weeks in advance, the writers need some time for rewrites."

Lacey picked up the photographs and started to stuff them into her tote bag. "The show just won't be the same without him. If you see him, tell him his fans are pulling for him."

"Sure." He turned to me. "By the way, Ms. Charles, we'd like to film Nick's scene with Ardis after breakfast on Saturday, if that's all right with you."

"Sure, I'll check with Nick and get back to you." At the director's sharp look, I laughed and said, "Just kidding. Nick will be available whenever you want him."

"Ah," Colgate said. He shook his head and muttered something under his breath that sounded suspiciously like "women" as he left the tent.

I thought about muttering "directors" under my breath, but thought better of it. After all, someone had to be the bigger person.

• • •

Promptly at twelve the cast and crew rolled in for their lunch. Everyone seemed more subdued than usual, understandable under the circumstances. I noticed Ardis Malone standing off to one side and went over and offered her a smile. "Rough day?"

She looked up at me and I could see her eyes were red-rimmed, as if she'd been crying. Her lips puckered and she expelled a short breath. "You can say that again," she muttered. She stole a glance at the center table, where Kenny Colgate sat, shoveling ziti into his mouth. "Forbes was tough, but Kenny's a real piece of work. Talk about a slave driver!"

I picked up a plate, spooned some ziti and stir-fry onto it, and handed it to her. "Surely it's not as bad as all that?"

She took the plate. "No, it's worse. I thought Kenny had a heart, but he's worse than Anton ever was. All he talks about is timing and budgets. He has no compassion whatsoever for what I've been through."

I was tempted to remark that she wasn't the only one going through a crisis but thought better of it. Instead I picked up another plate and started spooning salad onto it. "I noticed you were very upset over what happened with Mark Emerson. I take it the two of you are close?"

"Not as close as I'd like." She gave her lustrous raven locks a toss. "We've played lovers on the show for several months now, and there's always been a certain amount of chemistry between us." She let out a huge sigh. "He's only ever had eyes for Emily, and she was crazy about him too until Forbes came into the picture."

I picked up another plate and spooned some salad onto it. "Emily was that into Forbes?"

"Seemed that way. She started breaking dates left and right with Mark. He needed a shoulder to cry on, and I was there for him. I tried telling him that if she was that easy to lose, well, she wasn't worth having to start off with, but . . ." Ardis stopped speaking and bit down hard on her lower lip. "What happened to Mark yesterday was Forbes's fault, and Emily's too. He'd never have fallen off the wagon if not for them. He's better off without either one of them."

I took the plate from her hand and set it next to the one with the salad on the tray. "Are you that certain Mark and Emily are over?"

She gave a vigorous nod. "Oh, yeah. He wants nothing more to do with her now. It's too bad that Emily let herself get sucked in by Forbes. I imagine she was flattered by all the attention. I tried to tell her she had a gold mine in Mark and Forbes was just using her. Did she listen? Heck, no. Forbes was only out for one person. Number one, himself. And God help anyone who stood in his way."

"I take it you didn't care for him."

She barked out a laugh. "That's putting it mildly. Who did? But we all put on a big, happy face and did our jobs. As long as we did that, he left you pretty much alone. But if you went against him, watch out." She glanced around and lowered her voice to a mere whisper. "He was getting forgetful, too. I think it was from those meds he took."

"Forbes was ill?"

"He suffered with Ménière's disease, and sometimes he'd get bad vertigo attacks. He didn't want anyone to know but it's hard to keep secrets on a set like this. Colgate knew, and so did Reilly and God knows who else." She speared a ziti with her fork, started to nibble. "My, this food is good," she said. "I've been trying to lose five pounds, so I've been skipping lunch and just having a protein shake, but no sense in doing that anymore."

I raised an eyebrow. "No? Why not?"

"Forbes told me he'd consider expanding my part if I lost some more weight. That's not gonna happen now." A giant sigh escaped her lips. "I have to face facts. Even though I've had a lot of camera time with Mark the past few months, my role is still regarded as supporting. The only way I'm ever going to get it expanded is if Little Miss Perfect leaves. With Forbes dead, that'll never happen." She leaned in a bit closer to me and whispered, "No one knows, but Forbes was planning on taking a leave from the show to shoot one of those arty-type films in Europe. He wanted Emily to leave the show and star in the film. He told me that when Emily signed with him, he'd use his influence to convince the producers to make me the star alongside Mark, but now, kiss that goodbye." She picked up the tray with a huge sigh. "My character will be second string forever."

Ardis plucked a plump strawberry from the top of the fruit salad platter, popped it into her mouth, and sashayed off. I watched her go and considered crossing her off my suspect list. I started to turn and bumped right into Mamie Monroe, who also held a loaded tray.

"I see you were talking to *All the Days of Tomorrow*'s Queen of Mean," she said and chuckled. "She plays the prostrate costar well, doesn't she?"

"Oh, I don't know," I said. "She's a bit on the selfish side, that's for sure, but she does seem to be really upset about Mark."

Mamie sniffed. "Yeah, maybe. I'll grant you that she cares about Mark, as much as she's able to care about someone other than herself. I'd bet money she's not one bit sorry about Forbes. Although, to be perfectly honest, she's not alone in that respect."

"Ardis told me she was trying to get her role expanded. Forbes told her that if she lost some weight, he'd see what he could do."

"Hah! And she fell for that?" Mamie let out a loud hoot. "I wouldn't put it past Ardis to be the one who offed Forbes. That girl has it in her, trust me. You know, a woman scorned and all that."

"I'm not so sure. She has no motive I can see."

Mamie arched a brow. "What do you mean?"

"She said that Forbes was planning on leaving the show and taking Emily with him, and when that happened, he was going to recommend

Ardis's role be made front-burner. So Forbes was worth more to her alive than dead."

Mamie cocked her head to one side, considering. Finally she said, "I'd tend to agree with you, if I thought all that were true."

"You think Forbes lied to her?"

The expression on Mamie's face clearly told me she considered me the daft child in a sea of overachievers. "Honey, producers and directors lie all the time. It's what they do, it's how they get actors caught up in their web." She set her tray down and started to tick off on her fingers. "First off, this so-called arty film he wanted to direct wasn't a sure thing. The funding was spotty. Secondly, he'd never have gotten Emily to agree to leave *Days of Tomorrow* to star in his film."

"What makes you say that? I would imagine a starring role in a film would be a mighty big incentive."

"Maybe so, but the part involved several very graphic nude scenes, and that isn't Emily's bag." Mamie leaned in close and whispered, "Emily's not like Ardis, she's not comfortable showing off her body. She'd never agree to a scene without a stitch on. Why, she'd die first."

"Really?" I recalled the exchange outside Forbes's trailer. That conversation made a bit more sense now. Reilly's words came back to me too. "Do you think Emily could . . ."

"Kill Forbes over a role?" Mamie's face screwed into a pensive expression. "If you asked me two months ago I'd have said no, but she's changed so much over the past few weeks. It's hard to say. Of course," she said with a laugh, "I can see Ardis, Colgate or Mark offing Forbes too." She eased one hip against the table and her voice rose slightly as she warmed to her subject. "Colgate's the type who'd do just about anything to get ahead, and he's been assistant director on this show for, well, like forever. He thought when Griswold retired, he had a lock, and then the producers went after Forbes. Did. Not. Sit. Well." She punctuated her words with little jabs in the air. "Colgate felt he was entitled to become director, and it made for a lot of tension on the set. They picked on each other constantly."

"Why Mark Emerson? He hardly seems the murderous type."

Mamie reached out and patted me on the cheek. "Oh, darlin'. They're actors! They can play any sort of role. Mark knew Forbes was putting the moves on Emily, and Emily was falling for his phony charm. It made him sick, and maybe just desperate enough to do something about it. In that state he was in, I wouldn't have put anything past him. I tell you, if the police hadn't already arrested someone and let him Mark the hook, he'd be on my list." She turned her head and stared out across the tent. "And so would he."

I followed her gaze and saw she was looking at Ned Reilly. "Ned Reilly? Why him?"

"He's a snitch, for one thing. Rumor has it he was reporting back to someone big at the studio on everything that went on here. That's how he got this job." She sniffed. "Plus, I've seen him talking a couple of times to that buttinsky reporter who made such a big scene at the wake."

"Blaine Carmichael?"

"That's the one." She bobbed her head up and down. "He's been first with all the news about what's been going on. Where do you think he's getting all this info? A crystal ball?"

I frowned. Reilly had said he was running an errand at the courthouse, but he'd been very interested in the details of Remy's hearing. Was Mamie right? Was Reilly playing snoop, reporting details back to Blaine? "Why would he do that?" I asked. "Wouldn't he get in trouble?"

She shrugged. "Maybe Carmichael promised him a big payoff if he helped him." She glanced at her wrist and let out a cry. "Sorry, got to run. I've got to report to wardrobe in twenty minutes. See ya."

Before I could utter another word, Mamie grabbed her tray and walked swiftly out of the tent. And when I turned back to have another look at Ned Reilly, the table where he'd been sitting was empty.

Chapter Seventeen

Once the lunch service was done and everything cleaned up, Lacey and I gathered up all our pots and pans and packed them into the back of the van. I dropped Lacey off at her girlfriend Debbie's so she could fill her in on all the latest *Days of Tomorrow* gossip, and after extricating a promise from her not to be out too late, I headed back to Hot Bread. As I let myself into the kitchen, two furry faces peered out from underneath the table at me.

"Well, hello there," I said. Two pairs of feline eyes, one gold and the other blue, stared back at me. I knelt down on the kitchen floor. "What's up, Nick? Have you been playing nice with Valentina?"

Nick crawled all the way out from underneath the table and rested his paw on my knee. He was followed a minute later by the thin orange and white cat. Valentina squatted on my other side, cocked her head and almost appeared to be grinning at me. "How was your day?" I asked them.

Both cats meowed loudly.

"Yeah? Mine kinda sucked."

"Really? How so?"

I looked up into the eyes of Alexa Martin. Violet Crenshaw's niece and my friend Lance's main squeeze looked like a Miss America finalist, but she was a gal who was as nice and down-to-earth as you could ever imagine. Her full lips parted in a wide smile and her eyes twinkled as she said, "I can't imagine you having a boring day, not with all those television stars around. Although I guess the atmosphere over there is pretty tense, huh?"

I nodded. "You can cut it with a knife. I don't think they're as upset over Forbes's death, though, as they are about Mark Emerson."

Alexa put down the dishrag she'd been holding. "How is he, anyway?"

"According to Kenny Colgate, he's stable, but he's going to have to be off the show for a while."

"Oh, wow. Did they say what was wrong with him?"

I was half tempted to confide what Colgate had told me about Mark's drinking problem, then thought better of it. I shook my head. "I guess he just had a breakdown," I said at last. "Probably Forbes was working him too hard."

"It can't be easy for those people, the director being murdered and then one of their lead stars taking ill like that," Alexa said. "Although I still have a hard time believing Remy Gillard is guilty."

"Well, you're not alone in that. I have a hard time too. I've known Remy practically my whole life."

"Lance said pretty much the same thing. He doesn't buy it either."

I glanced around the neat kitchen. "Where is Lance, anyway?"

"He went over to the Poker Face right after the lunch crowd thinned out. He's got some sort of thing there tonight. The Elks, I think?"

"Oh, right." I nodded. "They always have their monthly meeting on the fifteenth."

Alexa untied her apron and laid it across the back of the chair. "There's only about fifteen minutes to closing, so would it be all right if I went over there? He didn't ask me to, but I know he still doesn't completely trust Jose's cooking, even though the guy has improved by leaps and bounds."

I laughed. "Go right ahead. I appreciate your watching Hot Bread for me today. No problems, I hope."

"Well, Elvina Biddle complained about the turkey salad. Too much salt. Ramona Hickey echoed her sentiments."

I laughed. Those two women were two of my best customers and biggest complainers. "Sounds about right. Anything else?"

"Mr. Hofstedder still wants to know when you're getting a 'darn smoothie machine' and Gladys Coffey almost jumped over the counter when she saw both Nick and Valentina in the back of the kitchen. Went on for fifteen minutes about how adorable they were."

The two cats in question, who'd been busy grooming, lifted their heads in unison at the word *adorable*. Then they both yawned.

I chuckled. "They've been told that so many times I guess it's old hat now."

"Gladys got real excited when I mentioned Nick having an upcoming part on the show. That was okay to say, right?"

"Sure."

Nick straightened, turned around twice, then dropped to all fours and immediately began grooming very heavily. Valentina walked over to Nick too, and started licking his face.

Alexa burst out laughing. "It's almost as if they understand what we say. It's so cute."

She scooped up Valentina in her arms. The cat didn't protest, but she did wriggle around so that she could look down at Nick. "He was batting his Scrabble tiles around a bit," she said as she headed toward the door. "I think they're probably still under the table."

Once Alexa and Valentina had gone, Nick stretched his forepaws out, then trotted over to the table. He stuck one white-tipped paw underneath and then pulled it out again. I knelt down. "Do you want me to see what you spelled out?"

"Merow"

"Okay." I lifted the edge of the tablecloth and peered underneath the table. Sure enough, there were several Scrabble tiles scattered around. I wiggled underneath the table to retrieve them, no easy feat as they'd gone in all directions. Finally I emerged, all the tiles clutched in my hand. I straightened up and laid them on the table. Two A's, an L, an I, and an S.

I scratched at my head. "Alias, huh? Meaning someone isn't who they appear to be. Well, that certainly could apply to Forbes, all right. But who else?"

Nick gave me a slow blink. "Merow."

I nodded. "Right. Make a list, like they taught us in PI class."

I went over to my middle drawer, pulled out a notepad and pen, and then sat back down at the table. As Nick stretched out and lay his head on his paws, I brandished the pen and divided the notepaper into two columns. The first column I headed *Suspects*, and the second, *Motive*. I leaned back in the chair, chewing thoughtfully on the end of my pen.

"Well, first we've got Remy Gillard. He knew Forbes, and something happened between them years ago he's reluctant to talk about." I wrote Remy's name in the Suspect column. I hesitated, my pen poised over the Motive column. What could I put there? I wasn't sure what motive Remy had, if any. In the end I put a question mark. I sat writing for several minutes, and when I was done, pushed the pad back so Nick could see too and surveyed my handiwork:

Suspects/Motive

Remy Gillard / ?–Depends on his past w/Forbes
Ardis Malone / Wanted her role on show expanded–
Forbes lied to her
Kenny Colgate / Wanted director job–only one way to get
it. Knew about Forbes having Ménière's disease.
Mark Emerson / Forbes seduced his girl–revenge?
Emily Van Horn / Thought Forbes loved her, but he only
wanted her to star in racy movie

"Well, Ned Reilly did say *cherchez la femme*, right?" I added another name in the Suspect column–Millicent Martin. Under motive I wrote, *Article she wrote seems to indicate bitterness toward Forbes–why?*

Nick reared up and batted at the paper with his paw. I pointed to the name. "You spelled out alias," I told the cat. "We know Millicent Martin isn't her right name. It's an alias. Maybe her true identity figures into all this somehow."

Another slow blink, and then a yawn. Swell.

I chewed at the top of my pen as I looked at Nick. "I hate to say it, but these motives all seem pretty weak. They're good motives for hating Forbes, but not for killing him, even though I heard all four wish him dead at one point or another. I have my doubts about Reilly's *cherchez la femme* theory too. In spite of what Mamie said about her wanting revenge, I'm tempted to cross off Ardis. I just don't get that kind of vibe from her, or from Emily Van Horn either. Millicent Martin might be a possibility, but until we get a handle on her real identity, she's a big question mark. I wish I knew the details of Remy's grudge against Forbes."

Nick let out a loud yowl and swiped his claw across the top of the page, making a hole in the *R* in Remy.

"If I knew what was behind their feud, it might explain a few things, like why Remy snuck around Forbes's trailer, and why he lied about not talking to Forbes. On the downside, it might also give Remy an excellent motive for murder, but how do I confirm this? And do I even want to?" I let out a huge sigh and set the pen down. "If Remy did kill Forbes, it will destroy Chantal. She really loves her brother."

"Mrrr," said Nick.

After a minute, I picked up the pen again and wrote down another name in the Suspect column—Ned Reilly. Nick peered over my shoulder as I wrote, and seemed to give a little nod of approval once I finished. My pen wavered over the motive column.

"Mamie seems to think he's a snitch who can't be trusted, and that he's also pretty chummy with Blaine Carmichael. What sort of errand was he running there in the Records office? Or was he just snooping around, trying to find out details for Blaine? If so, I guess I played right into his hands. He certainly was eager to point the finger of suspicion toward a woman, maybe to direct it away from himself more than Remy?"

Nick gave a loud yowl.

"Right," I said and nodded. "We should find out a bit more about Mr. Ned Reilly."

Suiting action to words, I crossed over to the back counter and picked up my laptop. I took it back to the table, booted it up, and then typed, "Ned Reilly—PR executive All the Days of Tomorrow" into the search engine. The official website for *All the Days of Tomorrow* came up, and I scrolled all the way to the bottom until I found a tab marked *Cast and Crew.* I clicked it and looked through the names. No Ned Reilly. I went back and pulled up the website for the cable network that televised the show and found their crew listing: no Ned there either.

Interesting. Where had the guy come from? Out of thin air?

My cell rang and I picked it up and saw Hal Frey's number on the screen. He didn't mince any words. "Remy's trial has been set for next Wednesday."

I felt my heart plummet into my stomach. "So soon?"

"The DA figures he's got a pretty airtight case. I'm doing my best to prepare a defense, but when you have a client who's shut up tighter than a clam, it isn't easy. I've tried every gambit I can think of—he refuses to talk." He hesitated and then said, "I hate to ask, but do you think you could try getting him to open up? You've got a knack for it."

A mental picture of Samms flitted in and out of my head. "Sometimes. I've been out of practice for a while."

He sighed. "Could you at least try? Maybe you can convince him that keeping silent about whatever happened between him and Forbes in the past isn't in his best interests or his sister's either. I've got a meeting with him at my office at six. I'd sure appreciate it if you could drop by, see what you could do."

I knew Chantal would be heartbroken if Remy did go to prison, and I knew she'd be angry at me for not at least giving it the old college try. "Fine. I'll talk to him. But I'm not making any promises."

I hung up and glanced over at Nick. The cat had been sitting on the chair next to me, his head cocked as if he'd been listening intently to every word. "Hal's right," I told him. "Remy needs to own up to whatever this feud was between him and Forbes. It's the only way he can prepare a halfway decent defense."

Nick meowed loudly.

"I know, I know . . . the truth might hinder rather than help Remy, but that's a chance we'll have to take." I tapped my finger on the tablecloth. "We'll talk to Remy, but first I think we need to make a little side trip. I think we should take Ollie's advice. Let's check out the gazebo."

Chapter Eighteen

I drove my SUV down the back road that led to the gazebo, Nick sprawled comfortably in the passenger seat beside me. As I pulled into the parking lot, I caught a flash of yellow up on the hill above. The police tape still graced the area. I stole a glance at Nick and saw that his eyes were glued to the same spot.

"Looks like the police still aren't done with the crime scene. Good thing we're not going up there, right?"

He looked at me and then started licking the splash of white fur on his chest.

"Your close-up's not until Saturday," I chided him. "Come on, let's do what Ollie suggested and search the perimeter, see if the murderer might have dropped anything incriminating the police might have overlooked."

Nick looked up and blinked, almost as if to say, *Anderson miss something? You're kidding?* Then he stretched his forepaws out in front of him on the seat, turned around twice and resumed his grooming ritual. I got out of the car and paused, waiting for Nick to rise and hop over the console and out onto the ground, but he just sat, apparently *very* busy with his ablutions. "Okay, you want to stay in the car, fine," I said. "But *stay* in the car." I slammed the door and peered in the window.

Nick still sat, unfazed, grooming his front paws now.

"Okay, then. Be that way."

Cats! Who could ever understand them?

The late-day sun slanted through the trees as I picked my way up the side of the hill toward the gazebo. Normally I relished walking in the woods this time of year, inhaling the crisp air and watching the multicolored leaves start to fall to the ground. Not so today. Today I was a woman on a mission. Ten minutes later I was standing in the clearing directly behind the gazebo. It was impossible to tell if the police had searched this area or not; I figured they most likely had. Anderson was pretty thorough, she'd have given her men explicit instructions.

How thorough they'd been, though, remained to be seen.

I made a wide circle, stopping every now and then to examine something on the ground. After a half hour the most I'd come up with was a sodden napkin, a plastic fork, and a lump of black wax with a burned wick. What that was doing here I shuddered to imagine. Nothing I'd found, though, could point to any of my suspects as Forbes's murderer. I paused to scratch at my eyebrow with the edge of my nail. Forbes had been strangled with a length of floral netting that Remy special-ordered. Somehow, someone got their hands on it, but who? And how? I started to walk the perimeter around the trees again when, out of the corner of my eye, I saw a black and white blur streak past and around the edge of the gazebo.

"Nick!"

I'd left the rear SUV window open enough for him to squeeze through, just in case my cat changed his mind about wanting to come with me. I'd long since learned that there was no rhyme or reason to the things that Nick could, or could not, do. I walked around the gazebo, and sure enough there was Nick, pawing at the ground at the base of the structure, the yellow crime scene tape flapping overhead. He looked up at me and blinked his golden eyes. "Merow."

As I approached him, I saw he had something underneath his paw. "What have you got there, buddy?" I asked. Nick shifted his body slightly and I saw what had been tucked beneath him. A medium-sized medallion. I picked it up gingerly. It was silver, and pretty tarnished. The front depicted a spray of flowers surrounding a rose quartz stone. The back was pretty badly scratched up, but it looked to me as if something were etched into the metal. "Not a bad find," I said to Nick. "I wonder where it came from. It looks pretty beat up." I turned it over in my hand.

"Merow!"

I looked down. Nick was sitting, shoulders hunched forward, his head raised, ears flat against his skull. I knew that stance. His kitty ears had heard something. I rose and slid the disk into my jacket pocket just as a figure emerged from the woods. I couldn't see him very clearly, but I could tell from the build it was a man. He moved out of the protecting circle of trees into the clearing, and I let out a soft moan as I recognized the familiar features.

Blaine Carmichael. What was he doing in the woods? His arrogant features were twisted into a frozen mask that definitely resembled fear. Impulsively I stepped behind a large elm. I had a feeling it was best if Blaine didn't realize he had an audience. He was walking very rapidly, and every few feet he paused to glance over his shoulder, as if he were afraid someone were following him. Midway across the clearing he stumbled over a rock and went down, arms flailing. He lay there, motionless, and I hesitated, debating whether or not I should leave my hiding place to check and make certain he was all right. Just as I was about to do so, he moaned softly and struggled to his feet. He paused, brushing dirt from his expensive-looking jacket, and then turned to give one more look back at the woods before taking off toward the parking lot at a much faster pace. Once he'd vanished from view, I stepped out from behind the tree, Nick at my heels.

"Something spooked him," I murmured. "I think maybe we should take a look, see if we can find out just what did."

I glanced down. I was talking to air. Nick was gone. I started to call out his name when I saw him a few yards away. He was over by the rock Blaine had stumbled over, and he was pawing at something on the ground. I hurried over to where he crouched. "Find something, buddy?"

Nick's head swiveled and he blinked his golden eyes. "Mrrr."

I could see something clenched between his paws, and I knelt down next to him for a better look. Nick shifted slightly, and I could see his prize clearly now: it was a small, soiled, jagged edge of paper. I reached out and disengaged it from his paw, held it up for a better look. There were four words on it, printed in a crude style:

Come alone to gaz

Since the jagged tear was right after the z, I was going to take a wild guess that the fourth word was *gazebo*. I gave Nick a pat on the head. "Two finds in one day. You're turning into quite the bloodhound, Nick." The cat's eyes narrowed as I said the word *bloodhound*, but he sat up a little straighter. It was hard to tell if the paper had fallen out of Blaine's pocket or if it had been on the ground all along.

Nick let out a soft *grr*, then sat up straight, ears flicked forward, lips peeled back. His backside wiggled like a bowl of jelly; the next minute he launched himself forward and took off into the woods like a black and white streak of greased lightning. I shoved the paper into my pocket and took off at a swift canter after him. I walked for what must have been a good half mile before I finally caught sight of him. He was perched on a large rock, sitting ramrod straight, ears flattened against his skull, his tail swishing to and fro like a banner waving in the wind. His gaze was fixed on something just beyond the rock, and as I drew closer I saw what had captured his attention.

The edge of a man's shoe.

Steeling myself, I peered cautiously around the side of the rock. Yep, it was a shoe all right, and what's more, it was attached to a body.

Ned Reilly's body.

Chapter Nineteen

Nick looked over at me and meowed loudly.

"Yes, Nick, I see him," I said. I picked my way carefully over to where Ned lay slumped against the rock. His eyes were closed, and his neck sagged to one side. I knew he was dead even before I reached to feel for a pulse, but I fought back my rising feeling of nausea and touched the side of his neck with two fingers. His skin felt cold to the touch, and I could feel no sign of a heartbeat. As I drew my hand back, though, my fingers brushed over a tiny bump the size of a pimple on the back of Ned's head, behind his right ear.

I straightened up and stared down at Nick. "You know," I said, "you should have quit finding things when you were ahead. You know what we have to do now, right?"

Nick rose from his sitting position and took a few steps toward the body. I bent down and twined my fingers into his ruff, stopping him.

"Uh-uh. You know better, Nick. No touching. If Anderson thinks we tampered with anything, she'll have our heads."

Nick swiveled his head to glare at me. "Merow," he said. Then he raised a paw and pointed at Ned's jacket.

I squinted down at the body and shook my head. "What is it, Nick? I don't see anything."

I swear he sighed, then waved his paw more imperiously. I leaned over a bit farther, and then I saw what had attracted his attention: a jagged piece of paper peeping out of the pocket. I leaned in for a closer look and saw a series of numbers scrawled near the page's gilt edge. I reached into my bag and pulled out my iPhone, switched it into camera mode, and snapped a few pictures in rapid succession. Then I switched back to phone mode and punched in the number of the Cruz police station from memory. Maybe if I was real lucky, Anderson would be busy elsewhere.

• • •

It wasn't fifteen minutes later that a police cruiser pulled up behind my SUV. I'd been sitting on a nearby rock, Nick at my feet, and we both rose as two officers alighted from the car and started to pick their way up the trail. I let out a slow breath as I saw Anderson wasn't one of them. One was a guy who'd been in Lacey's class in high school, Denny Miller, and the other one was obviously one of Dale's new recruits. The second officer looked to be a good bit older than Denny, and as he approached I saw that he sported a buzz cut and a serious expression. He carried himself ramrod straight, making me think he might possibly have some sort of military background. Denny's serious expression softened as he recognized me.

"Nora, hey," he said. "You made the call?"

I nodded and gestured toward the rock with my thumb. "Yes. He's over there."

Denny moved past me to check on the body and the other officer stopped in front of me. He gave me a curt nod. "Good afternoon. Ms. Charles, right? Mind telling me how you found the body?"

Before I could answer, another dark sedan came careening down the road, pulling to a stop beside the police cruiser. Samms slid out from behind the wheel and started toward us. He was wearing charcoal trousers and a gray and white sport coat over a white shirt and a gray-and-white-striped tie.

He looked pretty darn good.

Samms didn't look at me, but focused his attention on the other officer. "Kendricks! What's the situation?"

"We just got here, sir," Kendricks answered. He indicated me with a brisk wave of his hand. "I was just about to ask Ms. Charles how she found the body."

Samms looked at me. "Another body?"

I nodded. "Ned Reilly. *Days of Tomorrow*'s PR guy."

"Reilly?" Samms's eyes narrowed, and his lips slashed into a thin line. "Nora, I need to speak with the officers. Would you mind waiting by the police cruiser?" His tone was more indicative of an order rather than a request.

"Sure." I turned and started down the trail, Nick at my heels. When we reached the bottom I bent down to pick Nick up and took a quick glance over my shoulder. Samms was speaking to both officers, and his expression was granite hard. After a few minutes he turned and came down the trail and walked over to me.

"Okay. What happened?"

I inclined my head toward the top of the hill. "Nick and I were exploring around the gazebo . . ."

"The gazebo!" Samms interrupted, his face dark. "What were you doing there? It's still a crime scene."

"I know that," I said patiently. "I said we were exploring *around* it. It's a good thing we were, too, or we would have missed seeing Blaine Carmichael come out of the woods. Shortly after that, Nick took off like a shot. I followed him and found Reilly just like that, propped up against the rock."

"You saw Blaine Carmichael, you said?"

"Yes. He exited the woods right around the spot where we found Ned." I paused and then added, "Mamie Monroe told me she'd seen Ned Reilly with Carmichael a few times, that they were thick as thieves. It's a possibility that Blaine was meeting Ned in the woods."

"She did, eh? Who's Mamie Monroe?"

"She works in wardrobe on the soap. She's a very chatty sort."

"Oh." Samms scratched at his forehead. "I think I just might have to have a little talk with Mr. Carmichael."

"I think that's a very good idea. Oh, and before you ask . . ." I smiled sweetly and thrust out both my hands, palms down, and then rolled them over so Samms could see them. "I didn't touch anything here."

A ghost of a smile played across Samms's full lips. He took both my hands in his and leaned over, scrutinizing them. He held on to them a moment longer than was really necessary before releasing them and taking a step back. He rubbed absently at the back of his neck and glanced at Nick. "What about him?"

"Merow," said Nick. He squatted on his hind legs and pawed the air in front of Samms. Samms's expression softened and he dropped to one knee in front of Nick. He reached out and Nick allowed him to examine both his front paws. I noticed that during the examination, Nick seemed to be intently studying Samms's face. Samms rose and cocked his head at me.

"Okay," he said. "You're both clean. You and your cat can go."

"Great. But before we do, I've got something to show you." I ignored both his raised eyebrows and reached into my pocket for the slip of paper Nick had found. "Nick found this near the spot where Carmichael stumbled. I'm not certain if he might have dropped it or not."

Samms took it, looked at it, then motioned to Kendrick. As the officer approached, he held out the slip of paper. "Put this in a baggie."

Kendrick took the paper and for a minute I thought he was going to salute Samms. "Yes, sir."

"Oh, and there's a paper in Reilly's pocket," I said quickly. "I don't know if it's significant or not, but you might want to check that out as well."

Kendrick raised a questioning eyebrow in Samms's direction. Samms barked out, "You heard the lady. Bag both papers." He turned to me. "Well, thank you very much for all your help here, Nora. If I need anything further, I'll be in touch."

Impulsively I touched his arm. "I do have some thoughts," I began, but he cut me off with a brusque, "I've got to get going," turned on his heel and started picking his way back toward the crime scene. I watched him go, and my fingers closed over the medallion in my pocket.

"Well, what do you think about that?" I crossed my arms over my chest and looked down at Nick. "It appears Special Agent Samms doesn't want our help, Nick."

Nick cocked his head at me, raised one paw, and pointed straight at my pocket. "Er-up?"

My fingers closed over the medallion. "Yes, I probably should have showed this to Samms, but, after all, we've no proof that it's evidence in either murder. For all we know, it could have been lying in the ground for weeks."

Nick blinked twice, then shook his head ever so slightly.

I sighed. "I know, I don't believe that either. But without a definite connection, it's not like we're withholding evidence so we're free to investigate it on our own. Come on, let's brainstorm with someone who'll listen to our theories. We're going to Ollie's."

• • •

Twenty minutes later Nick and I were seated in Ollie's comfortable, if Spartan, kitchen. Ollie, whose culinary skills are relatively nonexistent, had managed to brew a decent pot of coffee. Nick got a small saucer of milk, which he slurped up eagerly. As Ollie and I sipped our coffees, I recounted the day's events to him in more detail. When I finished he sat quietly for several seconds, his face impassive, eyes narrowed. Finally he took a large gulp of coffee and asked, "You still have that medallion?"

I nodded and reached into my jacket pocket. I laid it on the table in front of us. Ollie set his mug down and picked the disk up, turned it over in his hand. "It's too big for a charm bracelet. It must have come from a necklace." He laid it back on the table, got up, walked over to a drawer and returned a few moments later with a magnifying glass. He held the disk in one hand and peered through the glass at it. "It's scratched up pretty badly," he said at last, "but there's definitely one initial, possibly more."

I sighed. "I sure could use Daniel right about now. He could take this to one of the FBI labs. With all their advanced equipment, they'd be able to decipher what's under the scratches."

Ollie set down the magnifying glass and looked at me. "Do you miss Daniel himself, or just what he could do for you?"

I cocked my head. "Does it make me a terrible person if I say both?"

Ollie laughed. "You know, Samms probably has a few FBI contacts himself by now."

"Yeah, but it's a safe bet he wouldn't be half as accommodating." I grimaced. "Now that I think on it, I'm glad Samms didn't give me a chance to say anything about the medallion. He would have commandeered it, told me I have no business getting involved, and I'd never find out anything." I pulled out my cell phone and snapped a few photos of the disk. "Maybe Hank will be able to shed some light on what's under those scratches. He's got lots of contacts, too."

"Good idea," Ollie said. "If you don't mind leaving the disk with me, I'll canvass a few jewelry stores. This looks like a made-to-order piece. Maybe we'll get lucky and get a bead on the owner that way."

I reached out and impulsively covered Ollie's hand with my own. "Would you do that? You're a dear."

"Yeah, well, it's not like I have anything better to do." He tossed me a rueful smile. "The sister-in-law owned up to purloining the cocker spaniel, so my services weren't required."

"Oh, Ollie, I'm sorry. But you know you're better than a case like that, right?" I reached into my bag and whipped out a sheet of paper. "I did as you suggested. I wrote down my suspect list, complete with motives. Guess I can cross Reilly off now."

Ollie took the list and studied it. He tapped at one of the names and frowned. "Millicent Martin? That's rather a stretch, isn't it?"

"Maybe, but that article was pretty scathing, and one doesn't write that strongly unless there's something driving it. Forbes did mention a reporter who'd done a hatchet job on him, and I'm positive he meant her. Then there's the fact Millicent Martin isn't her real name. Forbes said he was having a hard time tracking her down. There has to be a reason."

"Ah, so you think she's really some disgruntled lover of Forbes's with an axe to grind?" Ollie tapped at the paper. "I hate to burst your bubble, but all the motives seem a bit weak for murder to me."

I twirled an auburn curl around one finger and toyed with the edge of the list. "I know. When you look at them, it doesn't seem as if any of them had a good enough reason to kill Forbes. There's a missing piece to this puzzle. I have the feeling once we find out just what that is, everything will fall into place."

"And you think the missing piece has something to do with Dean Harriman, don't you?"

"Call me crazy but yes, I do."

"And Reilly's murder? Does that trace back to Harriman's as well?"

"A good question. It might. It all depends on whether Reilly's and Forbes's murders are related—and I think there's a good chance they might be."

Ollie got up, refilled his coffee cup and came back to the table. "Let's get back to the current murder. How was Reilly killed?"

"That's another interesting question. I didn't see any evidence of a gunshot or knife wound, but when I went to feel for a pulse I felt a bump behind his ear."

Ollie swiped at his nose. "He could have just fallen and hit his head on a rock."

"Or he could have been pushed, slipped and hit his head."

"And you think Blaine Carmichael might have pushed him?"

"No," I said after a moment. "I don't. Blaine's an arrogant, self-serving PITA, but I can't see him in the role of murderer. I'm not even certain he stumbled over the body. After all, he's after an anchor slot. He'd have stayed and called in a camera crew."

"I disagree," drawled Ollie. "Murders aren't exactly his normal bailiwick. I think if he came across a dead body he wouldn't be able to get out of there fast enough."

"Maybe. I can tell you this, I'd sure like to be a fly on the wall when Samms hauls him in for a grilling."

Ollie steepled his fingers underneath his chin. "Samms is awfully interested in these murders, for someone who gave up homicide for the FBI. Frankly, I'm surprised they're letting him help out Dale."

"Me too." I sighed. "But Samms said his caseload is slow right now, and his boss likes to maintain good relations with the local police, or at least he did when Daniel was in charge."

"Hm." Ollie looked skeptical. "Maybe, but it just makes me wonder if there isn't something bigger simmering below the surface somewhere."

"I wouldn't hold my breath for Samms to confide in me." I pushed my chair back and stood up. "I'd better get going. Remy's trial date has been set for Wednesday. I promised Hal I'd try and get him to open up about his past with Forbes."

"Think you can?"

"I don't know, but for Chantal's sake I'm willing to give it a try."

Ollie reached across and covered my hand with his. "I wish you luck. Maybe once the truth about what went on between him and Forbes comes to light, it will eliminate him as the number-one suspect."

I shot him a thin smile. "Either that or it might just give him the best motive of all."

Chapter Twenty

Nick and I said our goodbyes to Ollie and headed out to Morgantown, where Hal Frey's office was located. Twenty minutes later I parked in front of the two-story red-brick building and Nick and I hurried up the short walk. Hal must have been watching for us out the window, because the front door flew open as soon as we reached it and Hal stepped outside. He closed the door behind him and smiled at me. "Thanks for doing this," he said. "I'm getting nowhere with the guy. He refuses to speak. Even telling him he might face the death penalty doesn't seem to have made an impression on him. All he'll say is that he's innocent."

I nodded. "Well, like I said, I'll try, but I can't promise anything."

Hal squeezed my hand. "That's good enough for me. He's in my office." Hal opened the door and Nick and I followed him inside. Hal pointed to a closed door and then glanced down at Nick. "Maybe Nick would like a saucer of milk while you're in with Remy."

While Nick eagerly followed Hal down the hall, I squared my shoulders and pushed open the door leading to Hal's office. Remy was seated in one of the straight-backed chairs in front of the desk. His eyes widened slightly when he saw me, but he didn't say anything. I circled the desk and slid into Hal's buttery-soft leather chair.

"Hey, Remy. How are you doing?"

His expression was bland as he looked at me. "That's a rather moot question, isn't it, Nora?"

I settled back a bit in the chair. "I suppose so. Hal wanted me to have a word with you. He's trying his best to prepare a defense for you, but without more to go on, it's difficult. His hands are tied."

Remy stared at me for a long moment, and then he slumped down in his chair. "I know," he said. "But what can I do?"

"Well, for one thing you could tell him the truth about what went on between you and Forbes. You know that whatever you tell your lawyer is confidential."

"I know that. I have nothing to say. The idea that I could kill someone, even a lowlife like Forbes, is ludicrous."

"Look at it from the police's point of view. You lied to Chantal about working all day and snuck around outside Forbes's trailer. You have a history with the deceased you're reluctant to share, but which apparently isn't friendly. And you lied about not seeing or speaking to Forbes that day. Throw in the floral wire as a murder weapon and you can see why they think the way they do."

"I lied to my sister because Chantal can get a trifle dramatic, shall we say, and I did not want her worrying about me. I lied about not seeing or speaking to Forbes that day because I knew it would throw suspicion on me, and quite frankly, I had no idea anyone had seen us. As for the floral netting, I have no idea how anyone could have gotten their hands on it."

"Is it possible someone could have gotten hold of something similar?"

He shook his head. "No. It was a special order, just for me. I ordered it for Bruce and Maya Gillespie's wedding. She wanted a certain color netting and I managed to find just the right shade. I'd picked it up the day before, and I hadn't had a chance to take it into the shop. It was on the back floor of my van."

"And where was the van while you were keeping tabs on Forbes?"

"I'd parked it behind a clump of trees near the back of Forbes's trailer. It was pretty well hidden."

"Was the van locked?"

He passed a hand over his eyes. "I want to say yes, but the truth is, I was in such a hurry when I got out that I honestly don't remember if I locked it or not."

"So anyone could have gotten into it, if they knew it was there."

"Who would know the netting was there? It was on the back floor of the van, under a covering."

I took a deep breath. "They said they found traces of your blood on the netting."

He frowned. "They did? I do recall when I opened the package with my pocketknife, I did jab my finger. Some of my blood must have spilled on the netting."

"Did you tell the police that?"

"Yes." He frowned. "Now that I'm thinking of it, the bundle did appear to be tied a bit sloppily, but I can't say for sure." He licked at his lips and suddenly leaned across the desk and took my hand in his. "I know what you're trying to do, and I appreciate it, but what happened between me and Forbes all those years ago was a private matter. It is no one's business except mine."

"You do realize, though, how your reluctance to talk will look to a jury."

He shook his head. "I cannot help that. My story, if I were to tell it, would no longer be of any value. The only reason for me to reveal it would be to ensure that Forbes would get what was coming to him all these years, but since that's a moot point also, there is no reason to drag innocent people's names through the mud. I tried to secure justice many years ago, but Forbes wrangled some legal mumbo-jumbo that made an innocent person appear guilty. This person, someone I cared deeply about, served time for something Forbes did. And while I hated the man with a passion, I did not kill him, even though the man deserved killing, deserved it badly." He picked up a pen from the desk, tapped it against the edge. "You know, when I did get up the courage to knock on that trailer door and speak to him, he didn't even recognize me. He had no idea who I was."

I nodded, and then, recalling Samms's remark about Remy's van, asked, "Did you give Forbes a ride to the gazebo that afternoon?"

He pushed an errant strand of hair out of his eyes. "Hell, no. I wouldn't give Forbes the time of day, let alone a ride. If anyone said I did, then they are lying."

"Did you hear him making plans to meet anyone? At the gazebo, maybe?"

Remy shook his head. "Forbes had his windows shut most of the time, so I couldn't hear a thing, except . . ."

"Except what?" I prompted as Remy hesitated.

"He opened them for a few minutes, and I overheard a bit of a spirited conversation. Forbes and that actor were arguing."

"What actor?"

"The one who collapsed at the wake."

My ears pricked up. "Mark Emerson?"

"Yes. Emerson was very loud. To be honest, he sounded drunk. I heard his words quite clearly, though, as I got into my van. 'You deserve to die, Forbes, and I'm the one to make sure that happens.' Now, if that doesn't sound like a threat, what does?"

Chapter Twenty-one

After saying my goodbyes to Hal and Remy, Nick and I returned to the SUV and headed back to Cruz. My first stop was the Cruz police station. I left Nick snoring in the passenger seat and hurried up the stone steps and through the plate-glass door into the reception area. Fortunately the officer on duty at the reception desk was Ada Collins, a customer of mine. She glanced up and smiled as I approached.

"Nora. Hey, what are you doing here?"

"I was hoping to catch Special Agent Samms. I understand that he's been helping Detective Anderson out."

"Yeah, I guess you could call it that." Ada let out a snort and rolled her eyes. "He's interrogating a suspect right now. It shouldn't be much longer, if you want to wait." She gestured toward the bank of chairs on the far wall.

"Sure." I started to turn away, then did an abrupt about-face. "Have you heard anything about Mark Emerson?"

Ada's brow furrowed. "The actor? Not much. He's still in the hospital, from what I understand. Why?"

"I was just wondering if they were going to question him any further, you know, about the confession he made at Forbes's wake just before he collapsed."

"From what I understand, Detective Anderson did question him. Of course, she was somewhat limited due to his condition. Between you and me, I don't think Anderson put much stock in his confession. She can't wait until those television folks leave on Saturday. Said they've been nothing but trouble. She wasn't too happy to find out another one of 'em kicked the bucket, either."

"You mean Ned Reilly." At Ada's nod, I leaned one elbow on the desktop. "I don't suppose they've pinpointed the cause of death yet, have they?"

"Oh, yeah. Reflex cardiac arrest as a result of asphyxia."

"Suffocation? Really?"

"You look surprised."

"It's just that when I leaned over to take his pulse, I felt a bump on the back of his head. I thought maybe he'd hit his head on a rock."

"Um, he might have, but it wasn't the cause of death." Ada turned to the computer, started tapping at her keyboard. "Here's the coroner's preliminary report right here." She angled her screen slightly so I could see and tapped at the screen with one long, red-tipped nail. "Lips, gums and tongue show bruising consistent with asphyxia. A few petechial hemorrhages detected in eyelids and pericardium. Blood-stained frothy fluid present in air passages."

I frowned. Ned Reilly had been suffocated; Anton Forbes strangled. Both methods of death were usually performed when there was a great deal of aggression toward the victim. Who would have hated both men that much? Had both murders been committed by the same person, or were there two perps? I hadn't really examined Reilly's body, but I didn't recall noticing any defensive wounds on his hands. It seemed neither man had fought off the attacker. Why?

I could think of only two possible scenarios: either a) they'd been drugged, or (b) they both knew their attacker.

"Well, one good thing," Ada said as she swung the computer screen back toward her. "At least Remy's off the hook for Reilly's murder. They can track his whereabouts with that ankle monitor, and apparently he was at Poppies at the TOD."

I was spared answering as the door leading to the offices opened and Blaine Carmichael emerged. His eyes narrowed when he caught sight of me standing by the desk. If looks could kill, I'd easily be six feet under. He swept past me and out of the station without so much as a backward glance.

"Wow," murmured Ada. "That was sure awkward. What'd you ever do to him?"

"That wasn't by any chance the suspect Samms was interrogating, was it?"

"It certainly was."

I spun around as a shadow fell across the desk. Samms lounged against the doorjamb, his arms crossed over his chest, an unreadable expression on his face. He straightened and walked over to the desk and splayed both his hands across the countertop. "What are you doing here, Nora?"

"I have something to discuss with you . . . in private."

Samms raised one eyebrow, then made a sweeping gesture with his arm toward the doorway. "Let's adjourn to my office then."

I followed him down the long hall to the cubbyhole at the far end. The office had belonged to Daniel first, when he was undercover as a homicide detective, and then to Samms when he'd taken over as the head of Cruz Homicide. Since the arrival of Dale Anderson, this office had been remodeled into an interrogation room. The beat-up desk and file cabinets had been removed, replaced by a long table with uncomfortable wooden chairs. All that remained of the original furnishings was the beat-up coffee maker, which now sat on a folding table next to a beat-up water cooler. Samms eased his frame into one of the chairs and motioned for me to take the one opposite. Once I was seated he asked, "Can I get you coffee? Or water?"

I shook my head. "No, I'm fine. Thanks."

There was an awkward pause as we both regarded each other warily; then Samms said, "Okay, Nora. What is it you need to talk to me about?"

I cleared my throat. "I was just wondering if you planned on questioning Mark Emerson any further regarding Forbes's murder."

Samms leaned back in the chair and steepled his fingers beneath his chin. "Why would we do that? We have a suspect charged with Forbes's murder, remember?"

"Yes, and your key witness, the one who claimed he saw Forbes and Remy together, is dead now. Emerson practically confessed. You're not even going to follow up?"

He regarded me with a hooded expression for several seconds before replying. "We did interrogate him, as soon as his doctors gave the okay. He was pretty much out of it. He hardly even remembered his dramatic confession. It was pretty obvious that the combination of liquor and his medication had a lot to do with what happened."

I bit down hard on my lower lip. "What if I told you there was a witness who could testify that Emerson threatened Forbes right before he was killed. Shouted at him that he deserved to die, and he was going to make sure that happened."

He was silent for several seconds and then barked out, "And who is this witness? Remy Gillard?"

I squirmed a bit in my seat. "I'd rather not say at this time."

He started to chew at his bottom lip, and I imagined he was mentally counting to ten. The fingers of one hand drummed a swift tattoo on the tabletop, while the other hand raked through his mop of ink-black hair. "It still doesn't change anything," he said finally. "Remy's blood was found on the netting, as was the victim's—"

"Remy jabbed his finger with his pocketknife opening the netting," I blurted out. "He can't swear his van was locked when he had it parked near Forbes's trailer. Anyone could have gotten in there and stolen a piece of netting."

"Sure, because wire floral netting is the obvious choice for someone looking to strangle someone." He looked at me for a long moment. "Look, Nora, I know you find it hard to believe Remy's guilty, for Chantal's sake, if nothing else. But facts are facts. Remy's blood was on the murder weapon, he had a history with the victim he tried to conceal, he lied about seeing the victim. Shall I go on?"

I leaned back and blew out an exasperated sigh. "Fine. If you won't question Mark Emerson, then I'd like to. Unofficially, of course."

Samms silently watched me for a few moments. I could tell from the line of his jaw he was clenching his teeth. Finally he bit out, "And what good would that do? You really think Emerson is a murderer?"

"He was under the influence. People do strange things under the influence. I agree he doesn't seem the murderous type, but I've got to exhaust every possibility. At the very least, maybe I can jog his memory about what happened that afternoon. He might remember something significant."

Samms rubbed his hand across his chin. "You want to talk to Emerson? Okay. I'll call the hospital and clear you to visit. But I think you're wasting your time."

"It wouldn't be the first time." I pushed my chair back and stood up. "Thanks."

He just nodded. I turned toward the door and then paused, my hand on the knob. "By the way, what happened with Blaine? I saw him leaving and he didn't look too happy."

Samms snorted. "That's an understatement. For starters, he tried to deny being anywhere near the woods, until I told him I had an eyewitness who could place him at the scene. He admitted he had an appointment to meet Reilly in the woods, but according to him, the guy never showed. He thought he heard footsteps and he called out, but no one answered. Finally he said he had to get back to take an important call from his studio, so he left. And we did confirm that he did talk to the studio manager about an hour later."

I shook my head. "That may be true, but I still think he's holding something back."

"I agree completely. He's a 'person of interest' as far as I'm concerned. I'm going to keep a close eye on him." Suddenly he reached out and grabbed my hand. "You might do well to steer clear of him. I got the impression he thought it was you who blew the whistle on him. Ideally, I'd like you to just stay out of this investigation, but you're not, are you?"

I gave my head a brisk shake. "I can't."

He blew out a long sigh. "I can't pretend I like the idea, but I'm not going to try and discourage you, because I know you won't listen. But if you find out anything significant, at least promise me you'll let me know."

I hesitated then nodded. "Fine."

He took a step nearer to me, so close I caught a faint whiff of his cologne. "I think I know why you keep refusing my help. You're afraid you might actually have to figure out a way to thank me for it."

His gaze was fixed right on my lips. I swallowed, turned and walked out of the station without a backward glance.

• • •

Nick was not happy at all when I dropped him back at Hot Bread. I fixed him a bowl of his favorite yellowfin tuna and added in a few fresh sardines for good measure. "Sorry, Nick. But animals aren't allowed in the hospital, and I'm not sure how long I'll be."

Nick made a sound in the back of his throat that sounded like a disgruntled *hmpf*, then turned and pushed his face into his food bowl. I picked up my purse and car keys and started for the door. Nick lifted his head, let out a soft meow, then returned to his slurping, his mood apparently mollified by the sardines. I drove to Cruz General, parked and hurried inside to the reception area. True to his word, Samms had indeed put my name on the "approved persons" list to visit Mark Emerson. The actor was lying in the bed, eyes closed, when I knocked tentatively on the doorframe. His head turned and those blue eyes opened and fastened on me, and he managed a weak smile. "Ah, we've got company. Come in, Nora," he said.

I stepped over the threshold and realized for the first time that Mark wasn't alone in the room. Emily Van Horn sat huddled in a chair on the other side of his bed. She rose as I entered. I noticed that she looked even paler and more drawn out than Mark, and I couldn't help wondering just how long she'd kept up this bedside vigil.

I pulled up a chair and sat down on Mark's other side. "I just wanted to drop by and see how you were doing," I said.

Mark leaned heavily back against the pillows. "As good as can be expected. When one acts like a horse's ass one must pay the price."

"Don't say that." Emily's eyes gleamed. "If anyone is responsible for you being here, and for acting like a horse's ass, it's me." She turned to look me straight in the eye. "I'm sure you know about my affair with Anton Forbes. I have no excuse for getting involved with that man, other than stupidity, naivete, and a giant ego."

"Hell, the guy was a con artist," Mark chimed in from the bed. "Anyone could see that. I wasn't angry with you, not really. I was more angry with him for taking advantage of your vulnerable state."

Emily must have noticed my look of confusion because she said quickly, "I should explain. Mark and I weren't really seriously involved. It was all studio hype. I was actually involved with another man. Another actor, who dumped me for another woman right around the time Anton Forbes joined *All the Days of Tomorrow*. Mark warned me against getting involved with him but I didn't listen. Anton paid me so much attention, and he was so flattering about my acting talent—he bolstered my ego in a way my former fiancé never had. Anyway, the day he died, Anton and I had a big argument. He wanted me to quit the show. He said that he was planning on leaving also, to film a movie in Europe he wanted me to star in. I was very tempted, until he let me read the script." Her cheeks flushed a bright scarlet. "I would have spent more time with my clothes off than on, and that's definitely not my style. I yelled at him, told him I'd rather die than do that part, or else I'd rather see him dead. He was furious with me. Accused me of leading him on."

"As if anyone could ever lead him on," spat out Mark. "Anyway, Emily went immediately to the trailer where I was getting ready to film and told me what happened. She was so upset, I knew she'd never be able to do her scenes that day, so I told Colgate that she was sick. And then I got so mad myself, I took one of the studio vans and drove into the next town and got shit-faced drunk, something I haven't done in a long, long time." He let out a sigh, reached out and clasped Emily's hand. "It appears I was never totally honest with Emily, or with myself either, for that matter. I couldn't bear the thought of Forbes touching her one more second. I guess I'd been in love with her for months, I just didn't realize it."

"Oh, Mark," Emily murmured, pressing his hand to her cheek.

"Anyway, I drove back to the park and over to Forbes's trailer. I was determined to have it out with the bastard. When I got there, I heard voices inside. I banged on the trailer door and all of a sudden there was complete silence. Then Forbes came to the door. He saw I was drunk and he leered at me, called me a loser. He said that I never deserved Emily, and that he might not have her, but neither would I. I told him he deserved to die, and I was the one to see to it. Then I started to get dizzy, so I stumbled out. I crawled back inside the van and fell asleep for, oh, I don't know, a couple hours. When I woke up, everything was hazy."

"I see. And you don't know who it was inside the trailer with Forbes?"

Mark shook his head. "No, sorry."

"I have an idea who it might have been," Emily piped up. "Ned Reilly."

I turned to look at the actress. "Why do you say that?"

She shrugged. "It's nothing I can put my finger on, it's just a feeling. Reilly was always hanging around Anton, doing him favors, filling him on set gossip. Anton regarded him as his personal snitch, but sometimes it just seemed the other way around. Reilly had a way of worming information out of people. As cagey as Anton was, I'm willing to bet Reilly got more information out of Anton than he ever revealed." She clasped her hands in her lap. "Ned always acted affable around Anton, but there was this undercurrent. I could just tell he despised him, and he really had no reason to."

"I'm not so sure about that," Mark cut in. "I overheard Ned on the phone one day, and I got the impression he went farther back with Forbes than he wanted most people to know."

"Did you get the same sense as Emily? That Reilly disliked Forbes?"

His lips twisted into a rueful grin. "Oh, yeah. There was something there, some sort of animosity all right. And it seemed to be all on Ned's part. Anton was definitely unaware of how he felt toward him."

Emily nodded. "I think both of them had more than one skeleton in their closets, and truthfully it wouldn't surprise me if Ned were the one who killed Anton. But now that they're both dead, I guess we'll never know the truth."

Chapter Twenty-two

Nick was sprawled out, belly up, in front of the refrigerator when I let myself in the back door of Hot Bread. His head turned slightly as I dropped my keys and purse on the table, and he opened both eyes and blinked at me.

"Yes, it's been a very enlightening evening," I told him. I eased myself into one of the chairs and patted the one next to me. "Come on up and I'll tell you all about it."

Nick twisted his body around and got to his feet, stretched out both forepaws, and then made a graceful leap into the chair. He turned around twice, then settled himself, tail wrapped around his forepaws, and cocked his head at me expectantly. I recounted my meetings with Samms and with Mark and Emily. When I finished, I reached out and scratched the top of his head. "Any thoughts?"

Nick squinted at me, almost as if he were pondering the question; then he leapt off the chair and disappeared underneath the table.

"Yeah, neither do I." I leaned both elbows on the table and rested my chin on my folded hands. "Both Emily and Mark seem to think Reilly knew Forbes before he joined the show and there was some animosity there. What could that be, I wonder?"

I felt something hit my foot and I looked down. There were several Scrabble tiles scattered at my feet. I bent down and picked them up. An A, an L and an I. No sooner had I laid them on the table than more tiles came flying out. I picked up another A and an S and laid all the letters in a straight line. A-L-I-A-S.

"You're repeating yourself, Nick. You spelled this out before."

Nick's furry face peeped out from underneath the table. "Rrow."

I ran my hand through my hair. "For you to repeat a word, you must think it's important. I glanced at the cat sharply. "You think Reilly was using an alias? Reilly wasn't his real name?"

"Yowl!" Nick wiggled all the way out from underneath the table, sat up straight and waved his paw in the air as if to say, "Now you're catching *on, human."*

I got up, retrieved my laptop from the back counter, booted it up. I called up Google and typed "Anton Forbes—director—work history" into the search engine. The first two sites I called up just gave generic information, but the third one went into painstaking detail about each of Forbes's cinematic efforts—including the cult classic *Werewolf Zombies from Planet Hedron.* There were over a dozen horror films credited to Forbes, most of which, thankfully, I'd never heard of. There were a few other, more artistic films, the list of which included his debut film, *The Mysteries of Maya*—the film he'd inherited upon Dean Harriman's untimely demise. On impulse, I called up IMDB and typed in "Mysteries of Maya." The movie's summary described it as a thriller: an actress has psychic impressions of a killer stalking her, and hires a private detective, who she summarily falls in love with, to protect her and smoke out the killer, who turns out to be her director. There was a brief mention at the end of the summary about how ironic it was that the original director of the movie should have been accidentally killed in the climactic suicide scene. I scrolled down to the cast listing. Marilyn Montell and Edmund Clarkson were the two lead actors, portraying the actress, Maya Duke, and the ill-fated director, Joe Haskell. There was a photograph of Marilyn Montell, a sexy-looking blonde with a killer smile and blue eyes. I sucked in a breath as I recognized her—the woman who'd been in the photograph I'd seen on the collage at Forbes's wake. There was no photograph of Edmund Clarkson, but for the heck of it I called up Marilyn Montell's biography. The lone paragraph was succinct. She'd come from a poor family, gotten her big break while waitressing when she was discovered by none other than Harriman. He brought her to Hollywood, where she starred in a few movies directed by him, and according to one critic, had been on the "fast track to superstardom." Dean Harriman's death seemed to have a great effect on her. She finished *Mysteries of Maya* and then, for all intents and purposes, dropped out of the Hollywood scene entirely. She hadn't made a movie since, and no one could say exactly where she was at the present moment. The general consensus was she'd left show business entirely. The fact I found most interesting, though, was that she and Edmund Clarkson had been rumored to have had an affair during the filming of *Maya*, a rumor both she and Clarkson summarily denied.

"Hm," I said, tapping my chin with my nail, "I bet she was having an affair, only not with Clarkson. How much you want to bet it was with Anton Forbes?"

Nick looked me straight in the eye. "Yurgle."

I clicked on Edmund Clarkson's bio. He'd been groomed for leading man status, and *Maya* had been regarded as his big break. He, too, had been affected by the death of the man he regarded as his mentor, Dean Harriman. He hadn't done a movie since that one either.

Interesting.

I went back to Google and typed in Forbes's name again, this time with a different goal in mind. I found several fan sites devoted to the director, notably for his most recent work, the nighttime soap *All the Days of Tomorrow*. Finally I clicked on one called *Everything Anton*. This site only briefly touched on Forbes's time with the nighttime drama, focusing instead on his earlier career. I clicked on the page marked "Photos". There were over a dozen photo albums there, and the instruction "Click on album to view photos" was at the top of the page. I clicked on one entitled "Early Years" and found myself staring at a collage very similar to the one that had been on the memorial poster at Forbes's wake. I scrutinized each photo carefully. Finally, down at the bottom I saw one of Forbes, surrounded by a group of men. One I recognized from other photos as Dean Harriman, so I assumed this photo must have been taken on the set of *Mysteries of Maya*. I clicked on that photo and a slightly larger version filled the screen. The photo was a bit on the blurry side, but my attention was drawn to the man standing in back of Harriman. His face was thinner than Reilly's, and his hair was longer and darker, but . . . dammit, there was a resemblance. I looked at the legend below the photograph:

Group shot–Mysteries of Maya–from left to right: Josh Clarke, Paul

Matson, Edmund "Ned" Clarkson, Dean Harriman, Anton Forbes.

Edmund "Ned" Clarkson.

Something furry brushed my ankles and I looked down. Nick stared back at me, an expectant expression on his face.

"Looks like you're right again, Nick. Ned Reilly might really be Edmund Clarkson, one of the actors on that Dean Harriman film. But even if he is, there are still lots of questions."

Nick tipped his head up. "Er-ewl?"

"Well, for instance, what happened to cause the animosity between them? Did it have something to do with Dean Harriman's death, or something else entirely?"

Nick stood on his back legs and stretched upward so that his paws reached the strap of my tote. Before I could react, he gave the strap a sharp tug. All its contents went spilling across Hot Bread's floor.

I let out a little cry. "Nick, for goodness sakes. What was that all about?"

Nick held out his paw and gave a pitiful meow.

I shook my finger at him. "Don't give me that. You're not hurt."

He ducked his head and meowed again. I reached for him, and he gestured with his paw. I saw he was pointing at something that was peeping out of the zipper lining compartment of my tote. I reached in and pulled out an old necklace of my mother's. I'd been meaning to take it to the jeweler's for a few weeks now to have the clasp tightened, but I'd forgotten about it. The necklace wasn't an expensive piece but it had been my mother's favorite and I was reluctant to part with it.

I held it up and extended it toward Nick. "Is this what you were after? Mom's necklace?"

Nick tipped his head back. "Yurgle."

I turned the bit of jewelry over in my palm. The chain was stainless steel, and the medallion that dangled from it was made of the same metal. On the charm was an etching of my mother's favorite flower, roses and a small white quartz stone, meant to simulate a diamond for her birth month, April.

I narrowed my gaze at Nick. "This charm looks something like the one we left with Ollie, doesn't it? Do you think Reilly's the one who dropped it? Or that Reilly might have known who did?"

My cell chirped, and I saw Hank Prince's number pop up. When I answered, he said without any preamble, "That was some picture you sent me. I haven't seen anything that beat up in a long time."

"Tell me you have good news about it."

"Well, you are a lucky girl, Ms. Nora Charles. One of my best buds is an expert with photos just like that. He cleaned it up pretty nicely. I'm sending it to your phone right now."

"I owe you big-time, Hank Prince."

"Don't you forget it. I'll be out there to collect soon."

Hank hung up just as my phone pinged the arrival of an email. I opened it and quickly downloaded the picture. Nick lofted next to me and put his paw on my shoulder, craning his neck at the phone.

I was frankly amazed at the job Hank's pal had done. The back of the medallion was clear of scratches now, and I could see letters etched there that looked like initials. *ARI.*

My phone chirped again, indicating a text. I saved the photo and then pulled the text up. It was from Ollie, and my heart started to beat faster as I read the message:

Found store where medallion was ordered. Custom piece, made two years ago. Ordered by Anton Forbes. No other info available.

I set down the phone, leaned back and scrubbed my hands over my face. I had a lot of clues, but none of them made any sense. The note, the paper with the string of numbers in Ned Reilly's pocket, and now the medallion that had been specially ordered by Anton Forbes two years ago. I was pretty sure they all added up to something, but what could that something be?

Nick made a mewling sound in his throat, and I reached out and patted him on the head. "I know, I'm frustrated too. Know what I wish? I wish we could find something that would help us make sense out of all this."

What I didn't realize was that . . . I already had.

Chapter Twenty-three

I searched around the Internet for another good half hour but could come up with no more information on Edmund Clarkson or Marilyn Montell. I read over two dozen articles on Forbes too, but could find no mention of any woman he was involved with who had the initials *ARI.* At last I pushed my chair back, stretched my arms wide, and stood up. Nick, sprawled on the table next to the laptop, regarded me with a curious glint in his golden eyes.

"The solution is right in front of me, I can feel it. I just can't see the forest for the trees, for some reason."

Nick cocked his head. "Owrr?"

"Motive. The key is motive. Who had the best one? Let's drill down our suspects' motives, like they taught us in PI class. Why do people kill?"

I walked over to the middle drawer and pulled out a ruled pad, brought it back to the table, sat down and started to write down all the possible reasons people committed murder we'd gone over in PI class. After a few minutes I set the pen down and surveyed the list.

To keep a secret
Revenge
Frustration/hate
Money/Greed
Sex/Jealousy
Property Dispute
Personal Vendetta
Politics
Class Conflict
Narcotics
Other Felonies
Urge to Protect

I drew a big fat circle around the first one. *To keep a secret.* Had Forbes known something about his killer, something he'd possibly threatened to reveal, or had it been the opposite scenario? The only person I could think of who might fill that bill was, unfortunately, Remy. I bit down hard on my lower lip as I realized that quite a few of the motives might actually apply to Remy's situation. Depending on whatever it was between him and Forbes that he seemed determined not to reveal, it could fall under secret keeping, revenge, frustration/hate, even money/greed or sex/jealousy. I doubted it was a property dispute, political or narcotics-related, but personal vendetta was also a consideration. And then there was Ned Reilly. If he'd been the one to off Forbes, why had he done so? What secret could he possibly have known? The only thing I could think of was that the secret had to do with Harriman. There had to be some connection between Harriman's death and Forbes and Reilly. But what could it be? I couldn't help thinking about what Millicent Martin had alluded to in her article. Harriman's "big reveal." Did it have something to do with Forbes? Did it figure into the murders?

My gut was telling me a resounding *yes.* But how could I find out what it was?

I threw down the pen. I felt like I was spinning my wheels, covering and recovering the same ground. Funny thing, backtracking. Sometimes you spotted something important you missed the first time, and other times . . . you didn't.

Abruptly I pushed my chair back, startling Nick. "Sorry, fella. I'm getting nowhere." I let out a long sigh. "I do miss Daniel, and the way he always acted like the perfect sounding board. I bet he'd come up with a fresh angle."

Nick cocked his head. "Owwr?"

"No, I can't ask Samms for help. He'd lecture me on how I should stay out of the case and out of trouble. Anyway, he seems pretty convinced Remy's guilty, if you ask me. And we both know Remy's innocent, right?"

Nick raised one paw. "Er-up!"

"Yes, I agree. What we need is a change of scene. Maybe it'll help recharge my batteries." I tapped at my temple with my forefinger. "How does a drink at the Poker Face sound? Your pal Lance is on tonight. I bet there's a saucer of milk with your name on it. Maybe if we're real lucky, Samms and his girlfriend Dale Anderson will even pop in."

Nick made a disgruntled sound and wrinkled his nose.

"Yeah," I said, reaching for my tote. "My sentiments exactly."

• • •

Twenty minutes later Nick and I walked through the front door of the Poker Face. It had originally been a fire station, which the original owner had converted into a bar. When Lance and his brother Phil took over, they made some additions, but to me, the best improvement was the bar itself: a large sheet of scarred cherrywood that took up most of one side, flanked with high-backed leather stools, and to top it off, a forty-two-inch flat screen similar to the one that hung above the counter at Hot Bread. Lance's righthand man, Jose, was behind the bar, and he gave me a two-fingered salute as I slid onto one of the stools.

"Hey, Jose. Lance or Alexa around?"

"You just missed Miss Alexa. She left not five minutes ago." Jose gestured toward the back room. "Mr. Lance is just finishing up with the private party. They were having some sort of officer election, so they stayed later than normal. He should be out soon, though. Can I get you something in the meantime?"

"I'll take a Bud on tap."

Jose slapped a foaming mug of Bud in front of me before I could blink, and then he glanced down at Nick, who hunkered under my stool. "How about a saucer of milk for Mr. Nick, eh? Coming right up, if he'd like to follow me?"

Nick happily trotted into the kitchen after Jose. I sipped my beer and looked around the bar. For a Thursday night it was pretty crowded.

A group of guys all wearing plaid shirts clustered around the television, eyes glued to some sports program; at the far end of the bar a group of girls who looked to be in their twenties sat drinking Cosmos and giggling, presumably over boys; many of the tables were filled, either with singles or couples. I started to turn back to my beer when a movement from one of the corner booths caught my eye. I casually picked up my mug and twisted in my seat to get a better look, peering casually over the rim, and almost dropped the glass as I recognized the booth's occupants.

Dale Anderson and Leroy Samms.

Well, that'll teach me, I thought, taking a long pull on my beer. *Be careful what you wish for, even in jest.*

Dale must have felt my eyes boring into her back, because she turned and glanced over her shoulder. Her happy expression faded as her eyes locked on me. She leaned over, said something to Samms, and then she was up and out of the booth and making a beeline straight for me.

Oh, swell.

"Well, well, Nora. I didn't expect to see you out here tonight."

I took in her attire—tight-fitting skinny jeans, a purple fitted V-necked top, and cute heeled ankle boots—and realized that they must be off duty. Maybe this was the continuation of the "date" that had been interrupted with Forbes's murder. I managed a small smile. "Well, you're the last person I expected to see in here myself."

She thrust her hands deep into the pockets of her jeans. "Just relaxing a bit. We've all been putting in a lot of overtime lately. But I don't have to tell you that." Her eyes narrowed and she leaned in a bit closer to me. I got a whiff of perfume, Chanel No. 5, no less. "Lee told me you found Reilly's body."

I nodded. "That's right."

Dale let out a low whistle. "Two in one week. That's something of a record, huh?" Without waiting for me to answer, she went on, "Need I ask what you and Nick were doing out in the woods?"

I smiled sweetly at her. "Why, didn't Samms tell you? We were looking to see if we could find any clues your men might have missed when they canvassed the area."

Dale returned my smile with a frosty one of her own. "I thought I made it clear to you that it would be in your best interests to stick to your cooking and leave the detective work to us."

"You did, and I had every intention of doing so, until you arrested my best friend's brother for the crime."

She crossed her arms over her chest. "You act like I plucked Remy's name out of thin air. I didn't do it on a whim, you know. All the evidence points to him."

"He's explained how his blood got on the netting, and your eyewitness who put him and Forbes together is dead now, so really, how good of a case do you have?"

Dale arched a brow. "There is Gillard's past with the deceased. You know, the one he doesn't want to talk about."

I tapped one finger against my mug. "Yes, there is that. But is it enough to warrant murder?"

Dale eased one hip against the bar. "I guess we'll have to see, won't we." She eyed me. "You really believe Gillard's innocent, don't you? Is that why you went to the hospital to question Mark Emerson?"

"I went to question Mark Emerson because someone told me they heard him threaten Forbes. And since he practically confessed to the murder during Forbes's wake . . ."

Dale leaned over so her nose was level with mine. "You're not a professional detective, Nora. You don't get to question suspects."

"I beg your pardon. I've got a PI license that says otherwise, and Chantal did hire me to look into things."

Dale snorted. "There's a world of difference between a PI and a homicide detective. We both know Chantal only hired you so Lee would share information with you."

I shrugged. "What about Ned Reilly? According to Blaine Carmichael, Reilly was working on bringing Forbes down. It's not out of the realm of possibility that whoever murdered Forbes also murdered Reilly, and Remy would have no reason to do that."

"True," said Dale, "if the murders were related."

Now it was my eyebrow that winged skyward. "You don't think they are?"

"Reilly's body was found without jewelry or wallet. There was a lump behind his ear. It might just have been a random mugging."

I narrowed my gaze. "You really believe that?"

"I believe whatever the evidence points to. Right now it points to Reilly being in the wrong place at the wrong time, and Remy being number one for murdering Forbes."

I bit back the retort I wanted to make and said instead, "Did you get the tox report back on Forbes? Were there any drugs in his system?"

"The normal ones a person takes with Ménière's disease, Dyazide, dexamethasone, but what was really strange was the overload of sodium chloride."

I frowned. "Salt?"

Dale opened her mouth to say something, but before she could get a word out her pocket started to vibrate. She uttered a soft groan and pulled out her beeper, glanced at the number. "As fascinating as this conversation has been, I'm afraid my off duty time's come to an end." She started to turn away, stopped, swung back to me. "Look, Nora, I admit you've got a knack for tracking down clues. This time, though, I think you really should take a step back and let the pros handle this."

"I can't do that as long as Remy's under suspicion."

"If Gillard is innocent, then everything will work out," Dale said. "Just leave it alone, okay?"

She spun on her heel and marched back to the booth. I watched her go, then felt something furry brush my ankles. Nick, a white mark above his lip, stared up at me.

"Enjoy your milk?" I asked him.

"Merow."

I took another sip of beer and glanced casually around the bar.

Samms was just dropping a bill on the table. He saw me looking in his direction, and for a minute I thought he was going to come over and say something to me, but Dale tugged at his arm and he turned and followed her out the side door of the Poker Face without a backward glance at me. I looked at Nick and sighed. "Anderson read me the riot act. She thinks we shouldn't investigate Forbes's and Reilly's deaths."

Nick made a sound that sounded suspiciously like *Hmpf.*

I nodded, pushed my mug off to one side. "Yeah, that's just what I said."

"What? Keep Nora Charles from investigating? Can't be done."

I froze. Even though the words were slurred, I knew that voice. I gave a little cry of annoyance and looked up into the eyes of a very drunk—and angry—Blaine Carmichael.

Chapter Twenty-four

Blaine started to lean his elbow on the bar, missed, stumbled back a step. "Fancy meeting you here," he said. This time his hand shot out, gripped the underside of the bar. "Can I buy you a drink?"

I held up my half-full mug. "No, thanks, I've got one. What are you doing here, Blaine? I would think you'd be out trying to scrounge up some dirt for your broadcast."

He leaned over and wagged his finger in my face. "You've been a bad girl, haven't you, Nora? Telling on me to the police."

I waved my hand back and forth, trying to dispel the odor of alcohol that emanated from Blaine's mouth. "All I did was tell the truth. I saw you leave the woods near the spot where I found Reilly's body."

"What you saw. Ha!" He let out a snort. "You don't know the half of it."

"Really? Then why don't you enlighten me?"

Blaine glanced over his shoulder first right, then left, then he leaned down close to me again and wagged his finger under my nose. "You want me to share info, then you gotta do th' same. Maybe together we can get to the bottom of all this and figure out who dunnit."

"Really? You want to work with me?" I set my mug down on the bar and looked him up and down. "You're drunk," I said flatly. "How do I know this magnanimous offer of yours will stand up when you're sober?"

A shadow fell across the bar. I glanced up and saw Lance, his eyes narrowed into slits as he regarded Blaine. "Everything all right here? This guy bothering you, Nora?"

Blaine's head reared up and he turned around and barked at Lance, "I'm not botherin' Nora, am I? Tell him I'm not botherin' you."

Lance waved his hand. "Wow, how many have you had, fella? You're cut off as of right now." He slid his gaze to me. "Say the word and I'll throw this clown out on his ass."

I made up my mind. "No. I think I'll talk to him." I gestured toward the booth Samms and Dale had just vacated. "Can you bring a pot of your strongest coffee over there?"

Lance gave Blaine a quick once-over. "Judging from his condition, it might take two pots. But yeah, I'll be right out." He threw a dagger look at Blaine before turning on his heel and stomping off toward the kitchen. I took Blaine's arm and led him over to the booth. Nick followed and jumped onto the bench next to me, folded his paws beneath him, and lifted his head so that his golden gaze bored into Blaine's.

Blaine started at the sight of Nick, and he raised a finger and pointed at him. "Is that the same cat from your shop?" He squinted. "He looks . . . smaller."

Nick let out a soft grr. I gave him a quick scratch behind his white streak and he settled back, eyes still wary. I turned to Blaine and laced my fingers under my chin. "Okay, you wanted to talk so . . . talk."

He shot me a bleary-eyed stare. "You never liked me, did you? When we worked in Chicago together you thought I was a loser, didn't you?"

"Not really. I thought you were an opportunist, and I didn't like the fact you'd cut corners and step on someone's back to get a story, but personally? I've nothing against you."

He let out a soft snort and swiped at his nose with the back of his hand. "Funny. I always admired you. You're smart, sassy, tough. You succeeded in a profession where few women do. I have to admit, I was surprised when you left, at the peak of your career. I wondered why."

I held up my hand. "We're not talking about me, or my reasons for leaving the *Trib*. You said you wanted to share information, so I'm listening. What have you got?"

Lance appeared just then. He set two mugs and a large pot of black coffee in front of us, placed a small pitcher of milk next to the pot. "Strong black coffee." He looked at me. "Don't worry, Alexa had Jose make that pot before she left. If you weren't here, though, I'd have made Jose brew a pot for him anyway." Lance jerked his thumb at Blaine.

Blaine sniffed at the pot. "No Kahlúa?"

Lance rolled his eyes, turned on his heel and strode back to the bar. He picked up a dish towel and started cleaning glasses, his gaze trained on our booth. Blaine reached out, grasped the pot, poured coffee into the mug. He swished the contents around with his spoon, and then took a long gulp. "Oh, man! That *is* strong!"

I waited until he'd finished his first cup and poured his second before saying, "Are you ready to talk now?"

He took another sip of coffee, set the mug down. He glanced around furtively and then said in a hoarse whisper, "Reilly contacted me a few weeks ago. He'd heard the station was sending me out to cover the *Days of Tomorrow* shoot, and he told me about Forbes being the reason behind Emerson and Emily Van Horn's breakup. He wanted the story broken, but in such a way that it couldn't be traced back to him. I told him he was taking some chance. What was to stop me from breaking that story myself? He said that it was small potatoes compared to something else he was working on. Harriman's legacy, he called it. He said that if I played ball with him, he'd see I got the exclusive on that story. He promised it could be a real career changer for me."

"Harriman's legacy? Did he explain what he meant by that?"

Blaine shook his head. "No, but I figured it might have had something to do with that 'big reveal' Harriman teased the press with a few days before his death. Anyway, I said I'd help. I arranged to have info he gave me delivered anonymously to a reporter I knew who was more than happy to leak the story."

"So you don't believe Reilly had anything to do with Forbes's death?"

"Of course I don't know for certain, but I tend to doubt it. Anyway, yesterday he called me, asked me to meet him in the woods. Says he's got something important to give me, something that'll change the whole direction of the story."

"The whole direction? In what way?"

Blaine shrugged. "Dunno. He never said. Anyway, I went to the appointed spot, but he never showed. I heard a noise in the trees, like

179

someone stumbling through the foliage, and I followed it straight to Ned's body. That's when I thought maybe I was being set up, so I got out of there, fast. You know the rest."

"You heard a noise? Did you see anyone? Anderson seems to think Reilly might have been a random mugging victim."

He shook his head. "I guess that's possible, but no, I didn't see anyone. Then again, I wasn't looking very hard."

I drummed my fingers on the table, then raised my gaze to his. "Did you remove anything from the body?"

He looked horrified. "Hell, no! I wouldn't touch a corpse, not if my life depended on it."

I continued to drum my fingers on the table. "He said he had something to give you?" At his nod I continued, "Then what happened to it? I was there. They didn't find anything on Reilly's body, except . . ."

I dipped into my bag and whipped out my phone. I scrolled to the photo I'd taken of the paper in Reilly's pocket and showed it to Blaine. "That was sticking out of Reilly's pocket. Does it look familiar to you?"

Blaine took the phone and squinted at the screen. "Looks like a string of numbers."

"Could this be what Reilly wanted to give you?"

His brow puckered. "Maybe, but I have no idea what it could mean." He set down his mug and then his hand dipped into his pants pocket and he pulled out his wallet. He started to withdraw a bill, but I waved him off.

"My treat. Can you make it back to the Cruz Inn all right, or do you need me to call you a cab?"

"I'll be okay. It's not that far, and a walk in the fresh air will do me good." He rubbed absently at his temples. "Although I suppose I'll have a bitch of a headache tomorrow."

"Try some Alka-Seltzer or aspirin," I advised. "I haven't had a hangover in a while, but they always worked for me."

"Thanks."

I watched him go, and then I enlarged the photo of the list of numbers so I could see it more clearly. Then I fished a pen out of my bag and wrote down on a napkin what I thought the string of numbers was: 7145556981. A phone number, maybe? I switched my cell to phone mode and punched in the number. A few minutes later a crisp female voice answered.

"Drug Enforcement Administration. How may I direct your call?"

Chapter Twenty-five

I disconnected and leaned my head against the back of the booth. So Ned had been in touch with the DEA. I mentally reviewed what I knew about that agency. The DEA is a U.S. federal law enforcement agency under the U.S. Department of Justice, and their primary task was to combat drug smuggling and use within the U.S. of A. Not only was the DEA the lead agency for domestic enforcement of the Controlled Substances Act, sharing jurisdiction with the FBI and Immigration and Customs, it was also tasked with the responsibility for coordinating and pursuing U.S. drug investigations abroad.

Had Ned somehow connected Forbes to smuggling drugs? More important, had Dean Harriman done the same? And had Forbes killed Harriman to protect his secret, and had Ned figured that out as well?

Had Reilly been reporting on Forbes's activities to DEA agents? My jaw set as I suddenly realized why Samms had been hanging around, "helping" Dale out. The FBI was probably assisting, and Samms had drawn the assignment. I also realized what was probably behind his and Dale's repeated assertions to me that I should stay out of this case and stick to cooking. They didn't want me nosing around in what was potentially very dangerous territory. Random mugging victim, my behind.

Nick butted his head against my elbow. I reached out and stroked the top of his head. "Let's think this out," I said to him. "What if this big reveal of Dean Harriman's was that he'd discovered his protégé, Forbes, was involved with drugs? He was going to make a public show out of it, inform the authorities, and Forbes couldn't let that happen, so he decided to silence him. But how would he have known that Harriman would want to demonstrate that scene and go for the gun, unless . . ."

I lapsed into silence, frowning as I thought. Nick nudged his head into the crook of my elbow, purring like a race car. Suddenly I straightened and slapped my forehead with my palm, jarring Nick from his comfortable position. He let me know it, too, with a sharp meow of annoyance.

"Sorry, buddy," I apologized. "Forbes knew Harriman was a perfectionist, and he knew if the scene was flubbed, Harriman wouldn't be able to resist demonstrating how it should be played, so he deliberately instructed Clarkson how to play the scene in a way he knew would irritate Harriman." I slid Nick a glance. "How'm I doing so far?"

"Merow," he said, wrinkling his nose.

"Okay, we're on the right track. So, continuing on, Forbes decided Harriman had to be silenced, but how did he do it? None of the security tapes show anyone tampering with the gun, and the desk itself showed no sign of being broken into. The prop master admitted he hadn't checked the gun once it was locked away, so it might have been switched before, but that's doubtful." My eyes met Nick's. "There's only one answer, bud. Forbes had help."

Nick blinked, and then his head moved in a perceptible nod.

My fingers beat a swift tattoo on the scarred tabletop. "He had to. But who? It had to be someone familiar with manipulating a security camera, right? Although, maybe not. Maybe all he needed was someone who could manipulate the prop master himself."

Nick tipped his head to one side. "Er-ewl?"

"Think about it. The prop master would know how to manipulate a security camera, wouldn't he? So what if he were approached by Marilyn Montell for an assignation, maybe right on that very desk, even. He'd make damn sure they weren't caught on camera. So now, with the cameras turned off, Marilyn swipes the key and gives it to Forbes, who makes a clean switch."

Nick waved one paw in the air.

"Yes, I know. Montell was supposed to be an item with Harriman. But the way she looked at Forbes in that photo . . ." I whipped out my phone and called up my Google app. "You spelled out *alias*," I murmured. "Unless I'm mistaken, a synonym for *alias* is *nickname* . . ." I typed "nicknames" into the search engine. A few seconds later I had a site open entitled, appropriately, Nicknames.com. I typed in "nicknames–Marilyn" and a few seconds later a list came up. Mari-Lyn-Lynnie–and my eyes popped at the last one.

"Ari. What do you know?" I rested my chin in my palm and slid Nick a look. "We need to find Marilyn."

Nick regarded me silently for a moment, then let out a yowl that I took as approval.

I rubbed at the back of my neck. Of course, my theory wasn't perfect. Montell was supposed to be romantically involved with Harriman, and I doubted that even for a charmer like Forbes, she'd willingly agree to participate in a murder. Possibly Forbes told her he was planning to play a joke on the director, or maybe he hadn't said anything. I recalled the worshipful look on her face in the photo as she looked at Forbes. He might have asked her to jump off the Golden Gate Bridge and she might have done it. All the accounts I'd read said she'd been devastated by the director's death. So much so that she'd dropped out of sight shortly after *Mysteries of Maya* was completed.

What had happened to Marilyn Montell? Was she still alive somewhere, or had she also been a loose end that Forbes had needed to tie up?

That last thought was particularly chilling. There were still so many questions; but, at least it seemed as if I was finally starting to get some answers.

Lance came over to me, fresh coffeepot in hand. "Need a refill?"

I pushed my mug in front of me. "Yes, thanks. That last pot was pretty good. Jose's really getting better at coffee making."

"Yeah, Alexa's a good teacher." He topped off my coffee, set the pot down. "Everything work out okay with your buddy?"

"Blaine? He's not exactly my buddy, but I must say, it was a very interesting conversation."

Lance folded his arms across his chest. "You think you can trust that guy? He seems like a real jerk to me."

"He is a real jerk, and no, of course I don't think I can trust him. Let's not forget he was pretty drunk when he decided to ask for my help. I'll bet once he sobers up he's going to regret all of this, but it's too late now," I added with a grin.

Lance chuckled, then sobered. "How's Remy doing?"

"He's holding up."

"I heard that he won't tell any details of his relationship with that Forbes guy. Won't that hurt him when the case goes to trial?"

I took a long sip of my coffee. "I'm hoping that it won't go to trial. That the real murderer will be caught before then." I ran my finger around the rim of the mug. "Do you remember an actress named Marilyn Montell?"

"I'm not a big moviegoer, but I do remember her." He gave a low whistle. "She was one sexy babe. Say, whatever happened to her, anyway?"

"That's what I'd like to know. I sighed. "Apparently she dropped out of sight after making *Mysteries of Maya.*"

"Oh, you mean she quit show business, like Kim Novak?"

"It would appear so," I said dryly. "Although I'm thinking that maybe there was more to it than meets the eye."

"More to it? You think maybe she was pregnant or something?"

Hm, the thought Marilyn might have been pregnant hadn't occurred to me. I shook my head. "I guess that is a possibility, although I tend to think if it were something like that, some reporter somewhere would have gotten wind of it. That would have been a real juicy scoop."

A woman seated at the next booth with white hair who looked to be in her middle sixties turned around in her seat and smiled at me. "I'm sorry, I don't mean to eavesdrop, but I couldn't help overhear. Are you a fan of Marilyn Montell's?"

"Not really," I said truthfully. "I only recently learned about her, and her story just seemed so tragic, it piqued my interest."

"Yes, it was one of the more tragic Hollywood love stories, that's a fact." The woman thrust her hand out. "I'm sorry. I'm Amy Porter. I'm retired now, but a few years ago I was the entertainment reporter for the *Cruz Sun.*"

"Oh, of course." I smiled at her. "I recognize your name. I'm Nora Charles."

Amy waved her hand. "Oh, I know who you are. Besides making the most delicious sandwiches I've ever tasted, you used to be a reporter too. We gal reporters should stick together, don't you agree?" she said with a saucy wink.

"I do indeed." I motioned to the empty seat across from me. "Won't you join me for a cup of coffee?"

Amy indicated her empty wineglass with a wave of her hand. "I'll have another Merlot." She cut Lance a broad wink. "I'm sure if I get carried away and end up a bit tipsy, Lance will see that some kind soul walks me home."

Lance snorted. "Tipsy? Amy? She can drink any one of my customers under the table, that's for sure." He picked up the wineglass. "I'll be right back with that Merlot, on the house."

Lance left and Amy slid into the seat formerly occupied by Blaine. "You sound as if you are a Marilyn Montell fan," I said.

Amy nodded. "Oh, yes, I was a big admirer. I followed her career from the get-go. The girl was given the most schlocky roles, but she did an admirable job. If Dean Harriman had lived, he'd have seen to it that she got roles she deserved. I bet she'd have either won or have been nominated for an Oscar by now."

"I'm toying with the idea of possibly doing an article on her," I lied. "But I'm having a hard time getting some facts verified and I'm reluctant to write anything speculative."

Amy's lips curved upward. "That's one thing I always liked about you. You're a responsible journalist, unlike some others I could mention. Maybe I can help you. I know quite a bit about her. Not only am I a big fan, but several of my journalist friends were as well, and a few of them had personal contact with her when she was working on her last film." She gave a little shudder and then leaned across the table and said in a confidential whisper, "Marilyn wasn't pregnant with Harriman's child, or with any other man's either, for that matter, although maybe it might have been better for her if she had been."

"Why do you say that?"

Amy glanced around the crowded bar and then said, "What I'm going to tell you isn't public knowledge. I got this straight from the mouth of the president of the Marilyn Montell Fan Club shortly after Dean Harriman's death. She was extremely upset over a rumor she'd heard about Marilyn."

"What was the rumor?"

"That Marilyn knew more about Harriman's death than met the eye, and that she was all broken up over it. She blamed herself."

"How so?"

"Well . . . Marilyn was deeply in love with Dean Harriman, but she'd also been attracted to his assistant director, Anton Forbes. She'd told a friend that she'd been mentally unfaithful to Dean, and it bothered her, but she just couldn't seem to help herself."

"I see. What exactly was it that Marilyn was supposed to have known about Harriman's death?"

Lance arrived, set the Merlot in front of Amy and withdrew. She took a long satisfying sip before continuing. "No one really knows. Just that she knew something. Whatever it was upset her greatly." She glanced around furtively and then said in a stage whisper, "She had a breakdown."

My eyes widened. "Really? Was she hospitalized?"

"No one's quite sure. She collapsed at the afterparty. Only a few people knew, and I happened to be friends with the headwaiter at the café where the party was held, that's how I know. She collapsed, and was taken away. It was all very hush-hush. And that's the last anyone ever saw of her."

"That's such a shame." I took a sip of my coffee and then leaned forward. "You wouldn't happen to know if Marilyn had any nicknames, would you?"

"Oh, my, yes. Most of them were very unflattering, though." She took a sip of Merlot. "She didn't like all the comparisons to Marilyn Monroe. Some of her close friends called her Lyn or Lynnie."

"Oh." I tried to keep the disappointment out of my tone. "Not Ari? I read somewhere that's a popular nickname for Marilyn."

"I don't think—wait." Amy's brow furrowed and then she snapped her fingers. "I do recall hearing somewhere that she mentioned a special man in her life called her that. She wasn't fond of it, though." Amy wrinkled her nose. "Men are great for giving us nicknames we don't like, don't you agree? Rhonda Kaye's first husband used to call her Monkey Face, can you imagine? And Celeste Storm's college fiancé called her Fancy Pants . . ."

Amy rattled on, but I was thinking about something else. It was entirely possible the "special man" was Forbes. He'd ordered the charm right around the time all this happened. Had he used the necklace as an inducement to get Marilyn to help him murder her lover?

I had to find out.

• • •

The minute I got home, I made a beeline for my laptop. When I set it on the table, Nick hopped onto the chair and sat, squinting at the screen as I called up Google. Clearly he intended to help me with the research I needed to do.

I called up a listing of every exclusive rest and convalescent home in the greater LA area, private institutions where a person of Marilyn Montell's stature might receive the best care and utmost privacy. There were more than I thought: fifteen, to be exact. I looked up all the numbers and started dialing. On the fourth one I hit pay dirt.

A woman fitting Montell's description had been admitted two years prior, under the name of Lynnie Weston. The admission paperwork had been signed by a Monica Weston. Her sister. I hung up the phone and looked at Nick.

"So, let's say that Marilyn Montell, probably unknowingly, aided Forbes in killing Harriman. She had a breakdown from the guilt, and her sister admits her to a private facility, where she is today. But how did her medallion get to the gazebo?" I pulled my hand through my hair. "Maybe Marilyn isn't as sick as people think? If she found out Forbes was in the area, she could have also found a way to leave the facility, track him down."

Nick blinked at me. "Er-ewl?"

"Yep." I closed the laptop and folded my hands on top of it. "I'll have to put Lacey and Chantal on alert. They'll have to watch the shop tomorrow afternoon. Once lunch service is ended, I've got a date at Crestwood Sanitarium."

Chapter Twenty-six

When Mollie and I arrived at Cruz High Friday morning, I was met at the kitchen entrance by Kenny Colgate, who informed me that my services would only be required for breakfast. They were going to spend the afternoon filming some retakes at the Cruz Inn, and he'd arranged for Pasquale, the chef over there, to put up a buffet.

"But don't worry," he hastened to assure me, "we'll honor your contract. You'll be compensated for lunch today." He paused. "And also for the three days for your cat's scene, even though we're only spending one day on it. You do remember we're shooting that tomorrow after breakfast, right?"

I nodded. "Oh, yes. Nick is really looking forward to it."

He shot me a look that clearly said, *A cat? Looking forward to filming a scene for a TV show?* Clearly, Colgate had never owned an animal, or had an animal own him. However, I wasn't about to split hairs. Colgate's new shooting schedule fit in nicely with my plans for the day. By ten thirty the cast and crew were fed, Mollie and I had everything tucked away in the van, and after dropping the teen back at her house, I was on my way to Crestwood Sanitarium. After an hour's drive I arrived and parked the van in the area marked *Visitors*. I locked the van and stood for a minute, taking stock of my surroundings.

The Crestwood Sanitarium was a large, weather-beaten brick building that easily fit every stereotype of "mental institution" I'd ever heard. The only thing missing were bars on the windows. I walked up the crumbling stone steps and pushed through the heavy wooden door, pausing to glance around the waiting area, with its institutional beige-colored walls that were brightened by a few framed posters dotted here and there, offering such platitudes as *Every Day is a Gift* and *Today is the First Day of the Rest of Your Life*. A short, squat woman wearing a purple coat and ill-fitting trousers passed in front of me, then abruptly turned and crossed back to lay her hand on my arm. "Are you a doctor?" she asked, peering up into my face. "I've been waiting for my doctor."

I shook my head. "No, sorry. I'm here to visit someone, though."

The woman jerked her thumb in the direction of the wide reception desk. "Then you gotta check in with Sally." Her fingers pressed harder into my forearm. "Ever'body gotta check in with Sally. Who ya here ta see?"

"A friend. Thanks." I gently disengaged her fingers from my arm and quickly covered the short space from foyer to reception area, which was situated right in front of a bank of elevators. The heavyset gray-haired woman barely looked up as I approached. A brass name tag dangled from her red cardigan—S. Moyer—so I assumed this paragon was Sally. She pushed her wire-rimmed glasses up farther on her beak-shaped nose and slid open the glass that separated the staff from the outside world. She looked me up and down—twice—before saying in a bored tone, "Can I help you?"

"I hope so." I leaned forward and said in a confidential tone, "I'm here to see one of your patients. Lynnie Weston."

The woman's thinly penciled eyebrows rose. "Lynnie Weston? Are you cleared?"

"Cl-cleared?" I stammered.

She eyed me. "Yes. All Miss Weston's visitors either have to be cleared through her doctor or through her sister. The rules are very specific."

I bit down hard on my bottom lip, then dipped my hand into my tote and pulled out my PI license. I held it up for the woman to see. "Nora Charles, private investigator. It's imperative I speak with Ms. Weston."

"Regarding?"

I lifted my chin. "I'm afraid that's confidential."

The eyebrows rose even higher. "You still have to be cleared." She shuffled some papers around on the desk in front of her. "I don't see a Nora Charles anywhere on the approved visitor list," she said, and then slid the glass window shut.

I tapped on it.

She ignored me.

Swell.

As I started to turn away, the elevator doors opened and a man in a white coat came out. He looked at me, and suddenly his face broke into a wide smile. "Nora? Nora Charles? What are you doing here?"

I peered at the man. His face seemed vaguely familiar, but I couldn't quite place him. I glanced at the name tag pinned to his white coat: Dr. S. Stanbee. Stanbee. I did a double take. "Stanley! Oh, my gosh. What are you doing here?"

Stanley Stanbee, one of the guys who'd had a huge crush on me in high school. And if you think we didn't make fun of Stan Stanbee (what were his parents thinking?), guess again. Stanley was one of those nerdy types that girls should date but don't. I confess that I'd taken advantage of his crush, getting him to write more than one biology and chem paper for me, and then broken his heart by going to prom with Lance. Ah, callous youth! But as Stan beamed down at me, it seemed that he'd forgiven my youthful indiscretions. He didn't even make fun of my stupid question as he tapped at his name tag.

"I work here," he said. "How about you? What are you doing here? You can't possibly be visiting someone, so—wait!" He waved his hand in the air. "I remember hearing you became a reporter. Don't tell me you're writing an article on Crestwood?"

I huffed an errant curl out of my eyes. "No, I'm afraid I'm not. Actually, I'm no longer a journalist."

"You're not? What do you do now?"

"I run Hot Bread."

"Ah, your mother's shop. I read about her passing. She was a very nice woman. I'm very sorry." His gaze raked me up and down. "You came back to Cruz after spending all that time in some big city. New York?"

"Chicago."

He clucked his tongue. "Those winters can be brutal. I see why you opted to come home again. How do you like being in business for yourself?"

"I like it. It's a far cry from reporting, of course, but I manage to keep my hand in. I write articles for *Noir* in my spare time."

Stan's brow wrinkled. "*Noir*? I don't think I've heard of it. Is it a magazine?"

I nodded. "An online true crime magazine. It's becoming quite popular."

"Well, I can easily see why, if you write for it." He glanced at my left hand. "I take it you're not married?" As I shook my head, he added, "Whatever happened to that jock you were dating senior year? Lance, right? Everyone always thought you two would end up married with a pack of kids."

I laughed. "You mean Lance Reynolds. He runs the bar in Cruz, the Poker Face. He's not married either, at least not yet. He's dating a very lovely girl right now. You should stop by sometime for a drink. We could all reminisce."

"Ah, I'd love to. This place keeps me pretty busy, though." He spread his arms wide. "I run it."

My eyes popped. "You run Crestwood?"

He nodded. "For the past three years. After I graduated Johns Hopkins I interned at Bellevue in New York, and then I just couldn't take the winters anymore. I was lucky enough to land a position at Metropolitan State. One of the Crestwood board members heard about my work, and when the last director retired, put my name in contention."

"That's pretty impressive," I said with an engaging smile. "If you run this place, then you must be familiar with all of the patients here, like Lynnie Weston, for instance?"

The affable smile faded, replaced by a guarded expression. "Why are you asking about her?"

I reached into my bag and brought out my PI license. "In addition to running Hot Bread, I recently became a licensed investigator. Do you remember Chantal Gillard?" At his nod I rushed on, "Well, her brother Remy's found himself in a bit of trouble, and I'm trying to help him out."

"But what does that have to do with Lyn—wait a minute." He snapped his fingers. "That director was murdered in Cruz, right. Anton Forbes." His expression darkened a bit and he nodded. "Ah, I see. You know that Ms. Weston is . . ."

"Marilyn Montell. Yes, I do know that."

His frown deepened. "And you think she might know something about Forbes's murder? That's impossible. Lynnie's not permitted to leave the facility. Her room is always kept under surveillance. For another"—he spread his hands—"I doubt she would last five minutes in the outside world in her condition, let alone be able to murder someone."

I leaned into Stanley and said in a low tone, "I have no idea if Lynnie is involved in Forbes's murder in any way, and I'm not here to accuse her of anything. I just want to talk to her."

He looked a trifle uncertain, and then his expression cleared. He let out a long sigh. "I never could say no to you, Nora. Not even when I knew you were just using me to pass biology."

I swallowed as I felt the heat rise swiftly to my cheeks. "I should offer you an apology. Granted, it's about twenty years too late."

He held up one hand. "Forget it. We're not kids anymore. Who knows, maybe if I'd been one of the cool kids, and you were the nerd, the shoe would be on the other foot." He reached out and jabbed the elevator button. "So, if you promise to keep it short, I'll take you to her room."

Stan dropped me in front of Lynnie's room and told me he'd be back to escort me out in fifteen minutes. Once he'd disappeared down the hall, I took a deep breath and knocked on the door. "Come in," said a soft voice. I turned the knob and stepped inside.

The woman sitting in the chair by the window might have once been considered beautiful, but the past two years had definitely taken a toll. The eyes had lost their glimmer, and her face was pale, her cheekbones sunken. The only resemblance between Marilyn Montell and this woman before me was the tousled mane of blonde hair that flowed across her shoulders like a waterfall. She cocked her head to one side as I approached her. "Do I know you?"

I shook my head. There was another hard-backed chair a few feet away. I pulled it over and sat down. "No, we don't know each other. My name is Nora Charles."

Her eyes widened slightly and her lips curved upward in a smile. "Nora Charles!" She clapped both her hands together. "Like in the movie *The Thin Man?*"

I leaned forward a bit in the chair. "Pretty much. My parents were big Bill Powell and Myrna Loy fans."

"Hard not to be." She gave me a once-over. "You do kinda look like Myrna Loy, only prettier." She burrowed deeper into the chair and tucked one leg under her. She sounded almost coy as she asked, "Is there a Nick Charles?"

I laughed. "There is." I opened my bag and fished out a photo of Nick, which I passed over to her. "Only my Nick Charles is a tuxedo cat."

"Ooh, he's so cute. He's as handsome as Bill Powell any day." She passed the photo back to me and then crossed her arms over her chest. "I don't get many visitors. So why are you here?"

I reached into my pocket and pulled out the square of tissue. "I have something that I believe belongs to you."

I pulled the medallion out of my pocket and held it up. She stared at it for a long moment. "It's very pretty, but it's not mine," she said.

"Are you sure?" I nudged the medallion closer to her hand. "Take a close look. See. It's inscribed with Anton's pet name for you."

She pushed my hand away. "No it's not. It's *her* name. Why do people insist on bothering me with this?"

I stared at her. "People? Who else asked you about this?"

"The man who was here a few days ago." She flicked her wrist at the medallion. "He showed it to me, and I told him what I told you. It's not mine."

My pulse started to race. Someone had shown Marilyn this recently? There were only two possible people who might have done that. I leaned forward and rested my hand on the arm of her chair. Excitedly I asked, "Do you remember the man's name, or what he looked like?"

She brought her hands up, pressed them to her temples. "Oh, my, oh, my," she murmured, her eyes closing. "I feel dizzy, and sick. I have a migraine coming on."

I bit down hard on my lower lip. Dizzy and sick beat out frustrated as all hell, which is how I felt right now. The door opened just then, and Stanley stood on the threshold. If he sensed the tension in the room he gave no outward indication, just moved forward and said in a gentle tone, "How are we doing in here?"

Marilyn looked at him with big doe eyes and pointed an accusing finger at me. "She's giving me a headache. Asking me the same question *he* did." Her eyes darted around the room. "Do you have my pills? I need my pills."

"Yes, of course," Stan said soothingly. "I'll get them for you." He rose and took my elbow, pulled me off to the side. "What happened?"

"Not much. We started to have a nice conversation and then I showed her the medallion. She said that someone else had shown it to her, and that it wasn't hers." I looked Stan right in the eye. "Has she had another visitor recently?"

Stan frowned. "Not that I'm aware of. Because of her condition, her sister and I scrutinize every one, just in case the press might try to sneak by, although her sister hasn't been around much lately." He crossed over to the dresser, opened the center drawer and removed a bottle of pills. He went into the bathroom, filled a paper cup with water, and then brought it over to Lynnie. He placed two pills in her hand and tipped the cup to her lips. She swallowed the pills and water and then shrank back in the seat, one leg tucked underneath her. Stan knelt next to her and took her hand in his. "Lynnie, have you had another visitor lately?"

She nodded, her eyes big as saucers, and pointed to the medallion in my hand. "Yes. He asked me if Anton had given it to me. I told him it wasn't mine."

I pulled out my iPhone and called up one of the photos of Edmund Clarkson. I held the phone so Lynnie could see. "Is this the guy?"

She squinted at the screen. "I'm not sure," she said at last. "It looks kind of like him but I can't say for sure." Her shoulders lifted in a shrug.

I'd figured that was a long shot, but I wasn't ready to give up. "Did he happen to mention his name?"

She let out a snort. "Oh, yes. Ted or Fred or something like that."

I leaned forward. "Could it have been Ned?"

She shrugged. "Maybe."

I tapped at the screen. "And you don't recognize him at all?"

"He reminded me of an actor I worked with, years ago," Lynnie admitted. "But it couldn't have been him."

"Why would you say that?"

Her eyes held a glint of triumph. "He should have known that wasn't my charm, that it was *hers*. *She* always wanted everything I had. Everything." A tear rolled down her cheek, and she balled her hand into a fist and brushed at it. "I don't want to think about my sister. It's because of her Dean is dead, and I'm in here. I don't want to talk about *her*."

I started to say something but Stan moved forward and said in a soothing tone, "Then we won't. You don't have to speak about her if you don't want to."

She flashed him a grateful look, then rose out of the chair in a graceful movement and stretched her arms wide. "I'm tired," she murmured. "I need to sleep now."

"That's a good idea," Stan said soothingly. He gently steered her toward the bed. "I think it's time for a nap, right? Visitors tend to wear you out. Ms. Charles and I will let you rest."

Lynnie lay down on the bed and burrowed down beneath the thin blanket. Stan turned out the light and motioned for me to precede him out of the room. Once we were out in the hall Stan's expression turned grim. "I'll have to have a few words with security," he said. "Her room is supposed to be under surveillance. How the hell did that guy get in here?"

"I don't know," I said, "But I'm confused." I held up the medallion. "The back is inscribed *ARI*, which is a nickname for Marilyn, and someone told me that a special man called her that."

"That's why you thought the medallion belonged to her?"

I nodded. "Anyway, why would she think this is her sister's? Her name is Monica, right?"

Stan swiped at his forehead. "Actually, her legal name is Arianna Monica Weston. She doesn't like her first name, so she just goes by Monica Weston, sometimes Martin."

My ears perked up. "Martin?"

"Yes. Martin was their mother's maiden name."

I felt a tingle race along my spine. "I have one last favor to ask." I flashed Stan a high-wattage smile as I pulled out my phone and called up the photo of Millicent Martin Hank had emailed me. "Would you happen to recognize this woman?"

Stan looked at the photo and then at me. "I've never seen her with glasses, but otherwise . . . yes. That's Arianna Weston. Marilyn's sister."

Chapter Twenty-seven

It was almost three thirty when I let myself in the back door of Hot Bread. Nick rose from his position in front of the refrigerator, stretched, and came forward to greet me, apparently not too upset that I'd abandoned him for most of the afternoon. I found a note from Lacey propped on the counter.

Hope you enjoyed your afternoon off. Everything went fine here. I'm going out with Sara, be back in time for dinner. L.

Hm, talk about a guilt trip. I crumpled the note, tossed it in the wastebasket and got my laptop from the back counter. As I booted it up, Nick leapt onto the table and butted his head against my wrist.

"Interesting development," I told him. "That charm you found isn't Marilyn's. It appears to belong to her sister, Arianna Monica Weston. Who, get this, is none other than our mysterious reporter with an axe to grind against Forbes, Millicent Martin. Stan Stanbee identified the photo Hank sent me as the sister."

Nick sat up straight. "Er-owl."

"Exactly. Forbes must have had a pretty big crush on Marilyn's sister to have an expensive medallion like that made especially for her. We need to find out more about her."

A page of sites on Marilyn Montell came up, but none of them referenced anything about a sister. I clicked on the one marked *Bio* and was taken to another fan site. This biography was a bit more detailed, listing all of Marilyn's credits from her high school drama club debut in *Our Town* right up to *Mysteries of Maya*. The only mention of family was that her father had died when she was twelve, and she'd been raised by her mother. I clicked on some other sites, but they had even less information. I pulled up the white pages site and typed in Amy Porter's name. Her phone number was, thankfully, listed. I punched the number into my cell and she answered on the second ring. We exchanged greetings, and then I said, "I hope you don't mind my bothering you, but I'm still working on that article about Marilyn Montell, and there are some things I was hoping maybe you could clear up for me."

"I'll be glad to do what I can," Amy said warmly. "Marilyn deserves a fair shake, and you're just the one to give it to her. What do you need to know?"

"Were you aware Marilyn had a sister?"

Amy was silent for several seconds and then said, "You're an excellent detective, Nora, to have found that out. Marilyn never put it in her official bio, or spoke about Arianna. As far as she was concerned, she was an only child."

"Relations between them were that bad?"

"Apparently." Her voice became a hushed whisper. "Sibling rivalry. Jealousy. Toward the end, it got worse. Marilyn was certain that Arianna was trying to take her man away from her."

"Her man. You mean Forbes?"

"Oh, dear Lord, no. Forbes wasn't Marilyn's man, that was only a crush. It was Dean. Dean Harriman. Arianna was madly in love with him."

Well, I hadn't expected that. "Arianna knew Dean Harriman?"

"Of course." Amy's voice dripped with scorn. "Arianna was trying to be a journalist. She got a job on one of those Hollywood scandal sheets—the name escapes me—and her first big assignment was covering the filming of that movie. She was on the set practically every day, making goo-goo eyes at Harriman and irritating her sister to no end." She choked out a laugh. "I heard that she went after Dean in a big way, and he turned her down cold. It made for a chilly atmosphere on the set, I can tell you that."

"I bet. Do you know exactly when all that happened?"

"Sure. About a week before Harriman's death."

"What about Arianna and Forbes? Anything there?"

"Funny you should say that. It was common knowledge that Arianna was crazy about Dean, but she spent a lot of time with Forbes, too. A *lot*. As a matter of fact, a reporter friend of mine caught them together one day in one of the back rooms on the set."

"In a compromising position?"

"Not really. They were huddled together, looking at something in a briefcase. When my friend came in, they slammed it shut and hightailed it out of there without a backward glance. Forbes paid Ari a lot of attention, but that might have been because of the article she was supposed to be writing. If push came to shove, Forbes would have chosen Marilyn over her any day."

"Which wouldn't have sat well with her, no doubt. You wouldn't happen to know where the sister is now, would you?"

"Far away, I hope," Amy said with feeling. "She was never anything but trouble for Marilyn. It wouldn't surprise me if *she* were the reason for Marilyn's breakdown, and not Harriman's death. Believe me, if that girl could have engineered her sister's trauma, she would have. She certainly benefitted from it. Right afterward, she started buying fancy clothes, fancy cars. She was rolling in dough, her sister's, no doubt."

I hung up from Amy and sat for a few minutes, letting my mind drift. I recalled Marilyn's earlier words: *She always wanted everything I had—everything.* And she'd certainly seemed upset. Something else Marilyn had said echoed through my brain: *It's because of her Dean is dead, and I'm in here.*

I swiveled my head toward Nick. "Forbes had help all right, but it wasn't Marilyn. It was Arianna."

I got up and began to pace around the kitchen. If Harriman had evidence that Forbes was involved with drugs, it would have ruined his career before it got started, particularly if the involvement was on the dealing end. Forbes probably had that necklace made for Arianna as an inducement to help him switch that gun, and somehow they'd managed to pull it off. If Arianna was in love with Harriman, and that love wasn't returned, she might well have jumped at the chance to not only end the life of the man who spurned her, but to make her sister miserable as well.

"It makes sense," I muttered, "but there are still a lot of loose ends. If the medallion belonged to Arianna, how did it get to the gazebo? If

Forbes had it, he wouldn't be carrying it around with him, would he? So the only logical answer must be that Arianna herself dropped it. Which would mean she's around here, somewhere."

I frowned. Forbes had hinted his quest to find the reporter who'd written the unflattering article might be at an end. Had he located Arianna, summoned her to Cruz, confronted her? I remembered my last conversation with him. It had seemed someone was with him. Could it have been Arianna? From her picture, she didn't appear to be particularly strong. How might she have overpowered a strong man like Forbes, unless . . .

I remembered what Ardis had said about Forbes suffering from Ménière's disease. I typed it into Web MD and read the page that came up. Nick peered over my shoulder as I read. "Isn't this interesting? Salt can override the effects of the medication and increase the vertigo. Anderson said a lot of sodium chloride—salt—was found in Forbes's blood."

I drummed my fingers on the table. Remy had said he wasn't sure if the van were locked or not, but the netting had looked disturbed. Was it possible that Arianna had come to Cruz and stalked Forbes, waiting on her chance? That she'd somehow managed to load his food with salt, then stolen the netting from Remy's van and met Forbes at the gazebo. Then, when his vertigo started to kick in, strangled him?

Well, it made about as much sense as anything else.

And then there was Ned Reilly. Why would she kill Ned Reilly? I pressed my hand to my forehead, struggling to remember what Blaine had told me. That Ned wanted to meet him to give him something important, something that would change the whole direction of the story. Ned had mentioned that he was working on "Harriman's legacy." To my mind, that had to mean that he was going to reveal Forbes was dealing in drugs, but what if Forbes weren't the only one?

Amy had said that right around that time, the sister started showing up in fancy clothes, fancy cars. What if Harrman's death weren't the only thing Arianna had helped Forbes with? And if Ned had somehow managed to connect the dots . . .

"Merow."

I glanced down at the floor. Nick lay there, his paws wrapped around a thick book—I let out a little cry as I recognized one of Nick Atkins's journals. I was constantly changing their hiding place, but the journals were just like the Scrabble tiles. Nick had an uncanny way of digging them up when he felt like it.

"What have you got there, Nick?" I asked. I reached down and wrested the journal out from underneath my cat's portly body. I opened the journal, started to flip idly through the pages—and suddenly stopped and stared. Then I grabbed my phone and pulled up the photo of the slip of paper in Ned Reilly's pocket, the one with the DEA phone number on it.

No wonder the paper had seemed familiar to me. It was the same type of journal paper, with that distinctive scalloping around the edges. So Ned had to have gotten that page out of someone's journal—Forbes's perhaps? And maybe he'd been going to reveal to Blaine that Forbes hadn't worked alone?

An excellent motive for three deaths: Harriman's, Forbes's and Reilly's.

But how to prove it? Aha, that was the million-dollar question, for which I had no answer.

Or did I?

I reached for my phone and punched in Samms's number. He answered on the third ring. "Are you staying out of trouble."

"That's the way you answer your phone?" I huffed.

"It is when your number pops up on my Caller ID."

"I just have a question. Has Forbes's trailer been cleaned out yet?"

"I would imagine so. That director was bellyaching about paying the rental, so Dale released it yesterday. Her men were done with it."

I bit back the curse word that rose to my lips. "Okay. What about Ned Reilly's hotel room?"

"Same deal. I think Colgate had someone over there today. Why all this interest in the dead men's belongings?" Samms asked. "Is there something you want to share with me?"

I hesitated, and then sighed. "As a matter of fact . . . yes." Samms listened as I reiterated the day's events and my theories. When I finished, he was silent for so long I thought we'd gotten disconnected, and then I heard a giant sigh.

"It's a nice theory, but that's all it is. A theory. You've got no proof."

"There's that paper found in Reilly's pocket. If you go through the dead men's things, I'll bet you'll find a journal missing a page."

"It's still no proof that this sister had anything to do with it." He blew out a long breath. "Let it go, Nora."

"Sorry, I can't. Not as long as Remy's under suspicion."

"I told you. If he's innocent there's nothing to worry about."

"Why? Because innocent men are seldom unjustly convicted of murder?"

Dead silence and then: "Do you remember what I told you when your sister was in jail for murder?"

"Yes. You asked me to trust you."

"Exactly."

"That's it? That's all you're going to say?"

"That should be enough," he said quietly, and hung up.

Chapter Twenty-eight

"Ooh, Nicky, are you excited? Today is your big day! Are you ready for your close-up?"

I couldn't suppress a grin as I watched Chantal and my sister ooh and ah over Nick. The cat seemed to be well aware that today was his shot at superstardom and he'd certainly gone all out, grooming for the occasion. Chantal had brought over a white collar with clear stones embedded on it, and for once Nick hadn't made a sound of protest or tried to wriggle away as she slipped it around his neck. Maybe the fact the collar was made out of fine lamb's leather might have had something to do with it.

"Look how handsome he looks!" Chantal clapped her hands in delight, while Lacey got a mirror and held it in front of Nick. He sat up straight and lifted a paw in his reflection in the mirror, almost as if inviting the other cat to come out and play.

"Nick, that's not another cat. That's you!" Lacey pointed at the reflection. "That's you looking so handsome!"

Nick looked at her over his shoulder and the expression on his face seemed to say, *Well, I know that, puny human.* He gave a pleased-sounding *merow* and swatted at the mirror again with his paw.

I leaned over and gave him a quick scratch on his white-streaked ear. "You are going to behave today, right, Nick? You're going to take direction from Mr. Colgate, and you're just going to sit quietly on Ardis Malone's lap while she says her lines, and then you're going to reach up and touch her cheek, very lightly, with your paw. No claws. And then—" I leaned over and whispered in his ear, "you're going to be just a tad difficult. Make sure you keep everyone distracted to give me enough time to do what I have to do. Find those boxes of Ned Reilly's, right?"

I swear he rolled his eyes at me.

"Oh, stop fussing, Nora," Lacey chided. "Nick's smarter than all of those TV stars put together. You wait. This might just be the start of a whole new career for Nick. Why, soon Hollywood agents will be knocking on our door, wanting him for commercials, TV spots, maybe even movies!"

"Dream on, little sister. How about giving me a hand with that tray of sandwiches while you're planning out Nick's future?"

"Look, if you want to keep on running Hot Bread, I'll be more than happy to act as Nick's agent," my sister said with a wide grin. "I've always wanted to be a hotshot agent, and this might be my chance. I'll make a cool fifteen percent on anything they pay Nick. We'll ask for top dollar, of course." She rubbed at her forehead. "How much did Lassie make per episode?"

Chantal arched a brow. "You're comparing Nick to Lassie?"

Nick looked up and bared his teeth.

Lacey waved her hands in the air. "You're missing my point, Chantal. I'm not comparing him. Nick is way smarter. He should get double whatever they paid that dog."

While the two of them argued back and forth over Nick, my cell rang. I saw Ollie's number and answered. "Thanks for calling. I'm sorry I had to email you so late last night. Were you able to find out anything about Arianna Weston?"

Ollie's rich laugh sounded over the wire. "First off, eleven thirty is just the shank of the evening for a night owl like myself. Secondly, yes, I did find out something, but I'm not sure how much help it will be." I heard papers riffling and then Ollie said, "Arianna Weston graduated Brown with a degree in English, a minor in Drama. She was a member of the Dramatics Club, but she didn't do much acting. She was relegated to duties like makeup and wardrobe, scenery making. After graduation she got a job on the staff of the *Star Chronicles*, and her first big assignment was reporting news from the set of her sister's latest film, *Mysteries of Maya*. After her sister's breakdown it's as if she vanished into thin air."

"Hm. And what about Millicent Martin?"

"Even less. She did a few freelance articles here and there, most notably that one on Forbes, but even she slips off the radar a few months ago."

Hm. Which could possibly mean Arianna slash Millicent had in all probability assumed yet another identity, one that would enable her to keep an eye on Forbes. She could be anyone, anywhere. Aloud I said, "That's pretty much what I expected, but thanks for checking, Ollie."

"I'll keep digging. I have a few more sources I can contact. What's on the agenda for today?"

"Ah, well, today's the last day of food service, and it's Nick's big scene with Ardis Malone. If you get a chance you should drop by. I'll leave your name with the guard."

"I'd sure like to see Nick work with Ardis Malone," Ollie said and chuckled. "I'll try and get down there later."

I hung up with Ollie and returned to the back room. I found Chantal and Lacey both on their hands and knees, trying to coax Nick out from his position underneath one of the cabinets. At the sound of my voice, he stuck his furry black and white head out with a pitiful merow.

"For goodness sakes, Nick, come out of there. Your fur is all messed up now. You'll have to regroom in the van. And he'll groom himself, thank you very much," I added, swiping the hairbrush out of my sister's hand with a steely glint in my eye.

"Geez," Lacey grumbled. "We were only trying to help."

"I think the two of you were a little too helpful," I remarked as Nick wiggled out from underneath the cabinet. He gave his bottom a brisk shake, flopped down, and proceeded to lick his manhood. "Nick's perfectly capable of whipping his own coat into a lustrous sheen—and other parts of his anatomy, too."

Nick paused in his ablutions to give his head a vigorous shake. "Merow."

"See, he's got it under control." *Now, if only I did,* I thought. Once again that niggling feeling tugged at the corners of my brain. The feeling that finding Arianna and the solution to this whole mystery was somewhere right under my nose, but where?

• • •

It was shortly after ten a.m. The breakfast things had all been put away, but so far I hadn't heard a word from Colgate as to when and where Nick was required to report for his big moment. I was impatient to get on with my own search, so I left the lunch prep in Mollie's capable hands and went in search of the director. After making a few inquiries, I found out that he was filming in the biology lab on the second floor. I climbed the familiar steps and walked halfway down the dingy corridor to the door marked *Lab*. Two young crew members functioned as sentries outside the door. A red bulb had been inserted in the overhead lamp and was illuminated, a signal not to disturb. One of the boys held up his hand as I approached. He looked to be about fifteen years old, with red hair and freckles. He reminded me of a young Ron Howard, circa his Opie days on the *Andy Griffith Show*. The badge he wore around his neck said his name was Chuck.

"Sorry, Ms. Charles." His smile was engaging, but his tone was firm. "They're shooting right now. You can't go in there. Colgate would have my head, not to mention my job."

I held up my own hand. "I wouldn't want to get you in trouble. I was just wondering when Colgate might be done. He said my cat was supposed to film his scene after the breakfast service."

"Oh, right." Chuck motioned to his companion, who handed him a clipboard. "We're running a little late. I thought Colgate sent someone down to tell you we'll film Nick's scene right after lunch, if that's okay with you?"

Okay? Hell, no, that was perfect. "Of course not. I take it someone will get us?"

"Or you can come over to the home ec room at two thirty. That's where the scene will be filmed. They've set it up like a bedroom."

"Okay, that works. Thanks." I started to turn away and then said innocently, "Oh, I noticed that Forbes's trailer had been removed from Sweeney Park. I take it they boxed up all his possessions?"

"Yeah." Chuck reached up to scratch at the back of his head. "Colgate had some of the crew box everything up and ship it back to the studio. It took 'em practically all day. There was a *ton* of stuff." He sighed. "I'm not sure if Forbes has any relatives or not. Who knows? Maybe the studio will auction some of his stuff off on eBay. He had a few nice electronic devices I wouldn't mind having myself."

"Hm. Such a shame. And what about Ned Reilly's things? Did they get packed up as well?"

"Hm, I'm not sure. Grace would know."

"Grace?"

"Grace Oliver. She's in charge of wardrobe and makeup, and usually when something needs to be shipped on location, she handles it."

"I see. Do you know where I might find her?"

"Wardrobe is set up in the gymnasium. South side."

"Thanks."

• • •

I was amazed at the transformation when I finally reached the gymnasium. The entire south side had indeed been transformed into a sort of mini beauty salon, with a wide counter flanked by glass-doored cabinets holding a display of hairbrushes, combs and scissors along with multiple bottles, cans and tubes of every sort of hair product known to man, and then some. A makeshift sink had been connected to the plumbing in the locker room, which was only a few steps away, and above the sink was a lighted mirror as well as a rack for styling appliances—hair dryers, curling irons, and so on. There were also a half dozen chairs set up before tables with lighted mirrors. The tables held trays and trays of different types of makeup—shadow, foundation, mascara. A bit farther down were racks and racks of clothing—suits, dresses, nightclothes. Two dressmaker forms flanked the racks, and I could hear the hum of a sewing machine as I drew nearer.

A woman standing in front of one of the tables glanced over her shoulder as she straightened a hair dryer. "Can I help you?"

She was a short middle-aged woman with a pitch-black beehive hairdo and bright red lipstick. She wore a blue smock that had *Janis* embroidered on the pocket, navy slacks and thick-soled sneakers. Another, slightly younger girl, in a red smock with *Jess* embroidered on the pocket, leaned against one of the makeup stations, sampling one of the many lip glosses. A measuring tape circled her neck, and around her wrist was an elastic band attached to a red pincushion.

I smiled at both of them. "Yes. I'm looking for Grace Oliver?"

Janis picked up a cloth and proceeded to wipe off a black leather styling chair. "Grace isn't here right now." She squinted at me. "Oh, I know you. You're the one who's been feeding us that primo food all week. Nora Charles, right?"

I nodded. "Right."

She made a circular motion over her stomach and smacked both her lips together. "Well, I'll be sad to leave your cooking, I can tell you that. What's the chances you'd relocate that shop of yours to our studio in LA?"

I laughed. "Very slim right now, I'm afraid."

"Yeah, that's what I thought. Too bad. The studio commissary could take a few lessons from you, that's for sure."

"That's very kind of you to say. Will Miss Oliver be here later?"

"Doubtful," Jess piped up. "She says she wrenched her back packing up Forbes's belongings yesterday. But if you ask me"—she leaned forward and put her hand up to shield her lips—"she just thought it was a good opportunity to get a day off. We might not look busy right now, but it's early yet. Trust me, by noon we'll both be running around like chickens with our heads cut off."

"I'm sure," I murmured. "Perhaps you can help me." My hand dipped into my tote and I flashed my PI license. "I'm working with the police on the murder cases. They'd like me to go through Forbes's and Reilly's belongings, you know, to see if I can pick up on anything they might have missed. Would you happen to know where they are?"

"Let me think." Jess's lips screwed into a poutish expression as she thought. "I think Grace had them put in that storage area behind the gymnasium." She waved her arm in the opposite direction from their makeshift wardrobe/makeup room. "They just renovated it, and it's really big and there were a *ton* of boxes. Over two dozen." Janis shook her head so that her heavily lacquered hairdo bobbed to and fro. "It's a good thing that Grace did the packing, though."

"Why do you say that?"

Janis laughed. "Because Grace, in addition to being methodical, is also very anal. She made a list of each box and every single thing that went inside 'em. That's why it took her so long. Colgate was pissed, but mark my words, he'll be grateful in the end."

"Sometimes you need people like that," I agreed, hoping I didn't sound as excited as I felt. "She kept the lists with each box, I suppose?"

"There's a list inside each box, and she kept a master copy. Here, you can see for yourself." Janis went over to a drawer and whipped out a manila folder and handed it to me. She peered over my shoulder as I thumbed through the pages. "Have you ever seen anything like this? I mean, she's really detailed. Look at this. One leather-bound journal with ripped pages. Can you imagine listing something like that?"

I said a mental thank-you to Grace Oliver and her love of lists. "She is detailed." I glanced at the top of the sheet. Box 6. "I see she's got each box numbered, too."

"Yeah, well, once a nerd always a nerd."

"Are Reilly's boxes listed here too?"

"Yep." Janis riffled through the papers, then frowned. "Say, weren't both sets of lists in here?"

Jess walked over to peer over Janis's shoulder. "They were, I'd bet my life on it."

"Did anyone else know those lists were in there?" I asked.

They both started to shake their heads, and suddenly Janis stopped and gave a little cry. "Mamie was in here before, and I saw her by the drawer. But why would she take the list?"

"Mamie?" I asked. "You mean Mamie Monroe?"

"None other," responded Jess. "She's always snooping around, looking for gossip to spread. Probably wants to get some sort of souvenir she can auction off online. Thank God she's not working today." She leaned into me and whispered, "Ned Reilly caught her snooping around Forbes's trailer after he was killed."

My ears perked up. "She was?"

Jess nodded. "I happened to be going past and I heard them. He told her that she was too late and she should get the hell out of there or he'd call the police."

"Too late? For what?"

Jess shrugged. "I don't know. She came flying out of the trailer, mad as a hornet. That was my cue to exit too."

"Did you mention that to Detective Anderson?"

"I told that nice-looking guy, Samms, I think his name was. But he didn't seem very interested."

I let out a sharp breath just as Janis, who'd been bent over the drawer, straightened and waved a paper aloft. "Oh, Ms. Charles, I found the list. It was buried in the back." She handed it to me and shook her head. "I'm going to have to have a few words with Ms. Monroe when she comes in tomorrow. I wouldn't be surprised if she's the one who hid it back there—not that I think she'll admit anything."

I thanked them for their time and, lists clutched in my hand, headed for the north end of the gym. The high school was an ancient building that had been erected in the early 1700s. There were all sorts of little rooms and crawl spaces tucked away throughout the building, many of which we'd explored as students. I was familiar with the spot Janis had mentioned, but truthfully, there were many places where two dozen boxes could easily be secreted. I made my way through a doorway that led in a separate direction from the main part of the building. I hurried swiftly down a long, dark corridor until I came to a door marked *Facility Personnel*. I reached out, twisted the knob. The door swung inward, revealing a low-ceilinged corridor that was practically devoid of light. I felt along the wall and found a light switch, and a moment later the fluorescent fixtures on the ceiling feebly flickered into life. I started to step all the way inside, then hesitated, my whole body tensing. Had I heard a footstep behind me? I whirled around, scanned the corridor beyond.

Nothing.

I turned my attention back to the dimly lit room. If my memory served, the storage crawl space where the boxes were most likely stored would be at the other end of this room. I gritted my teeth and moved swiftly through the room, down another dimly lit corridor until I came to another gray metal door, this one bearing a brass plaque with the word *Storage* on it. I pushed the door open and stepped inside, and almost clapped my hands at the sight of cardboard boxes, stacked on top of each other. I walked over and looked at the top one.

Ned Reilly–Box 1–Grooming Incidentals

Pay dirt.

I quickly ran my finger down the list of Ned Reilly's boxes. Box 9 also mentioned a leather journal, pages missing—what were the odds. I stepped back and counted the rows of boxes. There were three, with eight boxes per row. If they were all in order, that would mean that Box 9 was either at the top of the second row of boxes or all the way at the bottom. I didn't know which was worse. I spied a stepladder in the corner and dragged it over. I climbed almost all the way up and peered at the label on the top box.

Ned Reilly–Box 9–Personal Items

Ah, success. I grabbed the box, tried to lift it, found it heavier than I'd expected. I nibbled at my bottom lip. I had two choices. I could leave everything here, go back and get either Chantal or call Ollie to help—or I could just do it myself. I opted for option two. I gave the box a tug and said a quick prayer that there weren't too many breakables in it as it dropped to the floor with a loud *thunk!* I scrambled down the ladder and went over to examine the box. It had landed on its side, but Grace Oliver had apparently been a master with tape, because none of the flaps had opened. I righted the box, then realized I'd need something to slit that tape with. I felt in my pocket and pulled out my key ring. After three concentrated tries, the flaps opened and I peeled them back, viewed the jumbled contents of the box. A man's jewelry box had popped open, and I saw the broken chain that had been on the list peeping out of it, along with a chunky gold bracelet that I imagined must cost more than I made at Hot Bread in an entire month.

But the object I'd seen on the list—what I was really after—was on top, wedged in between the jewelry box and a gilded picture frame. My hand closed over the leather journal. I flipped to the first page and saw the words I'd hoped for, written in a bold scrawl.

Property of Dean Harriman

This was it! I pulled one of the boxes over and squatted on it as I flipped through the pages. Harriman had used it mainly as a place to critique each actor's performance, as well as notes on various crew members and how their performances could be improved. My spirits rose, though, as I came to the last page.

> *Today I found out disturbing news about my protégé, Anton Forbes. It seems that he's been involved in smuggling large quantities of opium into the U.S. from Europe. And it seems he's not alone. This would kill Marilyn if she knew . . .*

A shadow fell across the page, cutting off my light, and I heard the distinct click of a revolver.

A hand shot out. "I'll take that," said Mamie Monroe.

Chapter Twenty-nine

I stared at the gun, and the journal slid from my hand onto the floor. Mamie reached down and snatched it up, the revolver still pointed right at my heart.

"I guess I should thank you for being such a nosy Nellie. You've saved me a lot of time looking for this." Mamie slid the journal into the pocket of the oversized houndstooth jacket she wore.

"It's a nice cover, Arianna," I said quietly. "The wig's a nice touch, and the false teeth. No one would ever suspect snoopy, frumpy Mamie Monroe was really Marilyn Montell's sister."

Her lips curved upward, and her eyes, glittering behind the massive glasses, held a glint of triumph. "A perfect disguise. Not even you suspected, and I thought for sure you might, especially after you went to see my sister. Oh, yes, I've been following you," she said as I gasped. "You're one smart cookie. I had a feeling it wouldn't be long before you figured everything out. I had hoped to be out of the country by now, but"—she waved the gun in the air—"I got a bit sidetracked."

"I wouldn't say I've figured everything out," I said, keeping my eye on the gun. "There are still some things that are puzzling me. For instance, I'm still not quite clear on who actually killed Dean Harriman. Was it you or Forbes?"

Her lips twisted into a sneer. "Who do you think? Anton had fabulous European connections for smuggling in drugs, but he hadn't a clue how to get rid of the one man who could have destroyed both of us forever."

"So it was you who killed Dean Harriman? Not Anton?"

"Are you deaf?" She waved the gun in the air again, this time a little too close to my face for comfort. "What did I just say?"

I swallowed. "Marilyn had no idea, did she, that her sister had a nasty little habit involving white powder? That's how you became involved with Forbes in the first place, right?"

"I never had a habit. Oh, I tried it once or twice, I won't deny that.

It didn't do much for me, but then I found out there was lots more money selling the stuff as opposed to taking it. I got some from a guy on the set of *Maya*, and I found out that Anton was the supplier. We hooked up. I got him plenty of customers, and I got a really, really nice cut. I could finally afford to buy all the nice things my sister could afford and I couldn't. And then the goon got careless, and Dean, paragon of virtue that he was, found his contact list."

"And you found out that Dean was getting ready to expose Forbes. So you killed Harriman to protect him?"

She tipped her head back and barked out a laugh. "No, stupid. I killed Harriman to protect *me*. My name was on that list, too. I had no doubt Forbes would be sure to spin most of the guilt in my direction in an attempt to save his own skin. So I convinced Marilyn to distract the prop master that night. Once he was out of the way, it was easy for me to disconnect the security camera, and then I just switched the guns. That look of shock on Anton's face when Harriman's brains blew out was real, let me tell you. And as for my sainted sister, well, that breakdown was only a matter of time anyway. I just helped it along a bit. Marilyn always did like playing the drama queen."

I couldn't believe my ears. "Ruining your sister's life meant nothing to you?" I asked.

Her lips slashed into a thin line. "I'm done answering your questions now." Her hand closed over my wrist and she jerked me to my feet, slammed the butt of the gun into my ribs. She gave me a push toward the far wall, and I saw the outline of a door. "Make yourself at home until I get back," she said. "Then we're going to take a little ride, just you and me." She gave the door a push, and it squeaked inward on rusty hinges. Arianna thrust her foot out and I tripped, went sprawling on all fours inside the room. As I struggled to my feet the door slammed shut, leaving me in cave-like darkness.

I turned in the direction I thought the door was. "Arianna! Let me out. You won't get away with this. The lunch service—people will start to wonder where I am."

"Don't worry, I took care of that little detail before I came looking for you," came a muffled voice from the other side. "I won't be long. Toodles."

I took a deep breath, exhaled slowly. The blackness I found myself imprisoned in was impenetrable. The door Arianna'd closed fitted so tightly not even a sliver of light shone through. My heart pounded in my chest, and I could feel myself swaying, or at least I thought I did. Tight enclosed spaces tended to give me a touch of vertigo, and I reached out, let my fingers touch the wall for support.

Think, I told myself. *Maybe there's a way out of here.*

Gingerly I slid one foot forward, then the next, my arms stretched out in a parody of an old mummy movie. My fingers touched concrete and I let out a breath. I'd found the wall, now where was the door? I inched my fingers downward in the direction of where the knob should be and . . . nothing.

Great. There was no way to open the door from the inside.

My hands fell to my sides, and then I suddenly remembered I'd put my cell in my jacket pocket. I pulled it out, and after fumbling for a few moments in the darkness, pressed the On button, then blinked as the sudden haze of illumination almost blinded me. I checked the bar level and groaned. No bars. No signal.

I was trapped in here, with no way to let anyone know where I was.

"Calm down, calm down," I whispered into the darkness. "Soon it will be time for lunch service. Mollie will start to get concerned. Nick has to be taken to the home ec lab for his big scene. Someone will be missing me. There has to be some way out." I called up the flashlight app on my phone, swung the beam over toward the far wall. I saw a series of conduits and panels, below a large sign that read *Danger High Voltage.* I swiped sweat from my brow and then tensed. Beneath the electric hum was another sound . . . a scrape, as if there were something moving behind the panel . . .

"Merow."

I stared as a black and white head popped up out of the darkness.

"Nick?" I stared at the cat. "How did you get here?"

Eureka. If Nick had gotten in here, then that meant there was another way out.

Nick stepped back into the shadows, bleating out another plaintive merow. Apparently Arianna hadn't counted on there being another exit. I followed Nick and found myself in a corridor that was so narrow I had to walk through it sideways. A few seconds later, I saw Nick trot into an area that seemed to be a connecting room. I followed, and then felt relief wash over me as I saw another door with a sign marked *Exit* right above it. I raced forward, tugged at the knob.

The door didn't budge.

"Great." I held up the phone to get a better look. This door was made out of wood. Maybe a good swift kick would open it.

"Merow."

I turned. Nick flicked his tail and trotted off again, and I realized that there was yet another room beside this one. I could see this space was more suited to a storage area. There were moving racks of folding chairs, and stacks of collapsible tables had been shoved off to one side. At the end of the room, I could see light seeping in from what appeared to be a gap. I moved swiftly toward it, and just as I reached it my phone went dead.

"Swell."

I moved toward the thin circle of light, and when I got closer, started to yell at the top of my lungs. "Help! Help!" It took me a few seconds before I realized Nick was no longer with me. Where had he gone? I heard a slight sound behind me and the next instant something tightened like a noose around my throat.

"Tut-tut. It's a good thing I remembered about that other exit. Someone as resourceful as you was bound to find it." Arianna's breath came hot on my cheek. "I'd much rather have done this in the woods, but I guess it doesn't really matter. By the time they find your body, I'll be far, far away."

I clutched at the narrow strip of cloth that dug into my flesh, wondering if this was how Forbes had felt when Arianna had surprised him in pretty much the same way. I whipped my head backward, let out a soft grunt as mine collided with hers. Arianna's grip loosened enough for me to roll away. I reached up to remove the material from my neck, but I wasn't fast enough. Arianna was on me in an instant, jerking the material and my neck back cruelly.

"You were smart enough to get out of that room, but not smart enough to know you should have disabled your opponent," she hissed. "Too bad. I rather liked you."

The noose around my neck tightened and my arms flailed helplessly as I gasped for air, and then . . .

"Er-owl!"

I jerked my head in the direction of the familiar sound and saw Nick, perched high on a beam above us. His claws extended, he dropped down, landing right on Arianna's hands.

"Ow! Where did you come from, you damned cat!" Arianna shrieked and loosened her grip on the noose. Nick took off and I availed myself of the opportunity to roll to the other side of the room. I removed the material from around my neck and flung it off to the side. Arianna so far hadn't paid any attention to me—she was hopping around on one foot, shaking her badly scratched hands in the air and muttering obscenities at Nick.

"Er-owl!"

I looked over. Nick was standing on top of a large burlap sack. He pawed at it, once, twice, and then launched himself at Arianna again, this time landing on her shoulder. The force of his attack brought her to her knees. As she howled in pain Nick scooted off and I quickly grabbed the burlap sack, raced over, and threw it over the wailing woman at about the same instant that the gap I'd noticed before suddenly got larger as a portion of the wall creaked back and Samms and Dale Anderson, guns drawn, stepped inside.

"Nora," Samms cried. "What the heck?"

I pointed to the squirming mass of burlap. "That's Mamie Monroe, aka Arianna Weston. She killed Forbes and Ned Reilly."

Samms raised an eyebrow. "This is your idea of staying out of trouble?"

I rose, brushing my hands on the sides of my pants. "Oh, for Pete's sake," I said. "Get a grip. If I stayed out of trouble, how would you have all this fun swooping in at the last minute?" I eyed the two of them. "How did you know where to find me, anyway?"

"Actually, we've had our eye on Ms. Monroe for a while, or at least Lee has." Dale pointed to Nick, who sat, tail curled around forepaws, on top of a nearby box. "As it so happens, we came here to question Ms. Monroe, but no one could find her. Then Mollie came up to us, said that Mamie Monroe had told her you'd remembered something you had to tell the police, and that she should take care of the food service and Nick's shoot. We all agreed you'd never have passed on Nick's shoot, so we started searching. The women in wardrobe said you told them you were going to look through the boxes in the storage area. We were headed over that way when we saw your cat, pacing back and forth by the bleachers. He led us here."

I went over to Nick and buried my face in his fur. "Once again, you save the day. Don't you get tired of being a hero, Nick?"

Nick lifted his head and stared at me for a long moment.

Then he yawned.

Chapter Thirty

"Well, Nick, tell me. Are you disappointed that you didn't get to do that scene with Ardis Malone?"

It was a little after four. I was seated at the table in the kitchen at Hot Bread, my hands wrapped around a steaming cup of chamomile tea. Nick was on the floor, hunched over his food bowl, which Lacey had filled with every sort of meat she could find from our refrigerator. The cat glanced over at me, shook his head, and then returned to slurping every last bite out of the bowl.

I laughed. "See, it doesn't bother Nick in the least," I said to my sister and Chantal. The two of them had been hovering over me like mother hens ever since Dale Anderson had dropped Nick and me off. "Actually, I think you're more disappointed than anyone," I said to my sister.

"Well, it would have been nice to have a TV star in the family, but I'm just glad the two of you are in one piece." Lacey shook her head. "Marilyn Montell's sister was one crazy chick. She killed not one but two men, and she would have done the same to you, sis."

Chantal set the teapot on the table and then eased into the chair across from me. "She really wanted that journal. Why did Forbes hold on to it, anyway?"

"Dean had made quite a few references to Marilyn in it, and Forbes apparently couldn't bear to part with it. Arianna tried everything. She even wrote that article under the name of Millicent Martin, hoping to start something up, and when that failed she played a waiting game. When Forbes joined the cast of *All the Days of Tomorrow*, she saw her chance. She disguised herself, got a job as a seamstress, and watched for her opportunity. Remy showing up that day gave her the opportunity she needed. She swiped the netting, then made sure she intercepted Forbes's lunch tray and loaded his soup with salt. She'd read up on his condition, knew it would counteract his medication and give him vertigo. She showed up at his trailer just as he was starting to feel the effects, and offered to give him a ride. According to her statement, he was swaying on his feet before they even reached the gazebo."

Chantal shuddered. "And Ned Reilly? Why did she kill him?"

"Well, Reilly'd always figured Forbes was the one who killed Harriman, and after Marilyn was institutionalized, he wanted desperately to prove it. He hired PI's to try and track something down, and then he got a hint that Forbes had once been involved with drug smuggling. He figured that was what Harriman planned to reveal, and so he got a job on *Days of Tomorrow* after Forbes was hired, hoping to find some evidence to support his theory. Emily Van Horn mentioned Forbes had a journal constantly with him. Ned was snooping around Forbes's trailer every chance he got, waiting for an opportunity to break in. He saw Forbes leave with Mamie in her car, and he went in and found the journal. As he was heading back, though, he saw Mamie racing away from the gazebo, and he went over there and saw Forbes's body. He also found the note Forbes dropped when he stumbled up the steps, but he overlooked the medallion that Nick found later. When Ned read the journal, he realized what must have happened and he tore out the page with the DEA's number on it, intending to contact both them and the FBI, but he wanted to confront Arianna first. That was his mistake. She figured he'd gotten his hands on the journal and she knew he was in her sister's camp, not hers. She figured he was going to expose her, so she lured him to the woods, knocked him out, and then suffocated him with a wool scarf."

"What a nice woman," Chantal said with feeling. "And she would have let my brother hang for her crimes. I hope they lock her up and throw away the key."

"Hal said she might get the death penalty," Lacey piped up. "Especially if she doesn't show any remorse."

"Well, she wasn't showing any when she had me trapped in that storage area under the bleachers," I said. "I won't shed any tears for her, but the one I do feel sorry for is Marilyn."

"I know." Chantal clucked her tongue. "Any chance Marilyn could make a complete recovery?"

"Stan seems to doubt it, but one never knows." I turned my attention to Nick, who'd finished his bowl of treats and had padded over to sit beside my chair. "I owe my life to Nick. If he hadn't burst in when he did . . ."

Nick sat up on his hind legs, eyes gleaming. "Yurgle."

"See, he does not have to be on TV to know he is a star," said Chantal. "It is a shame, though."

"He'll still get paid the seven hundred and fifty dollars, so it's not a total loss." I chuckled. "I did some Internet surfing, and I found a good used smoothie machine for six hundred. It'll be here next week, so we should start looking up some good smoothie recipes."

"That should make our customers happy," said Lacey. "I take it the TV crew is leaving town?"

"Yep," I said. "They've already cleared out, and I think they will check the references of people they hire on staff more closely from now on."

"Nick didn't want to be a star anyway," Chantal crooned. "He wants to be a little detective, just like both his humans. Right, Nicky?"

"Yurgle."

"So, now that the mysteries are solved and Remy's off the hook and we're getting our smoothie machine . . ." Lacey leaned forward and pinned me with a gaze. "What about Samms?"

I fidgeted in my chair. "What about him?"

Chantal tapped her forefinger on the table. "The universe, remember? If you don't make up your mind soon . . . trust me, the universe will help you along."

"Yes, and isn't it better to make your own decisions? At least that's what you are always telling me," Lacey said in an accusing tone.

"Samms doesn't need me," I said quietly. "He's got Dale, remember."

"He's only interested in her because he thinks he doesn't have a chance with you," my sister shot back.

I scrubbed both hands over my face. "I'm going to pull a Scarlett O'Hara. Can I think about all this tomorrow? Please?"

Both Chantal and Lacey rose. "We will let you off the hook for now. But tomorrow is another day," Chantal said with a wide grin.

• • •

After my BFF and my sister left, I pulled Nick onto my lap and stroked his soft fur. "I do realize there are some decisions I have to make but it's not easy. I care very much for Daniel, but it's true. He's not here, and who knows when he'll be back? Or if? I haven't heard from him since he went on this assignment."

Nick sat quietly in my lap, regarding me with his unblinking stare.

"On the other hand, Samms and I have never really gotten along. Sure, there's an attraction, but is it only physical, or something more? And how do I know the feeling is even mutual? Aside from what nearly happened the other day, he's never given me any indication that he'd like to pursue a relationship with me, other than one of sarcasm." I set Nick on the floor and rose. "That's what I need a sign for, if you ask me."

Nick wriggled around in my lap, raised his paw, and pointed at my cell phone. A second later it rang.

I looked at my cat. "How do you do that?" I grumbled. I picked up the phone and looked at the screen. It was Samms. I glanced again at Nick, who was busily engaged in washing his face. I hesitated only briefly before hitting the Accept icon. "Hey."

"Just thought you'd like to know that Arianna signed a full confession. The DA's ecstatic. I do believe he's going to push for the death penalty."

"Am I a bad person for not feeling sorry for her?"

"Hell, the woman was going to kill you. I'd be very surprised if you *did* feel sorry for her."

"You suspected her all along?"

"Not *all* along. When you mentioned her being such a fountain of information it kinda raised a red flag for me. I started digging deeper."

"Thank God you did." There was an awkward pause and then I said, "So . . . I guess you and Dale can finally have that date, huh?"

"Date?" He sounded genuinely puzzled. "What are you talking about?"

"You remember. The two of you were on a date when I found Forbes in the gazebo. I interrupted it."

"I remember, and you didn't interrupt anything," Samms said. "We weren't on a date."

My breath caught in my throat. "You weren't? The two of you seemed pretty cozy to me."

"I guess your definition of that word differs from mine," Samms remarked. "I have been seeing Dale, but it's in the capacity of friend slash confidante." He hesitated and then added, "She'd kill me for sure if she knew I was telling you this, but she'd been seeing a guy, and she thought it was pretty serious. Until he broke up with her in a text, that is."

"Oh, no! A text!"

"Yep. She called me, real upset, and wanted to vent."

"Just vent? Knowing Dale, I'm surprised she didn't go after him gun drawn."

Samms chuckled. "She wanted to, that's why I had to talk her down. That's what your 911 call interrupted."

I still wasn't satisfied. "She was dressed awfully fancy for just a pep talk."

"She was meeting some girlfriends for dinner, ones she went to college with. You know how that goes. Each one tries to look better than the next." He paused and then added softly, "Why, would it bother you if we were? Dating, that is?"

I hesitated. "Would you be pleased if I were bothered?" I asked finally.

He chuckled softly. "Honest answer? Yes. Yes, I would be pleased, and not because I have a giant ego. I know it might not seem like it, but

I like you, Red. I've always liked you . . . a lot."

"Oh." I could hear Chantal and Lacey's voices in my head, urging me on. *Go ahead. He likes you. You like him. Daniel isn't here. You haven't heard from him in weeks. You're not even sure if he's ever coming back. Bite the bullet.* I glanced over at Nick, still sprawled on the floor. He raised his head, opened his eyes and looked straight at me. Then, very deliberately, he blinked. Twice.

My heart was pounding. I swallowed and said in a rush, "Samms, I—there's something I need to talk to you about."

"Yeah? What's up, Red?"

I took a breath. "Not—I can't do it over the phone. Could you come over?"

There was a moment of total silence and then Samms cleared his throat. "I'm just wrapping up some case notes. How's half an hour, forty minutes tops?"

A little curl of desire fluttered in my stomach. "Make it twenty minutes," I said. I hung up before Samms could say anything else and glanced over at Nick. The cat was now in a sitting position, his tail wrapped around his forepaws. He looked me straight in the eye, and his lips parted, showing a bit of fang.

He blinked twice again.

From the Recipe Book of Nora Charles

Corned Beef 'n Swiss Mini Pot Pies

8 ounces thinly chopped corned beef
4 ounces Swiss cheese
1 can cream of celery soup
1 tablespoon mustard
1 can frozen biscuits, any brand, thawed

Heat oven to 375 degrees F. Grease or spray 8 regular-size muffin cups with cooking spray.

In large bowl, mix corned beef, cheese, soup, and mustard until well combined.

Separate dough into 8 biscuits. Press each biscuit to form 5½-inch round. Place ⅓ cup meat mixture in center of each round. Gently pull edges up and around filling, and place into muffin cups. Pull edges of dough over filling toward center; pleat, and pinch dough gently to hold in place, leaving some of the filling exposed.

Bake 20–22 minutes or until biscuits are golden brown. Cool 1 minute; remove from pan.

Preston McLintock Egg Scramble

3 eggs
1 teaspoon milk
1 teaspoon salt
3 slices of ham, any style
¼ cup shredded cheese
2 slices of your favorite bread
1 teaspoon mustard

Beat eggs, milk, and salt together in a bowl.

Heat a small nonstick skillet over medium heat. Cook eggs in hot skillet without stirring until set on the bottom, about 1½ minutes. Flip eggs and cook without stirring until set on the other side.

Fold in ham and cheese, let cook about 1 minute more. Remove from heat.

Toast bread while ham, cheese, and eggs are cooking. Spread mustard over each piece of toast. Place eggs on one piece of toast and top with remaining piece.

About the Author

While Toni LoTempio does not commit—or solve—murders in real life, she has no trouble doing it on paper. Her lifelong love of mysteries began early on when she was introduced to her first Nancy Drew mystery at age ten—*The Secret in the Old Attic*. She and her cat pen the Nick and Nora mystery series, and they also write the Urban Tails Pet Shop mysteries, which will be continued soon with book two, *Killers of a Feather*. Catch up with them at Rocco's blog, catsbooksmorecats.blogspot.com, or her website, tclotempio.net

CPSIA information can be obtained
at www.ICGtesting.com
Printed in the USA
BVHW030813150223
658552BV00001B/63